Herman W. Mudgett

Holmes' Own Story , 1895

Herman W. Mudgett

Holmes' Own Story , 1895

ISBN/EAN: 9783337377717

Printed in Europe, USA, Canada, Australia, Japan

Cover: Foto ©Andreas Hilbeck / pixelio.de

More available books at **www.hansebooks.com**

HOLMES' OWN STORY

IN WHICH THE ALLEGED

MULTI-MURDERER AND ARCH CONSPIRATOR

TELLS OF THE

Twenty-two Tragic Deaths and Disappearances

IN WHICH HE IS SAID TO BE IMPLICATED

WITH

MOYAMENSING PRISON DIARY APPENDIX

PHILADELPHIA:
BURK & McFETRIDGE CO.
1895.

PREFACE.

The following pages are written under peculiar circumstances, perhaps the most peculiar that ever attended the birth of a literary work. Incarcerated in prison and awaiting trial for the most serious offense known to the law, it has been written only after mature deliberation, against the advice of my friends, and in direct opposition to the positive instructions of my counsel, who have attempted in every way to dissuade me from its publication; but the circumstances under which I am placed, in my judgment, make it imperative that I should disregard all of these considerations.

For months I have been vilified by the public press, held up to the world as the most atrocious criminal of the age, directly and indirectly accused of the murder of at least a score of victims, many of whom have been my closest personal friends.

The object of this extended and continuous enumeration of alleged crimes has been apparently to create a public sentiment so prejudiced against me as to make a fair and impartial trial impossible. My friends have been alienated, my nearest kindred plunged in grief, and the world horrified by the bloody recital of imaginary crimes.

I feel therefore justified in the course I am now pursuing, and am impelled by an imperative sense of duty to publicly deny these atrocious calumnies. The following pages will therefore be found to contain a simple and complete narrative of my entire life, and a full history of my associations and dealings with Mr. and Mrs. B. F. Pitezel and their children, the alleged disappearance of Minnie Williams and the tragic death of her sister Nannie.

My sole object in this publication is to vindicate my name from the horrible aspersions cast upon it, and to appeal to a fair-minded American public for a suspension of judgment, and for that free and fair trial which is the birthright of every American citizen, and the pride and bulwark of our American Constitution.   H. H. M.

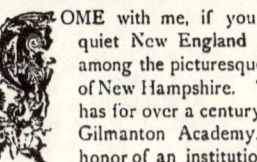OME with me, if you will, to a tiny, quiet New England village, nestling among the picturesquely rugged hills of New Hampshire. This little hamlet has for over a century been known as Gilmanton Academy. So called in honor of an institution of learning of that name, founded there by a few sturdy, self-denying and God-fearing men, over a hundred years ago, who, could they now leave their silent resting places in the church-yard near by, and again wander for an hour through these quiet streets, would, with the exception of new faces, see little change.

Here, in the year 1861, I, Herman W. Mudgett, the author of these pages, was born. That the first years of my life were different from those of any other ordinary country-bred boy, I have no reason to think. That I was well trained by loving and religious parents, I know, and any deviations in my after life from the straight and narrow way of rectitude are not attributable to the want of a tender mother's prayers or a father's control, emphasized, when necessary, by the liberal use of the rod wielded by no sparing hand.

On my fifth birthday I was given my first suit of boy's clothing, and soon after was sent to the village school-house where the school was "kept." I had daily to pass the office of one village doctor, the door of which was seldom if ever barred. Partly from its being associated in my mind as the source of all the nauseous mixtures that had been my childish terror (for this was before the day of children's medicines), and partly because of vague rumors I had heard regarding its contents, this place was one of peculiar abhorence to me, and this becoming known to two of my older schoolmates, they one day bore me struggling and shrieking beyond its awful portals ; nor did they desist until I had been brought face to face with one of its grinning skeletons, which, with arms outstretched, seemed ready in its turn to seize me. It was a wicked and dangerous thing to do to a child of tender years and health, but it proved an heroic method of treatment, destined

ultimately to cure me of my fears, and to incul-
cate in me, first, a strong feeling of curiosity, and,
later, a desire to learn, which resulted years afterwards in my adopting medicine as a profession.

When I was about eight years old, an unusual
occurrence took place in our village—the arrival of an itinerant photographer. He was a
man apparently suffering from some slight lameness, and gladly accepted my offer to act as his
errand boy, and in payment for my services he
was to execute for me a likeness of myself. One
morning upon going to his office I found the door
still locked. It was immediately opened, however, by the artist, sufficiently for him to hand to
me a small wooden block broken in two pieces.
He instructed me to take them to our village
wagon maker and have him make a new one,
which I was to return to him. I did this, and
upon entering the office again, I found the artist
partially clothed and sitting near the door, which
he at once locked. He then proceeded to remove the greater portion of one of his legs, and
not having known until then what was the cause
of his lameness, in fact, not ever having seen or

even known that such a thing as artificial limbs
existed, my consternation can better be imagined
than described. Had he next proceeded to remove his head in the same mysterious way I
should not have been further surprised. He
must have noticed my discomfiture, for as soon as
his mending process had sufficiently progressed,
he quickly placed me in a dim light, and standing
upon his whole leg, and meantime waving the
other at me, he took my picture, which in a few
days he gave to me. I kept it for many years,
and the thin terror-stricken face of that bare
footed, home-spun clad boy I can yet see.

In those days in our quiet village, so remote
from the outside world, that even a locomotive
whistle could scarcely be heard, daily newspapers were rare and almost unknown, our usual
source of information being the weekly papers
and a few periodicals; and in one of these I saw
a glowing offer, emphasized by a fine illustration
of a gold watch and chain, a few of which would
be sold at a comparatively trifling sum. Surely
this was for me the one opportunity of my life,
and although my entire wealth at that time

consisted mostly of pennies and other small coins,
almost every one having for me its own peculiar
history, all of which I converted into more trans-
ferable shape by exchanging them with our shoemaker, who was also my confidant in the matter,
was hardly more than sufficient to buy the
watch.

I was far more concerned lest, before my order
should reach the distant city, all would be sold,
than troubled over the depleted condition of my
purse. Then came anxious days of waiting and
later the arrival of the watch, and after going
alone to my room to wind it and deciding which
pocket was most suitable for its reception, and
still later going to the several stores and some
houses, bargaining beforehand with a little friend
that, in consideration of his accompanying me
and at each place asking in an unconcerned manner what time it was, that he should wear it the
greater part of the day, although I was to be
present that no harm befell my treasure; but
before it came time for him to wear it the wheels
had ceased to turn, the gold had lost its lustre,
and the whole affair had turned into an occasion

of ridicule for my companions and of self-reproach to myself.

My first falsehood and my first imprisonment occurred synchronously, and were occasioned as follows:—

One morning as I was driving our small herd of cows, which had a few days previously been increased by the addition of several others belonging to a neighbor, to their usual feeding ground, outside the limits of the village, an inquisitive neighbor met me and asked, "Whose be they?" I replied very proudly, "Ours." "What, all of them? "Yes, *all*, everyone, and that best one is mine, my own." An hour later upon returning to my home I found father waiting to receive me. He demanded why I had told Richard the lie about the cows, but before I could answer him my mind was most effectually taken up by the production of an implement, to which I was no stranger, and by its vigorous use. After this I was consigned to an upper room and strictly enjoined to speak to no one, and for the ensuing day I should have no food. My absence was soon noticed by my playmates and the cause ascertained, and not long after upon looking out of the window I saw my little friend perched upon the fence nearby, looking almost as disconsolate as I, and later in the day, after sundry pantomime communications he came with a liberal supply of food, which, with the aid of the ever present ball of cord, which you can find in almost every boy's pocket, I was soon enjoying. Accompanying the food was a note written in his scrawly hand encouraging me to "never mind," and that upon the following Saturday we would go down and let Richard's cows into his cornfield.

But this was not done, for late at night when the shadows in my room had assumed strange and fearful shapes, my mother came and taking me into her own room, knelt down and earnestly plead with me and for me, and it was many days before I forgot that lesson. This little note, however, with two others form a unique collection. The second was a joint production of my friend and myself, addressed to an unpopular school teacher one vacation upon our hearing that some slight financial calamity had overtaken him. This was done with the belief that a new teacher was to take his place during the coming year, but in this we were mistaken. I had abundant evidence during the first day of the following term that he had received our letter, when he changed my seat from one I had long occupied, and which was very favorably located for looking into the street, to the opposite side of the room. My seatmate was a very disagreeable and unpopular girl.

The third note was also a joint production, written upon brown paper and tacked upon the barn door of a village farmer, who had, as we thought, misused us. It was not a lengthy note, the words being " Who will pull your weeds next year?" This note was occasioned by the farmer engaging us for a stipulated price to rid a field of a large weed that is common there, and a great hindrance to the healthy growth of other products. The weeds were tall and strong, and the pittance we were to receive was ridiculously small for the amount of work. But when we had finished and held out our tiny, blistered hands for our pay, it was not forthcoming. We went again and again for it, and being convinced it was useless to go more, we returned quietly with two large baskets

to where we had piled the weeds, to be dried
preparatory to their being burned, and very soon
thereafter the seeds from all that we had pulled
were sown broadcast over the field again. It is,
perhaps, a small matter to speak of here, but it
so well illustrates the principle that many times
in my after life influenced me to make my conscience become blind, that I thought well to write
of it.

My first business ventures consisted of a pair
of twin calves that I raised, and later to bring
home, on a stormy winter day, a tiny lamb given
to me by a farmer, which, in time, together with
a few others purchased later, expanded into a
flock of about forty sheep. Both ventures were
failures, however, from a financial point of view,
but the failures were nothing compared with the
collapse of the innumerable air castles which had
depended upon the result of these speculations.

One day I found a purse containing about $40;
an immense sum at that time to me. In the
purse were other papers showing me plainly who
the owner was. I know that I hesitated, but only
for a moment; and having made up my mind

could not too soon return it to its owner, and because I had hesitated was adverse to receiving the reward offered me.

When I was about nineteen years of age (the preceding years having been filled in for the most part with six to nine months each year of preparatory studies and the balance of the time devoted to work and teaching) I was prepared to enter the Dartmouth College, but instead of doing so, I decided to commence a medical course at once, and, with this object in view, I matriculated at the University of Vermont, at Burlington, where I remained one college year, deciding, before it had expired, to complete my course at some larger college, and the following September found me at Ann Arbor, Mich. After having paid my college fees, bought my books and other articles necessary for my second year in college, I found myself hundreds of miles away from friends and relatives, and with about $60 in money with nine months of hard study before me, allowing but little time for outside work if I wished to keep up in my studies with the other members of my class.

About this time I first became acquainted with a Canadian, a fellow-student, and from then until the time of his death he was one of the very few intimate friends I have ever allowed myself.

The limits of this book will not allow me to write the many quaint and some ghastly experiences of our medical education were I otherwise disposed to do so. Suffice it to say, that they stopped far short of desecration of country graveyards, as has been repeatedly charged, as it is a well-known fact that in the State of Michigan all the material necessary for dissection work is legitimately supplied by the State. At the end of my junior year I entered into an agreement with a fluent representative of a Chicago firm to spend my vacation in the northwest portion of Illinois representing his firm as a book agent. In this venture I committed the first really dishonest act of my life.

The firm as well as the book itself, from the sale of which I had been assured I could earn hundreds of dollars during my vacation, was a fraud, and after the most strenuous efforts, having succeeding in selling a sufficient number to defray my expenses and pay my return fare to Ann

Arbor, I came back without making a settlement
with the firm there, and for the remainder of my
vacation earned what money I could in and about
the college city.

I could hardly count my Western trip a failure,
however, for I had seen Chicago.

The remainder of my medical course differed
very little from the first two years ; filled perhaps
more completely with hard work and study, and
almost wholly devoid of pleasure and recreation.
At last, however, in June, 1884, our examinations
were passed, our suspense was ended and I left
Ann Arbor with my diploma, a good theoretical
knowledge of medicine, but with no practical
knowledge of life and of business. After taking
a vacation of less than one week in my old New
Hampshire home, I went to Portland, Maine, and
engaged with a large business firm of that city to
represent them in Northern New York in the sale
of their products ; my prime object being to find
some favorable location in this way where I could
become a practitioner. Such an opening was not
easily found, however, and I accepted a winter
school to teach at Mooers Forks, N. J., and later

opened an office in that village. Here I stayed for one year doing good and conscientious work, for which I received plenty of gratitude but little or no money, and in the fall of 1885 starvation was staring me in the face, and finally I was forced to sell first one and then the last of my two horses, and having done this I resolved to go elsewhere before all of my means were again exhausted.

During my long years there in New York I had abundant time to work out the details of a scheme that my University friend, before referred to, and myself had talked over during our hungry college days as a possible last resort in case our medical practice proved a failure; and from certain letters I had received from him, I judged that he, too, had not found all his hardships at an end upon receiving his diploma. I therefore went to where he was located, and found that though his experience had been less disheartening than my own, it had from a pecuniary standpoint been far from successful. During this visit we carefully planned the following method of obtaining money:—

At some future date a man whom my friend knew and could trust, who then carried considerable

life insurance, was to increase the same so that
the total amount carried should be $40,000;
and as he was a man of moderate circumstances
he was to have it understood that some sudden
danger he had escaped (a runaway accident) had
impelled him to more fully protect his family in
the future. Later he should become addicted to
drink, and while temporarily insane from its use
should, as it would appear afterwards, kill his wife
and child.

In reality they were to go to the extreme West
and await his arrival there at a later date. Suddenly the husband was to disappear, and some
months later a body badly decomposed and
dressed in the clothing he was known to wear
was to be found, and with it a statement to the
effect that while in a drunken rage he had killed
his family and had shipped their dismembered
bodies to two separate and distant warehouses to
conceal the crime, first having partially preserved
the remains by placing them in strong brine.
That he did not care to live longer, and that his
property and insurance should pass to a relative
whom he was to designate in this letter.

At the proper time he was to join his family in the West, and remain there permanently, the relative collecting the insurance, a part of which was to be sent to him, a part to be retained by the relative, and the remainder to be divided between us. This scheme called for a considerable amount of material, no less than three bodies in fact. This difficulty was easily overcome, however, so long as it was supposed that they were needed for experimental purposes, but no doctor could call for three bodies at one time without exciting suspicion, and so it was arranged that I was to go to Chicago for the winter, and some time during the intervening months we should both contribute toward the necessary supply. I reached Chicago in November, 1885, but finding it difficult to obtain satisfactory employment, I went to Minneapolis, where I spent the winter in a drug store as a clerk. Meantime, my friend had promptly obtained his portion and placed it in the storage in Delaware, from which place it was shipped to me later in Chicago. I remained in Minneapolis until May, 1886, when I returned to Chicago. My own life I had insured meantime for $20,000, which, at a later date, I intended to realize upon. I had prior to this time made arrangements to furnish my portion of the material. After reaching Chicago, certain sudden changes in my plans called me hastily to New York City, and I decided to take a part of the material there and leave the balance in a Chicago warehouse. This necessitated the repacking of the same, and to accomplish this I went to a hotel (May, 1886), where I registered under an assumed name, and occupied a room and had the package, which had been shipped from Detroit, taken there, and carefully removing the carpet from one portion of the room I divided the material into two packages. In doing this the floor became discolored.

Later, one of these packages was placed in the Fidelity Storage Warehouse in Chicago, and the other I took with me to New York and placed it in a safe place. Upon my trip from Chicago to New York I read two accounts of the detection of crime connected with this class of work, and for the first time I realized how well organized and well prepared the leading insurance companies were to detect and punish this kind of fraud, and this, together with a letter I received upon reaching my destination, and the sudden death of my friend, caused all to be abandoned.

Soon after leaving New York I came to Philadelphia. where I sought employment in some drug store where I could hope to become either a partner or an owner. Not finding such an opportunity at once I took a situation as a keeper in the Norristown Asylum. This was my first experience with insane persons, and so terrible was it that for years afterwards, even now sometimes, I see their faces in my sleep. Fortunately within a few days after entering the Asylum I received word that I could obtain different employment in a drug store on Columbia avenue, which I at once accepted. About July 1st, one afternoon, a child entered the store and exclaimed, "I want a doctor! the medicine we got here this morning has killed my brother (or sister)." I could remember of no sale that morning corresponding to the one she hastily described, but I made sure that a physician was at once sent to the house, and having done this I hastily wrote a note to my employer, stating the nature of the trouble, and left the city immediately for Chicago, and it was not until nine years later that I knew the result of the case.

Later, when it became necessary to disprove the alarming statements that were made relative to various persons having been killed at 701 Sixty-third street, I placed in the proper authorities' hands a full collection of documentary evidence, consisting of railroad and storage warehouse receipts, letters, references and dates sufficient to show the truthfulness of my statements.

Upon reaching Chicago I found I could obtain no employment as a druggist until I had passed an examination at Springfield, Ill., and when I went there for that purpose I gave my name as H. H. Holmes, and under this name I have since done most of my business. Later, in July, 1886, I went to 701 Sixty-third street, Chicago, where I found a small store owned by a physician, who, owing to ill-health, wished to sell badly. A little later I bought it, paying for it for the most part with money secured by mortgaging the stock and fixtures, agreeing to repay this loan at the rate of $100 per month. My trade was good, and for the first time in my life I was established in a business that was satisfactory to me.

But very soon my landlord, seeing that I was prospering well, made me aware that my rent would be increased, and to protect myself I was forced to purchase at a great expense the vacant property opposite the location I then occupied, and to erect a building thereon. Here my real troubles commenced. The expense incurred was wholly beyond the earning capacity of my business, and for the next few years I was obliged to plunge deeply in debt in every direction; and, worse than this, when these debts became due, if unable to meet them to resort to all means of procuring a stay or evading them altogether. At last there came a day when Thomas Fallon, a constable, together with a lawyer named Sanforth, both of Chicago, came to my store to attach the same to satisfy the claim of some impatient creditor. And during the appraisal of the goods they came and asked me the contents of two small barrels.

I gave them some misleading answer, and bringing out other goods to attract their attention,

they were passed for the time being. They were
the two packages I had arranged more than a
year before at a certain hotel, and which had been
removed from the storehouses in Chicago and
New York, first to my former store, and later to
the new one.

A soon as possible after this attachment took
place, I resolved to permanently dispose of both
these packages, and to do so, I opened the
smaller of them and commenced its destruction
by burning in a large furnace, then in the basement. The experience was so unpleasant, owing
to the terrible odor produced, that I did not
think it safe to destroy more of it in the same
way, and therefore buried the remainder of that
package, as well as the fragments that were partially burned, in the places where they have lately
been found.

The other package was removed, unopened,
from the building, and so disposed of that it is
hardly probable it will ever be found, and I do
not feel called upon to bring it forth, as it would
only serve to add more newspaper notoriety to
the case.

If, however, my life is ever jeopardized, or my other statements discredited owing to want of additional proof in this matter, I shall at once cause it to be produced, and my so doing will result in showing that the portions therein contained are parts of the two bodies already found, and more important still that the package thus brought to light has necessarily occupied its present location for nearly seven years.

This will be corroborated by documentary evidence. freight, express and warehouse receipts, letters, etc., already in the hands of the authorities, together with evidence from workmen, if still alive and to be found.

Early in 1888, needing some extra carpenters, there came to me, in response to an advertisement, a tall, thin, muscular man, whom, at the time, I took to be a farmer from the Western plains.

BENJAMIN F. PITEZEL.

He assured me, however, that he was a carpenter, able to do as much and as good work
as anyone else, that his name was Benjamin F.
Pitezel, that he had a large family, was badly in
need of work for their support and begged me to
give him a trial. This I did, but soon found him
to be a dreamer.

Coming to him at his work I would find him
with a set of figures and perhaps a diagram illustrative of their use, or busy making a model of
some complicated contrivance. This proceeded
so far that for my own protection I had to cause
him to work by contract instead of by the day,
although I found him fully as improvident of his
own time as he had been of mine. Little by little
I grew to like his quiet ways, and to depend upon
him to take charge of the work at times when I
was obliged to be absent, and one day I said to
him, "Ben, with all your mechanical ingenuity you
should have been a rich man before now. How
is it?" His answer was that heretofore the world
had not seemed to be inclined to be kind to him.
This seemed so aptly to describe my own case,
that I talked with him further from time to time,

and a summary of what I learned was as follows :—

He, like myself, had been a country-bred boy, knowing few pleasures, but, unfortunately, receiving few school advantages. At a comparatively early age he had married and commenced life as a farmer in Illinois or Indiana. Later he had moved to Kansas, and, later still, had been forced to leave that State owing to some legal trouble with a bank there, to which he had given a worthless mortgage to secure a loan in money. After leaving Kansas he had wandered through the Western States, principally in the gold regions, and finally had settled in Chicago with his family, which, while he traveled, had remained in Kansas. Very soon after reaching Chicago he had commenced working for me, and from that time until September 2, 1894, when he died, he was continually in my employ, working as a carpenter and builder, and as a real estate dealer and as a wholesale lumber merchant, buying and shipping lumber from the South and West to Chicago and St. Louis, where I also sold the same products.

I think it was in 1889 that I was one day
waited upon by two gentlemen who wished to
sell me a gas machine, by using which I could be
forever independent of the regular city gas company. So great were the inducements held
out that I later met them at their office in La Salle
street, and before leaving them had bought one
of the machines, which a few days later was arranged in the basement of my building, and I
had notified the city company that thereafter I
should cease to be one of their patrons. For two
days the new machine performed wonders, and I
recommended it to many of my customers and
friends. The third evening when I was very
busy my store was suddenly enveloped in darkness. I was obliged to turn away my customers
and close for the want of light, and from then
until morning I wrestled with my gas machine;
and when Pitezel came to his day's work he found
me still perspiring, and, I fear, swearing over it.

The machine was to him as a new toy to a
child, although he soon assured me that as a gas
producer it was an absolute failure. That afternoon I instructed him to temporarily connect it

with the city gas to provide light for the evening, and next day I would go to the company and make a new application to again become a permanent customer. As he finished making the connection he remarked that he thought that it would be a good permanent arrangement without going to the gas company. His quiet remark resulted in my having him, next day, lead the gas from the city main to the machine underground in such a way that it would not be known without a close inspection, and this I did, not to defraud the city, but "to get even" with the company who had defrauded me. A few evenings thereafter the president of this company called upon me, and, after quietly studying my new light for a time, spoke to me of it.

I then told him that I had bought his machine for the purpose of trying a new gas that for years I had been experimenting with. Several other visits followed, and although I was apparently averse to disposing of my new discovery, I finally did so, taking in return first a contract so skillfully worded that there could later be no claims brought against me, and, second, a check for a

large sum of money. Had matters stopped here
as I had at first intended, all would have been
well, but I neglected disconnecting from the city
supply from day to day, until finally an inspector,
more energetic than his fellow-workers, became
aware of it, and this resulted in my very willingly
choosing to pay a five hundred dollar gas bill in
preference to being openly written up and perhaps prosecuted.

There have occurred other deals of a somewhat
similar nature, and generally inspired by the same
motive, but this one suffices as an example of
those that occurred later. Sometime previous to
this I had had occasion to employ an attorney to
transact some business in which certain papers
had to be signed in my New Hampshire name,
and to do this work I employed one I did not
know in order that my real name should not be
confounded with the name of Holmes, under
which I had been known and had done all my
work since commencing business in Chicago.

About a year after consulting this attorney, I
was called into court as a witness on some trivial
case, and while giving my testimony under the

name of Holmes, I saw him sitting in the court room apparently much mystified. Instead of denouncing me to the court, as he might easily have done, he spoke to me alone, and, later, feeling he had done me a most kind favor I gave to him the greater part of my legal work; but though he attended to this conscientiously for me as an attorney, he at no time encouraged me to acts that were wrong, nor was he a party to them, and the late newspaper comments reflecting upon his integrity are most unjust and uncalled for.

Aside from this one incident I know of no time during the nine years prior to my arrest that my two names conflicted the one with the other, or caused me trouble or annoyance.

In 1890 I added a jewelry store to my business, and placed Julius L. Connor in charge of that and my drug business, his wife, Julia Connor, assisting him as cashier for a time, who, after the sale of the store, lived in the building and supported herself and child by taking boarders. That she is a woman of quick temper and perhaps not always of a good disposition may be true, but that any of her friends and relatives will believe her to be an immoral woman, or one who would be a party to a criminal act, I do not think. She lived for her child, and her one fear was that she should lose her, and as soon as the daughter is of sufficient age to protect herself, I feel that her whereabouts will be made known. I last saw her about January 1, 1892, when a settlement of her rent was made. At this time she had announced not only to me, but to her neighbors and friends, that she was going away.

At this interview she told me that, while she had given her destination as Iowa, she was going elsewhere to avoid the chance of her daughter being taken from her, giving the Iowa destination to mislead her husband. I corresponded with her upon business matters later, and the so-called secreted letters lately found could only have been obtained from my Chicago letter files, in which hundreds of my business letters were stored away in alphabetical order.

In 1890 I opened an office on Dearborn street, Chicago, and organized "The Warner Glass-Bending Co.," the principal value of which consisted in certain not very clearly-defined ideas I possessed upon the subject of bending glass for mechanical purposes. This was a stock company, in which I had interested, among others, Osmer W. Fay, a most reputable and honest man (a retired minister), of whom I will speak later in this history. Suffice it say here that, when I found that he had invested the principal part of his savings in my company, knowing that it would not be a successful business venture to others, save myself, I returned to him his investment with interest. At this time Pitezel was in the same office with me, selling an invention he had lately patented, known as "Pitezel's Automatic Coal Bin." I later established him in an office by himself, where he opened a patent exchange similar to the one he was conducting in Philadelphia at the time of his death.

At about this time, Patrick Quinlan, a whole-souled Irishman, had left his farm in Michigan to come to the city to work during the winter months, and commenced his service with me. He soon became almost indispensable, owing to his careful management and supervision of help and general faithfulness, and for several years he worked for me continually, though during that time he did no illegal act nor committed any wrong so far as I know.

Early in 1891 I became interested in one of the most seductive and misleading inventions that has ever been placed before the American public; a device known as the "A B C Copier," which had been brought to this country from Europe by a prominent official of the World's Fair.

He had been swindled in its purchase, and, knowing this, was very willing to dispose of one-half interest in the invention to me for $9,000 worth of "securities." A company was immediately formed, and by using his name freely as the president of same, we were able to make over $50,000 worth of contracts for future delivery before our offices had been open sixty days, numbering among our customers many large insurance companies and prominent wholesale houses.

However, I was glad to sell my interests, clearing about $22,000 in cash upon the entire deal. It was at this time, while employing quite a large office force, that Mr. J. L. Connor asked me to give his sister Gertrude some work to do. Instead

of doing so at once I told him I would aid him in
furnishing her with the means to take a short
course in a business college, and if later she
proved proficient, I would give her employment.
Shortly after her commencing to attend this business college, she received an offer of marriage
from a young clerk in Chicago. She spoke to us
of it, and asked us to learn, if we could, of the
antecedents of the young man and of his pros-
pects. Our investigation resulted in learning that
he had a wife living in Chicago. Gertrude was
inclined to disbelieve this statement, and not
expressing herself as being willing to break the
engagement, Mr. Connor thought best to send
her to her home in Iowa. A statement from the
physician who attended her at the time of her
death, long after this, speaks for itself, effectually
disproving one of the most persistent and disagreeable charges that have been brought against
me. I have had many young ladies in my employ,
most of whom are still living in and about Chicago,
whose parents and friends know only too well
that far from being their seducer I have done
much to materially help them in their narrow lives,

owing to the enormous competitions in Chicago for positions.

At about this time I sent Pitezel South upon an extended lumber purchasing trip, and upon his return to Chicago he encountered some severe domestic troubles, the full details of which he did not tell me until long afterwards. But at the time they resulted in a neighborhood quarrel and some arrests, and thereafter he grew more morose, and drank more freely than he had done heretofore, but managed to do so during my absence or after working hours, as he knew me to be wholly intolerant of drunkenness in my employees.

It was about January 1, 1893, when I first met Minnie R. Williams at the intelligence office of Mr. William Campbell on Dearborn street, Chicago, whom she had engaged to provide her with a position as stenographer.

EMELINE CIGRAND.

I found her to be a bright, intelligent woman, an interesting conversationalist and one who I could see had seen much of the world. When she had been working in my office for a few weeks, knowing that she had a history, I asked her one stormy winter afternoon to tell it to me. After considerable hesitation she did so, in nearly the following words :—

" My earliest remembrance is of a poor home in the South. My father was a drunkard and my poor mother was not strong. One terrible day my father was brought to us dead, and very soon after this mother's strength seemed to leave her utterly, and she soon followed him, leaving me, a tiny child, together with a still younger sister and a baby brother, to the tender mercies of the world. An aunt in Mississippi took my sister to live with her, and another relative cared for brother, and an uncle, a physician, adopted me.

" During the short time he lived he was a loving and tender father to me, and at his death willed to me all of his possessions. A guardian was appointed to care for me, but I was not again happy until years later, when Mr. Massie was appointed to take his place, and since then I have looked upon him and his wife as my parents.

"When I was 17 years old I was sent to Boston to finish my education at the Conservatory of Music. At first, after leaving my warm Southern home, I nearly died from homesickness, and you will not wonder that having met at some place of entertainment in Boston a young gentleman, and having found that he was an honest clerk, occupying a position where he could hope for advancement, I allowed him to address me, and later became engaged to him.

"Soon after the engagement he introduced me to a gentleman who is prominently known throughout the New England States. He is much older than myself.

"From the first time I met him he seemed to exert a powerful influence over me. I loved his wife, and my visits to her made a pleasant break in the tedium of my school work, but as soon as he came home, or I was in his company, I was ill at ease, my mind being filled with an indefinable presentiment of evil. I avoided meeting him alone upon all occasions when it was possible for me to do so, but he would often insist upon accompanying me to my home, and this, owing to their continued courtesies to me, I could not well refuse. All too soon there came a day when I could no longer look into the eyes of either my lover or of those of my betrayer, and for more than a year thereafter I was wholly under the influence of my seducer; so much so, that any and all good resolutions I would make during his absence would vanish upon meeting him again, and my life became one of mental torture to me, for by nature I was a pure-minded girl.

" Our meetings for the most part took place at a hotel near his place of business, a portion of which was available for meetings of this kind, so long as the parties were known to the manager.

" During the year I broke my engagement with my lover, and by so doing apparently deserved his reproaches for heartlessness, although if he could have known it my motive was of an entirely different nature. As though my burden had not at this time been sufficiently heavy for me to bear, about the end of this year I became aware that another and still more terrible calamity was in store for me.

" For days I sat in my room until it seemed I should go mad, and fearing lest I should utterly lose my reason I decided to kill myself, but no one realizes how dear life is until, thinking it worth-less, they have tried to destroy it.

" I could not do it, and there was nothing left for me to do but to go quietly away in a strange place, under a different name, and bear my shame.

"I went to New York, engaged board under the name of Adele Covell, in a quiet portion of the city.

" Physically, I had never been strong, and now followed days and weeks of serious illness until, to save my reason, the life of my unborn child was sacrificed. As soon as I was able I returned to my Texas home, accounting as best I could for my terribly haggard appearance.

" Later, feeling that there was left little that I could do, and being wholly reckless of my future, I prepared for the stage, and for three years I was almost continually before the public. Becoming somewhat ambitious I organized a company, and for a time traveled through the New England towns and small cities under the name of Geraldine Wande.

"This venture cost me between five and ten thousand dollars, and in 1891 I went to Denver, Colorado, as a member of a theatrical company then playing a prominent engagement. There I staid until the burning of the theatre, which caused my engagement to end, and not being able to find another suitable opening, I decided to prepare myself for office work.

"Unfortunately, while in Denver, I attracted the attention of a young man engaged to be married to a lady whom I knew and liked, and rather than to cause them trouble I decided to go elsewhere, though against the wishes of the young man, who, if I had allowed it, would have married me. At about this time my brother, whom I had never seen much of, was killed, or rather died, as the result of a railroad accident at Leadville, Colorado, leaving sister Nannie, who is now teaching in Nudlothean, Texas, and to me, about $400 each, payable about one year after his death.

"I went to Leadville to attend his funeral, and later came here to Chicago, where, until I obtained my position with you, I have been at times really in need of money, as owing to my unfortunate theatrical venture all my ready money has been used, and I now have left only one piece of good real estate in Fort Worth, Texas, valued at $6,000 but encumbered for $1,700.

"A piece of land adjoining my property, of which Mr. Massey has recently written me, can be sold by him for $2,500, besides paying a heavy mortgage standing against it.

"I have also one small, unimproved lot near Dallas, Texas, worth about $200."

During the spring of 1893 I was, if possible, more busy than ever before.

Among other work, preparing my building to rent to a prospective tenant, who would use the entire five stories and forty rooms, at a good rental, if I could get it completed in time for World's Fair purposes.

This left me with little time to attend to my office duties, which gradually Miss Williams took more and more into her own hands, showing a remarkable aptitude for the work. During the first weeks she boarded at a distance, but later, from about the 1st of March until the 15th of May, 1893, she occupied rooms in the same building and adjoining my offices.

Here occasionally meals were served from the restaurant near at hand, and if any bones have really been found in the stove there I think it will later be learned, by microscopical examination, that they are the remnants of such meals. Certain it is that no human being was ever cremated there during my occupancy of the room, my own experience years ago being quite sufficient to show me the danger of such proceedings on account of the awful odor, if I had no other motive to deter me from such a course.

About the first of April I dictated quite a number of urgent letters to parties who were owing me, requesting them to make immediate settlement of their accounts, as I was much in need of the money at this time. Some days later Minnie brought me a draft for about $2,500 and asked me to use it until she should need it, explaining that this was the proceeds of the Texas sale she had previously spoken to me about. I could make good use of the money at that time, but declined to take it until I had explained to her, at some length, more of my business affairs than she had before known. And, finally, I caused to be transferred to her, by warranty deed, a house and lot at Wilmette, Ill., valued at about $7,500, in order that she should be well protected against loss in case of my death.

This money was returned to her about May 10, 1893, from money obtained for this purpose from Isaac R. Hitt & Co., Chicago, who paid it to Miss Williams personally. At about this time she expressed a wish that I should aid her in converting her remaining Southern property into either cash or improved Northern property. This was hard to do, and I finally advised her to execute a worthless deed (by having some one other than herself sign same) to a fictitious person and offer the property for sale at a very low cash figure, and years later, if she chose to do so, to demand an additional sum in exchange for the good deed.

This was done, forging the name upon the deed so made, which deeds are still in existence. When matters had progressed thus far in our various transactions, Miss Williams was taken seriously ill for several days at the house where we were stopping at the time. She suffered from the same form of acute mania that she had been troubled with in New York years before. She was under restraint at this hotel a few days about May 22d, but owing to careful nursing and good medical attendance, she soon became so much better that she could plan intelligently with me what steps were best to be taken for her safety.

It was decided that she should go to the Presbyterian Hospital, near the Clybourne avenue car limits in Chicago, to stay until I could determine if she were in further danger. She entered this institution about May 23, 1893, as a private patient, and her ailment being such that it was prudent for her to pass for a married woman, she was enrolled upon the records there as Mrs. Williams.

The greatest drawback to her improvement here was the fact that she knew she was in an asylum with other insane persons, and she soon begged me to take her to some private

apartments where she could receive special attention. To accomplish this, I hired a house at 1220
Wrightwood avenue, and early in June accompanied Miss Williams there, and during my
absences she was in care of a young woman
hired for this purpose.

Here she rapidly improved, and during the
following months exhibited only once any mani-
acal symptoms, when, owing to some trivial dis-
agreement with her attendants, she so frightened
her that she left at once. At this time Miss
Williams first spoke of inviting her sister to
spend the summer and fall months with us, and in
response to a letter Nannie came from Texas. I

NANNIE WILLIAMS.

met her at the train and found her to be a remarkably quiet and gentle woman—apparently not
very strong—certainly of a most kindly disposition.
The sisters had never lived together for any considerable length of time, and they anticipated
much pleasure in the society of each other.
Minnie had asked that it should appear to her
sister that we were married, and also that nothing
should be said of her recent illness, which she
now, day by day, seemed to be overcoming.

I cannot imagine a happier, quieter life than
they passed there during the month of June and
the first part of July, 1893. I was extremely busy
in the city, but was at the house whenever I
could conveniently arrange it. Minnie had so far
recovered as to attend to several business matters and to aid me in my writing. Among other
things, arrangements were made to convert her
own and her sister's interests in her brother's
estate into money, and to commence certain preliminary proceedings that would ultimately cause
her betrayer in Boston to pay her a considerable
sum, and, to make this easier, it was thought wise
that she obtain some evidence in support of her

claim by wiring to him for a small amount of
money.

This was done, and to this telegram he promptly
responded by sending to her, by wire, $100. At
the time it came to the Western Union office she
was not feeling well enough to go there for
it, and I executed the proper papers, signing
her name in her stead, and next day, to more
fully protect her attorney in the matter, she
executed a supplementary receipt in her own
name. Later in the year it was her intention to
return to Boston and go further with the matter.
Late in June, upon returning one day from my
business in the city, I met and was introduced by
Miss Williams to a Mr. Edward Hatch, whom
she had formerly known during her theatrical life
(he was at that time attending the Columbian
Exposition at Chicago). A few evenings later
he accompanied Minnie, Nannie and myself to the
Exposition.

Early in July it became necessary for Miss
Williams to leave the city for a day, and before
doing so she asked that I come home early and
not allow Nannie to remain alone during the

evening and night. I went with Miss Williams to the cars, and later accompanied her sister as far as the business portion of the city, upon her way to spend the day at the Exposition. That evening I returned to the house at about 6 o'clock, and soon after Nannie also returned. During the previous weeks of Miss Williams' illness, I had been unable to be away from the house at night, and wishing to go out that evening I asked Nannie if she would mind staying in the rooms alone, explaining to her that there were two other families in the house. She replied that she would have no fear, and that being so tired from her day's exertions among the crowds, she felt sure that she would sleep all night.

This being arranged I went away, agreeing to call on my way to the city next morning, and asking her if her sister returned before I did to refrain from telling her I had staid elsewhere, giving to Nannie as my reason for this that her sister would feel annoyed at my leaving her alone. Next morning I reached the house at about 8.30 o'clock, and shortly before Miss Williams returned.

Being in haste to reach the city I welcomed her,
and almost immediately bade them both good-
bye, and taking my bicycle from the hall started
down the street. At this time both sisters were
standing within the doorway of the house.

Quite early in the afternoon, upon returning,
I was surprised to notice the shades at the windows closely drawn. Entering the hall and passing
from thence into the parlor, I was greeted by Miss
Williams screaming to me :—

"Is that you? My God! I thought you
would never come. Nannie is dead!"

She was seated upon the floor holding her
sister's head in her arms, rocking back and forth
and moaning, much as a mother would over a
child that was dying or dead. I did not believe
it at first—I made no effort to do so—looking
upon it as one of the jokes which, when well, she so
liked to indulge in, but a moment later I noticed
the disordered condition of the room, and as my
eyes became accustomed to the darkness, Miss
Williams' terrified face, which good actress though
she was, I knew she could not so successfully
counterfeit.

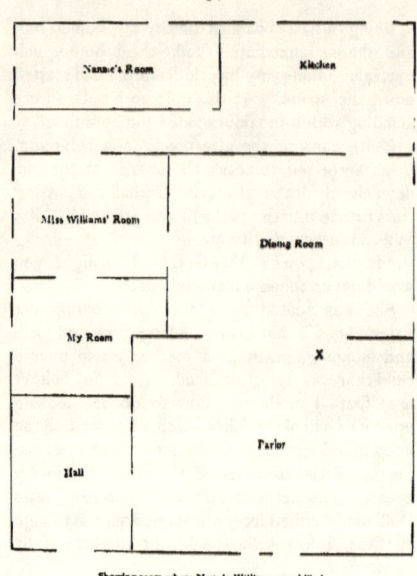

Showing room where Nannie Williams was killed

I was alarmed and instantly was upon my knees beside them, to find to my horror that Nannie had probably been dead for hours. By this time Miss Williams seemed almost as lifeless as her sister, and half leading, half carrying her, I took her to her room and did all I could to restore her, but it was hours before she was in a condition that would allow of her giving me an intelligent account of what had taken place during my absence.

In the meantime I had carried Nannie to my own room, where she lay, looking more like one asleep than dead. The only mark of violence discernable being a slight discoloration upon one of her temples, from which a small quantity of blood had apparently flowed.

Later, in answer to my questions, I gained the following knowledge:—

Upon my leaving the house in the morning, Miss Williams had seized her sister by the arm and ran romping with her through the rooms to the dining room, and without waiting to remove her hat had sat down at the table and drank some coffee, talking to Nannie the while. She had asked her what time I had reached the house the preceding evening, to which question Nannie answered that she did not know, as I was at home when she had herself returned, thus giving the impression that I had been there during the night.

After finishing her lunch, Minnie had passed into her own room, had exchanged her street costume for a house dress, and then, in going to the front portion of the house, had passed through my room, and in doing so had noticed that it had not been occupied during the night.

With this one thought in her disordered mind she had rushed into the adjoining room where her sister then sat, and in a voice, which only the very few who have been intimately acquainted with Miss Williams can appreciate and understand the tragedy of, had said:

"You devil! You have stolen my husband from me."

At the same time she had struck her sister with a small foot-stool, causing her to fall to the floor, where, with hardly a struggle, she had ceased to breathe.

Miss Williams had, at the first moment, run to the lower portion of the house for assistance, but the people being absent for the time being, she had returned, and at first thinking her sister had only fainted, had resorted to all the means of which she knew to resuscitate her. She soon found her efforts useless, and from then until I had arrived, had remained in the position in which I found her.

After this came the terrible question of what steps should be taken. It is useless for me to speak now of what should have been done. What was finally decided upon is as follows :—

I first wished to call in the authorities and explain fully, and also have it known that at the moment the act was committed Miss Williams was not accountable for what she had done. She would not listen to this. Next, I suggested that it should appear that death had resulted from an accidental fall, but to any and all propositions that necessitated a court investigation she would hear nothing, begging me to go to Englewood, and with Patrick Quinlan's aid take the body to some quiet place and bury it.

Finding that the discussion was worrying her into another serious condition, I gave her some medicine, and as soon as I could do so safely, I left her, intending to go to Englewood, and did go as far as Twenty-second street.

There were some reasons why this last mentioned course would have been advantageous, as it was not generally known that I was living with Miss Williams as her husband; and those who did know of it did not know my identity, and to have this matter known, as well as the death of her sister under such distressing circumstances, would have occasioned an amount of notoriety that would have been ruinous to me.

But as I rode towards Englewood, I could see good reasons for not using Quinlan in the matter. His loyalty to me was such that I should not have feared his making it public, but I did not think I had a right to burden him with so terrible a secret.

In fact, it was by never asking him to do any act that he could be held accountable for or that would jeopardize his property that the loyal feeling had been caused to exist.

Leaving the cars at Twenty-second street, I returned to the house, finding Miss Williams still asleep; later we clothed her sister in a light dress she had liked to wear, and taking the large trunk she had brought with her from Texas, I placed her therein as carefully as I could.

No funeral rites were observed; no prayers were said, for I felt that from either of us such would have been a mockery. I also took her small, well-worn Bible (this without Miss Williams' knowledge) and later consigned it with her to her last resting place, which was all I felt at liberty to do. I then went to a livery stable and obtained a covered conveyance, stopping upon my return at the car barns near by, where there were many workmen waiting to take the cars. I engaged one of them to accompany me to the house and help me place the trunk in the carriage.

I then drove to the lake-side, and waited until night had fallen, making it appear to parties noticing me, if any, that I was awaiting the return of some belated boating party. Afterwards, I procured a boat at some distance, and took it near my waiting place, and still later, with considerable difficulty, I placed the trunk in it, and proceeded about one mile from the shore.

There in the darkness, passed beyond the sight of this world, into the ever grasping depths of Lake Michigan, all that was mortal of this beautiful Christian girl ; but from my sight it has never passed, nor has there been a day, an hour, since that awful night that I would not have given my life if by doing so that of Nannie Williams could have been returned.

Upon coming towards the shore I thought it wise to deposit the trunk upon another and more remote portion of the beach. I did this, and, after returning the boat, drove away, and later came back for the trunk.

Upon reaching the house I found Miss Williams more at ease. She had occupied her mind during my absence by collecting and placing in Nannie's room all of her belongings, even those of her own things that her sister had used. She was inclined to talk to me and plan for the future, but for this I had no heart, and little by little, as often as I could do so without exciting

her again, I told her that our life together was
ended.

I did not do this with anger, and agreed to
guard her secret so long as it did not place my
own life in danger. The housekeeping was broken
up, and very shortly thereafter Mr. Hatch took
her to Milwaukee, where she remained in a
private institution until later in the summer. The
cause that had produced her unsound mental
condition had been removed.

Hatch did not know of her sister's death for
months afterward, and then against my advice
was it told to him, he supposing she had returned
to her Texas friends. All of the things that
Minnie had separated from her own were packed
and taken to Englewood and were placed in a
room in the second story, where they were kept
for several weeks until I could obtain time to
dispose of them, when I assorted some of them
and gave them to Pitezel, telling him that they were
some that Miss Williams had sent to his children.
All the others were burned in the large stove in
the third-story office, and this I plainly told the
Philadelphia authorities in the fall of 1894, and

all the subsequent excitement occurred as a direct result of a visit made there by their representative in verification of my statement.

Another trunk, containing pictures and books, was not taken from the express company owing to a mistake in charges, though Miss Williams supposed this had also been disposed of, and this was the one later returned to Fort Worth. Before going to Milwaukee, Miss Williams was in such a nervous condition that only one important step was taken, which was that her people in the South should suppose that she, together with her husband and sister, had gone to Europe or elsewhere, this being made easier inasmuch as some talk had been had earlier of a short fall trip abroad if money matters would allow it.

At about this time there occurred a very severe lake storm, July 18, 1893, doing much damage and it was hoped they would conclude that all had perished during this storm. Certain it is that Miss Williams wrote no more letters to her friends and did not appear publicly in Chicago, if possible to avoid it, in order to carry out this idea, but fortunately for my (our) present safety there are, as

I shall show later. several instances when she did appear and in my company.

While she was in Milwaukee, I did what I could to arrange our business affairs so that neither she nor myself should suffer loss, it being impossible for her to make new transfers of a later date or to go to Texas without abandoning the idea of deceiving her friends there regarding her existence.

I was determined, too, as soon as possible, to sever all my relations with her, deeming it unsafe to continue them, and from time to time I encouraged Hatch in his attentions to her, which he was more willing to bestow than she to accept.

Just here it would not be amiss to return to an exciting incident, which lasted some days, in connection with one of my insurance cases.

It happened shortly after the death of my medical friend and former college chum.

The sad announcement of his death—for to me it was a sad one—set me to thinking. I began to seriously consider the chances of my carrying out the plans which my old friend and I had spent so many anxious days and nights in perfecting.

The prospect was a good one, and I desired, and finally determined, to carry at least one of them to a conclusion, single-handed and alone. No person was to be in my confidence, and I set to work getting my scheme in order.

Some time previous to this I had, while in Minneapolis, insured my life for $20,000 in favor of my wife. Failure in this one instance, where my friend was concerned, made a desperate man of me. I determined to succeed at any cost. The prospective profits in the work were most alluring. The chance for detection, of course, must be guarded against, and the contingencies of all other serious accidents which might arise, and make exposure certain, had to be taken into consideration.

Upon figuring up what the gross proceeds had been in similar operations, the result showed me that, with the very modest outlay of $3.950, they aggregated $68,700. This work one can easily see was profitable beyond any legitimate work that might be entered into.

The assessments having been paid up on my recent $20,000 policy to and including the month of June. 1887, I thought that it was time to bring this case to a close.

In order to realize the $20,000 before September 1st, I accordingly went to Chicago and had a long conversation with an acquaintance of a year before, who was an assistant at —— Medical College, over certain details of my proposed work.

However, I found it more difficult to obtain a body that would prove a substitute for my own. I had a "cow-lick" which could not be imitated by artificial means, and it was absolutely necessary to get a subject so favored by nature, and I had a most gloomy wait, lasting about two weeks, going to the dead room of the college each morning to inspect the "arrivals," which had come in during the preceding twenty-four hours.

Finally, my patience was rewarded, about May 20th, when I was informed that a man had been killed accidentally falling from a freight car. The body in due time arrived, and after making a most minute and critical examination of it, I determined that it was just what I required for my purpose. Satisfactory arrangements having been made with the hospital for my possession of the subject, I started out to ascertain the best way to have it moved.

It was here that a chain of most extraordinary and gruesomely interesting circumstances began. All the precautions that the mind can conceive and the body execute had to be brought into execution. No chance for detection now could be entertained. No loophole for surprise and discomfiture was to be left uncovered; and I had to do all that was vitally necessary to this end alone.

Knowing that I had a most trustworthy friend in a certain expressman, I at once repaired to his abode. My surprise and discomfiture were great. He was dead. He had died some time previously. All hope for assistance in that quarter, naturally, had to be given up.

From inquiries I made of the janitor of the college, I learned that a certain expressman in the neighborhood could be employed for the purpose I desired, as he had on former occasions been hired for "outside work" by some of the men in the institution,

I called at this man's address, and after seeing him I stated my business. "How much
will you charge me for taking a body from ——
College to Polk Street Station?" I asked.

"Five dollars," was the reply this man gave
me.

This price being satisfactory to me, we started
for the place where I had ordered a trunk to be
made according to a special design. This trunk
was one of more than ordinary large size, and
externally it resembled one of those iron-bound,
burglar-proof arrangements jewelry salesmen call
sample cases. Inside, the construction was of a
very elaborate nature.

The greater portion of it being occupied by a
large zinc box of sufficient dimensions to allow a
man to occupy it by doubling his joints, where
doubling was necessary. This was fitted by a lid
of wood to deaden any sound that might be caused
through the possible rattling of the ice, which was
to surround the inner box. The entire trunk was
made water-proof, but who knows how it could
travel on a railroad train without undergoing
severe usage, and possible demolition?

The trunk was taken to the college, the body placed in it with the aid of the expressman, who did not seem to relish that sort of work. He seemed to weaken at times, and once or twice I noticed him grow pale. After the trunk was carefully packed and ready for conveyance to the station, we found that it was almost too early to remove it.

After standing about for some time, the Jehu grew more courageous, inasmuch as he gazed through a few inverted liquor glasses when their contents were amber-lined. He said :—

"I can't do this job for $5."

"Why not?" I asked, very much surprised.

"Because, if I make a hearse of my wagon and personally act as combination driver, undertaker and pall-bearer, I must have $35. If I don't get that sum, I shall inform the police that all is not right."

Of course I expostulated with the man, and resorting, as often before, to my sugar-and-fly policy, I placated him, gave him $5 in cash and promised the other $30 when we reached the station.

This was all right, for he said if I did not pay he would have me arrested instantly.

In due course of time the trunk was carted to the Illinois Central Station, and, after having it placed on the platform, the driver turned to me and demanded the $30 forthwith.

This was the chance I had been waiting for.

"I shall not give you another cent," said I.

"Oh, yes, you will!"

"Besides, I have a mind to demand the return of the $5 from you for attempting to extort money from me."

"You would stand a great chance of getting it, too. Now, give me $30 or to the 'cops' I go."

"You may go, but first listen to me and answer my questions. Did you not, in the presence of the janitor and myself, help place the corpse in the trunk? Did you not haul it here? Have you not assisted me in all this work?"

"Yes, I have."

"That man was murdered. Speak a word about it to any one, and I will have you arrested as an accessory to his murder."

The driver was evidently very much frightened, as his eyes widened and bulged, and his hair began to assume a perpendicular position.

"The body must go in the lake," I continued, "and let the waves bury it forever from human sight. I hope you understand me."

Then he told me that he did not want any more money, and as I knew his address, he would always be at my service at any future time.

Having purchased my ticket for the timber lands of Michigan, I checked my trunk, and it began its adventurous trip North.

Everything had gone along as well as I could have wished until our train was nearing Grand Rapids. My attention was attracted to a group of trainmen standing about a trunk in the baggage section which occupied the forward part of the smoker in which I was traveling.

I got up and looked closer, and was almost stricken dumb with horror when I saw that it was my trunk, and that the men were talking as though they suspected something wrong with it.

I immediately changed my plans about going North directly, and was in a feverish state of excitement when we reached Grand Rapids. As soon as the trunk was deposited in the baggage room, I went in as though to claim it. As I did so, I noticed a stranger looking at me and on the trunk in a manner which made me feel quite uncomfortable. I pretended not to notice him, and thereby got a better chance to study him. I soon concluded that he was a Secret Service man, and that I had been "spotted."

Realizing that some decisive and telling action was necessary at this time, I stepped to the telegraph office and wired myself at the hotel, as follows :—

"Holmes. Look after my trunk, which left Chicago this morning.
(Signed)   HARVEY."

The initial "H" was the same as that on my trunk, and when I got to the hotel, I showed the clerk the telegram, which he held for me, and engaged communicating rooms for Harvey and myself, with a bath attachment. I sent a porter for the trunk, and after seeing it in the rooms, I then learned the cause which attracted the attention of the trainmen to it. My suspicions had been confirmed, for an awful odor emanated from the trunk, and I then knew that the man had been dead longer than the college attendants stated, and, also, that I had been imposed upon.

Fearing that such a contingency might arise, I formulated a plan while on the smoking car of transferring the body from the Chicago trunk to another, which I should purchase.

After locking my room carefully, I started out to look for a suitable trunk, but stopped long enough to tell the clerk that my baggage would be on hand in the course of an hour or so. It was growing toward evening, and I had but little time to spare.

After looking about for a short while, I soon got a used trunk that suited my purpose quite well. I ordered the lock to be changed on it, and while this was being done I made several trips to a couple of plumbing shops and bought a considerable quantity of old lead pipe. I had this cut up into suitable lengths, and made into packages. I made several trips to the trunk store, and each time I placed a package of the heavy material in the new trunk, after which I had it sent to my room at the hotel. This was done to make it appear that it was filled with my effects.

The day had been warm, and the night also promised to be sultry. No time was to be lost in getting things in order and to guard against surprises.

During my several trips to the trunk store I noticed the man I first saw at the Grand Rapids Station was looking after me, and I was placed on my guard.

As I said, the night was going to be warm; I knew that it would be but a short time until all the floor I occupied would be permeated with the odor from my friend in the trunk.

I went out again and secured a water-proof hunting bag, and carried a considerable amount of ice to the room, which I placed in the bath tub.

I then took the lead pipe from my new trunk and laid it beside the first one in the adjoining room.

While doing this work the atmosphere became so stifling that I had to hoist the window. This window opened out on the roof of a porch, and by the time that was done it had grown quite dark.

I decided to defer further work until after I had eaten.

As I entered the dining room I could see the eye of that mysterious stranger watching me in the reflection of the mirror from the bar.

I was somewhat troubled at this, and I did not enjoy my dinner very well.

After my repast, I lounged out to the office and then went to my room.

I went to the bath room first, drained the water from the ice, and prepared a place for the dead man to lie in. When this was done to my satisfaction, I went to the trunk my supposed friend was to occupy and opened it. The usual balancing and cording precautions which I had taken were all right, but the face that met my gaze was drawn, colored and hideous, yet it somewhat resembled the outlines of my own when I first secured the body.

The sight was disgusting, yet when I looked upon it, and realized that at least $20,000 would come to me after a little further trouble, I gazed on it as a very good investment which was about to mature.

The monetary possibilities of this work set me thinking, and yet I knew I had in this instance to work rapidly. I loosed the cords, raised the body, and carried it to the bath tub, where I sought to freeze it hard enough for another day's transportation.

There, in the twinkling light of a solitary gas jet, lay all that was mortal of—I knew not whom.

I claimed him as my own, and as I studied the now rigid form, strange questions arose and floated across my mind.

Who was he? What had he been? Was he a father, a lover, or brother? Was his absence from home noted? Was he cared for? Or, was he, like myself, a wayward son? Such thoughts troubled me but little before, and yet, as he lay there on his frozen bed, I, seemingly fascinated by the awful solemnity of death, did not seem able to tear myself away.

The gas flickered, a door slowly opened, and before I knew what had transpired, I was given the opportunity of looking straight into the eyes of the mysterious stranger—the Secret Service man—over the glittering barrel of a death-dealing weapon.

Not a word was spoken, but our eyes instinctively turned towards the object in the bath tub.

"Consider yourself under arrest, sir," said the nocturnal intruder.

"I am at your service," I replied, knowing that it would be useless to try conclusions with that man in such a small room.

While he was getting some iron bracelets out of his pocket, I mentally determined to have him in the street, glad enough to get away from me and my rooms.

I was ready for him when he walked out into the next room ; he keeping his pistol leveled at me with one hand, and trying to get his handcuffs out with the other.

By the merry little twinkle in his eye I read his character as though it lay printed before me on an open page. It was part of my game, and I intended to play my hand as well as I knew how. He seemed to hold a good one, too, but as I had the greatest bower—money—I knew that it was worth the while to play it as best I could.

Desperate, indeed, did my situation become when I saw that he had a companion awaiting us in the room, and a glance at the window explained how their entrance had been effected.

As we got into the chamber the man with the pistol, who was much larger than his associate, looked at me and winked.

"John, go to the station house, and wait until I send for you; but do not say anything until you get word," my captor said to the other.

No sooner had the man called "John" gotten out on the porch roof than the other turned to me with:—

"This is a nice sort of a business, and I have entrapped you neatly in it. It looks very much like the rope for you."

"My dear sir, you will let me explain, I hope. This man was my brother. He has just died of a malignant and very contagious disease. He had been sent to a medical college for dissection, and when I learned of it, I determined to save the body from the demonstrator's knife. Come, look again, and see if you cannot discern a family resemblance?"

As I was talking, the man drew back, and, at my invitation, turned an ashen color. His hands trembled, and as they dropped listlessly the pistol fell to the floor and exploded with a loud report.

Critical as the moment was, it was time for me to act, and I made a successful effort to get the weapon, and as I did so, I ordered him to go to the window and save his life if it was of any value to him.

He lost no time, and as his form disappeared over the ledge of the porch I fired a shot into the air.

This of course brought the landlord and several guests to my door, which I opened in response to repeated knockings.

I was very much excited, apparently, and called out, " There, see, there he goes." The crowd of half-dressed men and women rushed to the window and gave me a chance to close the bathroom door. Heavens, but I did breathe more easily! The escape was a narrow one, but I succeeded in allaying suspicion by saying that the man had attempted burglary, and as I shot he jumped from the roof.

The figure of a running man was discernible in the darkness when they were at the window, which had the effect of verifying my explanations.

After they had gone the landlord offered me the use of another room, which I, of course, declined.

Now my real hard work was to begin. The man was apparently satisfied that I had told the truth, yet he had a suspicious look which I did not like.

As early as possible in the morning, I packed my own trunk with the lead pipe, and to leave that of the fictitious Harvey, while I took my dead friend from his frigid resting place, and repacked him in the new trunk. Upon going to breakfast, I explained that I must go to a place which was somewhat distant, on the early train; but would leave my friend's trunk in the room, as he was expected at any time.

Therefore I had the porter take the newly-packed trunk to the station, where he bought me a ticket and had the trunk checked to my pretended destination.

I timed myself to get to the station just as the train was going out, and as the coast seemed clear, I boarded the smoker.

I knew if the detective missed me, he would go at once to the hotel, and if he found my trunk there he would naturally wait around for an hour or so, thus giving me a pretty good start of him.

When about thirty miles from Grand Rapids I got off to get a paper. The newstand was next to the Western Union Telegraph office, and as I looked over the operator's shoulder, he received the following message :—

"Look out for man and black trunk. Left here this A. M. Arrest and hold him."

I may have looked queerly, but I inquired in a natural way, how far it was to ———, my destination.

"Forty-eight miles," was the reply of the operator; and without raising his eyes, he called a boy to take the message to the station policeman.

But he was too late. The train started, I swung on, and immediately got hold of the baggage porter. I showed him my ticket, and asked him to put my trunk off at the next station, which was but eight miles distant. This he did, and it was a dismal place, indeed. When I got off the train it was raining. It had been raining hard, evidently, all night. The mud was hub deep on the lumber wagons, and the prospect of stopping there was not a pleasant one.

I learned, upon making inquiries, that I could get to a little town fifteen miles distant, which connected with another railroad, and to do this I would have to drive. I determined to go, however, as the detective, no doubt, would haunt every station between Grand Rapids and my destination until he got some trace of me, when he would learn that I had gotten away from him.

It was with difficulty that I secured a conveyance, which I did in the evening, as I did not want a driver, because I knew the trunk had become troublesome again on account of the odor of my dead companion.

Having carefully attached the trunk to the rear of a back-number buck-board, a dismal trip was begun. As I said, I had considerable difficulty in getting the rig, and as it was I had to leave a deposit large enough to buy several of that particular kind.

After seven hours of the worst riding it has been my misfortune to endure, I reached a small town from which a combination freight and passenger train was about to leave. It was one of those accommodating trains. I "saw" the conductor, who agreed to hold the train for half an hour.

This delay was for the purpose of giving me a chance to freshen my subject up a little. Ice was not procurable, and as there was no drug store in the town, I went down to the grocery store, got the proprietor up and bought several bottles of ammonia, which, when combined with one or two other simple things, made a solution that rendered my quiet friend quite acceptable so far as one's olfactories were concerned.

This operation of attempted preserving was done in the privacy of the baggage car, and all went well until we got about three miles from town. Through the negligence of some section hands a rail was left without the fish-plate being bolted on, and the whole train was ditched.

The engineer was killed, and the conductor was badly injured, as also were two or three passengers. I escaped through a window, and after helping some of the injured who needed surgical attendance, I went to the baggage car. It was a wreck. So was most of the baggage. My trunk and one or two others were intact, and while awaiting the arrival of the relief train and wrecking crew, my thoughts again got to wandering.

There was a score of us. Some were injured, one dead, and all of us anxious. The morning was just breaking; the rain had ceased to fall; and, as I looked away down the railroad, I could just distinguish a cloud of steam and smoke, through the fog, which showed the approach of a train.

Something seemed to tell me that I was about to be confronted with some disagreeable occurrence, and, in anticipation of this premonition becoming a fact, I quickly hauled my trunk to a little shed used by workmen, and impatiently awaited the wrecker. Therefore, I was not astonished when I saw that the first man to alight was my friend, the detective of Grand Rapids. He also saw me, but seemed to pay very little attention to me, as he knew I could not escape, for by this time it was broad daylight, and no trains coming or going.

Finally he accosted me, and we entered into "an agreement" to have my trunk taken to the junction of the road, which was done to my entire satisfaction, and, I have every reason to think, to his also. Just what that little agreement cost me I am not at liberty to say, for that officer still lives.

It was a dark and dreary day when I got into the wild wildernesses of Northern Michigan's lumber tracts. I was soon established in a hut, and it shortly became known that I was a lumber operator of considerable means, and was regarded with much consideration by the hardy hewers of trees and strippers of bark. The men were all honest, it seemed. So one day I went out in the evergreen forest and failed to return.

A week or so later what was purported to be my dead body was found pinioned to the earth by a fallen tree. Money and papers were found in the clothes on the body which established my identity beyond the question of a doubt.

Thus, by case No. 5, after a great deal of trouble and thrilling escapes from the law's officers, I added the neat little sum of $20,000 to my bank accer. '. by September 1st, as I had anticipated.

When I had finished with the trunk I presented it to a friend, but at the time did not tell to what use it had been put.

Some years afterwards I met him at his home, and told him all about it. Then he and his wife declared that often they had found it open—no one having touched it—when both declared it had been closed and locked the day previous.

One day in July, 1893, I met an old friend upon the street. I had not seen him for nearly two years, and I noticed at once that he had not prospered since I last saw him. I asked him to accompany me to lunch, and upon inquiry, he told me that his only means of support at that time consisted of what he could earn as a solicitor for the Fidelity Insurance Company of Philadelphia, and he asked me if I could not carry some insurance in his company, to which I replied that I was carrying all I felt able to pay for.

I gave him, however, the names of several parties whom he was to visit, some of whom he later insured. I invited him to come to the office and accompany me to lunch whenever he was in that part of the city, and later, at his solicitation, I abandoned the company in which I had been insured, and allowed him to place a policy for me with his company for two reasons: *first*, that he might be benefited by the premiums I paid; *second*, upon his showing me the advantages they offered. Considerably later, having exhausted all my resources so far as finding him customers was concerned, we were standing within the Chamber of Commerce Building, Chicago, when Pitezel, just returning from a successful Southern lumber trip, came in; and not having seen my friend for quite awhile, they talked for some time together, and finally he asked Pitezel if he could not carry some insurance. Pitezel answered that he did not care to do so then.

Up to that time Pitezel's insurance record was as follows: Upon all long trips, his instructions

were to take out temporary insurance at the time
he bought his transportation ticket or mileage,
making the policies in favor of his family, and at
my expense. He had occasionally carried yearly
accident insurance, and upon one occasion some
regular life insurance in the Washington Life Co.
Soon after this meeting with Pitezel, my friend
asked me to try and induce him to take some in
his company. Pitezel was about to receive several hundred dollars, the greater part of which I
knew would, in a very few days, be wasted, and
considering the great help it would be to my
friend during the coming winter, I decided to
induce Pitezel to insure, telling my friend beforehand my reasons for doing so, and instructing
him to place no more insurance than Pitezel
would pay cash for at the time.

Later, a policy was issued for $10,000, for
which a cash premium was paid. This policy differed very materially from one I should have
chosen, if any fraud had been anticipated at the
time. After this I do not think insurance was
again mentioned between Pitezel and myself for
six months.

MRS. PITEZEL.

My first intimate acquaintance with Mrs.
Pitezel and her children began in the fall of 1893,
although I had often seen them prior to that,
especially the children, whom I liked and looked
upon as remarkably bright when they had come
to me from time to time upon errands. At this
time Pitezel had gone to Indiana on some lumber
business there among the farmers, and to aid him
in establishing a credit, had taken with him some
worthless checks to carelessly exhibit among his
money, thus having it appear that he was a man
of considerable means and worthy of credit in
his business.

While under the influence of liquor he either
lost or tried to use one of these checks or drafts,
resulting in his being arrested.

This necessitated my making three special trips
to Terre Haute, where his arrest occurred, and
during this time a part of his family being sick,
it was also necessary for me to visit them often
as well. In November, 1893, I met Miss
Williams by appointment at a hotel, where I
made some preliminary arrangements that resulted later, after several more visits, in her

accepting collateral security for all her real estate holdings in Texas, they being valueless to her for the reasons previously given.

The last of these visits took place in Detroit in December, 1893 (nearly six months after the death of her sister), since which time I have not personally seen her. At the time of this visit a final settlement was reached. I told her, after having reached such a settlement, that I was very shortly to be married. This created so severe a scene that she not only threatened my life, but that of my prospective wife as well. These threats ceased only when I told her I should, upon my return to Chicago, give to the authorities the details of the tragedy that had occurred there in July.

The next day she seemed as pleasant as usual, and planned her own future course, which consisted in opening a massage establishment in a London hotel, Hatch to help her in conducting the enterprise.

About the middle of February I sent to her, from Fort Worth, $1,750, which, when deducted from my previous indebtedness due her, left me

still considerably in her debt. This was secured
by the Wilmette property, the title to which it
was agreed she should hold until all was paid. I
left Miss Williams in Detroit, apparently well
pleased with her business arrangements, and at
least passably satisfied that the many other matters between us had been settled.

Early in January, 1894, I sent Pitezel to Fort
Worth, instructing him to sell the real estate
there which previously had been conveyed to
Benton T. Lyman, whom Pitezel was to personate,
it not being safe for him to act in his own name
on account of his recent trouble in Terre Haute,
Ind. He did not succeed in readily finding a
purchaser, and later in the same month, having
been married in the meantime, I joined him there
to aid him in his work. I had given Pitezel careful
instructions as to his conduct while away, but I
found upon reaching Fort Worth that he had not
been governed by them. My first duty was to
remove him from the boarding place he had
chosen to one in a more respectable quarter, but
the mischief had already been accomplished, and
he was known by that time throughout the town

as a liberal, free and easy drinking man, who, it
was understood, had considerable property.

A party owning property adjoining that which
we wished to sell had need of a portion of ours,
but would not buy, depending upon renting it at a
very small figure, as he had been doing heretofore. In order to force him to buy I directed
Pitezel to withdraw his offer, and remain wholly
away from him, quietly survey our lot, and proceed to excavate a portion of it, having it understood that he was about to erect a large building,
covering all of the ground. Our neighbor was
fully as crafty as ourselves, and not until we had
caused elaborate drawings to be prepared by an
architect, and some foundation laid encroaching
upon the portion he needed, did he conclude to
buy, and at a figure about twice what it was
worth. With a portion of this money, the old encumbrance of $1,700, that had existed against the
property, was paid. Then having had some tempting offers from prospective tenants, a larger loan
was made and the building later nearly completed.

While the building was in progress there came
to us a forlorn looking object, begging for work,

and out of charity we gave him some light labor to do. He grew stronger as soon as he procured food. Later he confided to me that he had recently been released from serving a ten-year term in a Southern prison.

I had at first called him "Mascot," which name clung to him thereafter, though I think his real name was Caldwell.

Early in March Pitezel came to me one morning to say that the day before while drunk he had been induced by some of the disreputable associates he had formed at his former boarding place to marry a woman of doubtful character, an adventuress some said, and that as soon as he became sober had come to me. He threatened to shoot both the woman and himself. I had him watched carefully for a few days, until I had reasoned him out of this idea. A little later I sent him home to his family in Chicago. He had in the meantime lived with this woman, and they were known as Mr. and Mrs. Lyman.

Upon reaching Chicago he did some work there, and in St. Louis where he afterwards went. He finally met me about May 1st, at Denver,

where I had gone to prepare papers with which
to secure a loan of $16,000 upon this Fort Worth
building. I needing his signature to the papers,
inasmuch as the property was (and still is) in his
fictitious name, Lyman, upon meeting him in
Denver, I wished to proceed at once to the Court
House to have the necessary papers acknowledged, but he told me had, while away, devised
a plan whereby he could not only gain $10,000,
but at the same time forever do away with any
fear of prosecution or trouble in consequence of
his marriage in Fort Worth—a matter which had
perpetually worried him.

I had times without number listened to his
visionary schemes for obtaining vast wealth upon
a day's notice, usually in connection with some
new patent, until such matters had become a joke
between us.

So I said to him, "Well, Col. Sellers, what is
it now?" He replied that it was one of my
own inventions, and if I would go to the hotel
with him, he would tell me of it. He seemed so
much in earnest that I, although in a great hurry,
went with him.

His plan was this (I should say here that several years before, while making a Southern lumber trip with him, he had taken up some of the tedious hours of the journey in telling me of his wild gold-mining experiences, and, in reciprocation, I had told him something of my medical experience, including a part of the frustrated insurance scheme): He wished to hire an office in one of the highest buildings in Denver, having it understood that he was to use it as a wholesale book agent's office; that he should buy an awning to protect the room from the sun, and while placing it in position upon the outside of the window it should appear that he had fallen into the area way below, wishing me to have shipped to him from Chicago, or elsewhere, a body which he could use to aid in the fraud.

I do not think we talked of the matter to exceed fifteen minutes. He was accustomed to accept my judgment upon matters of importance without much hesitancy. I proceeded to give him several reasons why his plan was not a feasible one, principal among which was the fact that at the present time insurance companies are too

well equipped and too much upon the alert not
to detect this kind of fraud, nearly all of them
having a corps of private detectives. Among
other reasons I gave him was one he very well
knew, that theretofore, when I had thought it
wise to indulge in business transactions that were
not strictly legitimate, I had always insisted upon
two conditions being carried out:—

First, that such proceedings should be outside
the regular beaten track followed by ordinary
disreputable schemers, for in consequence thereof
those engaged in them were closely watched.
Second, that all such acts should stop short of
anything that was punishable by either a large
fine or imprisonment.

There was another reason I had for not
entering into this fraud at that time, if no others
had existed, I did not tell him of it, namely,
that during the previous years he had been
worth to me much more than $10,000 per
year, and I could not afford to have him place
himself in such a position as would necessarily be
the case if this were carried out where I could
not further use him. His idea in regard to this

had been to go to South America and later have his family join him there.

Having dismissed the matter, I went on with my real estate work, and as soon as the papers were executed, returned to Fort Worth, Pitezel going back to St. Louis to attend to some work there.

Upon reaching Fort Worth, I found that some to whom money was owing had filed mechanics' and furnishers' liens against the property, and this so alarmed the party who was to have made the large loan that he withdrew from his agreement, and this resulted in a large number of the other creditors becoming alarmed, some two or three proposing to cause my arrest for having obtained the material for the building under false pretenses of payment.

I had never been arrested, and I had the same horror of it that I would of being shot. Especially terrible seemed the methods prevalent in the South, where I had seen, from time to time, convicts chained together, with hardly any clothing, and if I could believe the reports our "Mascot" had given us, with less food and more inhuman

treatment than was accorded the slaves of that
region forty years ago.

I therefore raised what money I could, paying
all of it, save $200, to the poorer laborers who
had worked for me, and immediately left the city,
intending to secure the loan in St. Louis or
Chicago.

From time to time, during my residence in
Fort Worth, I had bought from different parties
six good horses, paying for them, it is true, for
the most part with notes guaranteed by Lynam
as the owner of the real estate there. I make no
claim that these notes have been paid, but I do
claim that the transactions were lawful, that no
mortgage or other encumbrance existed against
any of the horses, but they were, however, subject
to attachment by any parties whom I was owing,
and to avoid this I instructed "Mascot" to take
them to Denison, Texas, and ship them from
there to St. Louis.

Upon reaching Denison he shipped five of the
horses, but failed to accompany them himself, or
to send $300 worth of other material, including
much of my clothing, one carriage, a watch I had

loaned him, and $80 cash given him to pay the freight upon the stock; nor did I hear from him again until July, 1895, when, as an inmate of an Arkansas prison, he was willing in exchange for his liberty to tell of matters of which he could not have known even had they existed.

After reaching St. Louis, I immediately tried to negotiate the loan I had failed to secure in the South. Pitezel was feeling much annoyed at my failure there, for he had expected a rather more liberal payment therefrom than he had received during the few preceding months, owing to the fact that while he had been in Texas it had been necessary, in order to appear that he was the owner there, that he should carry the bank account in his name, and before he had known it, during his drunkenness, he had been robbed little by little of nearly $1,000. Therefore, when I told him that we should be short of money for some time longer, he again advocated the insurance scheme, saying that it could be carried out in the Southern Lumber Co.

He felt sure, and finally, against my better judgment, I told him we would take a trip to the region he had spoken of, partly upon lumber business and partly to look over the ground in connection with the insurance work. He was as pleased as a child, and all his morose feelings vanished at once. We first went down the Mississippi River to visit a lumber tract that had been offered to me the year before upon very easy terms, hoping to buy it, using some Chicago securities as payment, and by selling at once to raise the money we so much needed at Fort Worth. We found upon reaching our destination that this tract had been sold. We then went East to the Tombigbee River in search of another similar tract, and here Pitezel wished to have it appear that while he was traveling upon horseback through the extensive swamps he had met his death accidentally, or had been killed for what money he was supposed to have carried. He was known in that locality under his own name, having transacted a number of legitimate lumber deals there the year before. After wandering with Pitezel for several days through those swamps, being eaten by fleas and terrified by snakes, he walking ahead, as he said, to drive

:hem away, but, as I later found, to escape their anger by passing out of their reach, leaving them for me to contend with, I flatly refused to go farther with the scheme, but told him instead that I would interest some of the planters in a canning factory.

With the machinery which I was able to furnish from Chicago I felt sure that, before sixty days, we could realize $15,000 in cash and lumber therefrom. He would not hear to it, however, and opposed me more strongly than I had ever known him to do previously. He told me that at that time he was liable to arrest in Kansas, in Terre Haute, Ind., and Fort Worth, Texas, and that since his domestic trouble some years before in Chicago he had cared less than ever, and he had been determined ever since he left Texas, where he had drank more heavily than before (which also worried him), that he would leave the country, and now, if he could not do so, he would, upon my refusal to go on, go through with his scheme alone. His words were, "I can furnish a body, and, the way I feel now, I do not care how quickly I do it." Seeing how downhearted

he was I complained no more, but talked with him
of other things, and finally told him that I would
next day go to Mobile, and if I could procure a
suitable body there, would return with it. If not,
I should go direct from Mobile to St. Louis, where
he must join me, and, after doing some work
there, we would go to Chicago and organize a
company among certain lumber firms we knew,
and return South later and make what money we
could by exchanging this stock and machinery for
the canning factory into lumber and other products. I therefore left him, as he supposed, to go
to Mobile. This I did not do, and have never
been in that city in my life. I returned at once
to St. Louis and, after a little delay, wrote to Pitezel that it had been impossible to obtain what I
needed South and for him to join me at once.
Nearly two weeks' delay occurred before he came.
His wife had been receiving letters from him that
he was sick during this time.

Later, after his death, I learned that upon receiving my letter that I could not do any more
in the insurance matter he had made an effort to
take his life at the hotel of Henry Rodgers, at

Perkinsville, Ala., and for days, as a result of this ineffectual attempt, he was sick there, as he was later at the Gilmer House, at Columbus, Miss. As soon as I reached St. Louis I found that all efforts towards securing a loan there were useless, and being nearly out of money, owing to my having paid out so much before leaving Fort Worth, I had to look sharply about for some immediate source of revenue. I finally bought and took possession of a drug store in that city, paying for it with notes secured by a chattel mortgage and some other securities. Owing to the negligence of the firm of whom I bought, this mortgage was not recorded, and upon Pitezel reaching the city I sold to him all my right, title and interest (this being the wording of the bill of sale) in the store, which he immediately mortgaged for a considerable sum.

For this transaction I was arrested and confined in the St. Louis jail for several days until, although I perhaps could, by a legal fight, have shown that I had a right to sell the store under these circumstances, it became clear to me that it was safer to settle the matter, which was done.

My arrest occurred on a Saturday evening, and from then until Monday morning I was confined in the receiving portion of the jail, below the level of the street, and these few hours of my first imprisonment were far more trying to me than my subsequent experiences of like nature have been.

Here, all through that long, hot Sunday, all classes of prisoners, both male and female, were brought together, and allowed to indulge in the most filthy and obscene talk.

And at the open windows, opening directly upon the sidewalk, all day and far into the night, a crowd was standing, more than half of whom were tiny children, eagerly drinking in each word that was said. The next morning I had handcuffs placed upon my wrists, and was taken into Court and later into the jail proper, where better discipline was enforced. Here I was consigned to a very small iron cage (I know no better name for it), one of about three hundred, ranged tier above tier around a large area in which all, or nearly all, the prisoners are allowed to exercise together during certain hours of the day. Here were to be seen many noted criminals, who were soon pointed out to me as "This is so and so, who is to be hung upon such a date." (About thirty murderers, one of whom was the prison barber, who if you paid him ten cents, would shave you with a very dull razor, while if you paid him more he would use a sharp one; and as I sat in his chair, I could not help thinking that which ever one he used was plenty sharp enough for him to commit one more murder with, if he chose, and I therefore directed him to use his sharpest razor at a price above his own figure, very much as I would have held out a tempting piece of meat to a vicious dog which I feared was about to bite me.)

Or, "That is the notorious forger or confidence man," as the case might be. Among others was one, a noted train robber then serving an eighteen years' sentence, and who a short time previously had become more notorious by a nearly success-ful attempt at escape from the prison. He is a young man, whom, to meet upon the street, one would suppose to be a bright mechanic or a farmer. He is very intelligent, and I took much interest in talking with him. He told me of the case that had resulted in his arrest; of his subsequent trial, and remarked that Blank & Blank in St. Louis were his attorneys ; to which I replied that but for the fact of the senior members of the firm being absent on a vacation they would have been my attorneys as well, I having first sent for them, and finding this to be the case had employed Judge Harvey instead.

He afterwards asked me if, upon leaving the prison, I could not contribute $300, which, together with some other money he could obtain, would give him his liberty by bribing one of the keepers, making a claim that he had successfully done so before. My answer was, that at the present time I had less ready money than had been the case for years previously, owing to my having invested so much in the South. I told him if I could arrange to aid him later I would do so, but I made no engagement with him to furnish me with an attorney for the insurance work as has been claimed, for I was already acquainted with the firm.

The balance of my short stay in this prison was taken up by my reading "Les Miserables," a peculiarly interesting volume to me under the circumstances, and I judge it was to all prisoners who cared for reading, as was evidenced by the condition of the book itself, which I obtained from the prison library. I was also entertained by watching a huge negro being prepared to meet his death by hanging, by having alternately administered to him spiritual consolation from his confessors, large quantities of cigars to smoke, food to eat and liquor or beer to drink. A so-called death watch was kept also, but not so stringent but that he was allowed to go alone to the front of the compartments occupied by his favorite companions, and talk at some length with them.

Next morning, upon looking from my laticed window across into the court yard, I saw him meet his death upon the gallows in the presence of a large and morbidly curious crowd of people. If I had been in need of any warning to deter me from almost immediately placing myself in a similar position, I know of no stronger one that I could have received than to witness this man's death struggles, to see the crowd making light of it, and almost before he was dead quarreling to possess small portions of the rope which sent his soul hence, and, I think, of his clothes. Gruesome relics they were, indeed.

Upon the day I was liberated from this place of confinement, I visited first my own attorney and later Blank & Blank, in the same street, at which time the following conversation took place. Entering the office, and having explained who I was, I said :—

"I have called on you to perhaps make some arrangements that will aid in securing the liberty of your client," to which one of the firm to whom I spoke, replied, "I guess you have made a mistake in the office; I know nothing in regard to the matter." I said, "I am sure I have made no mistake in the office, and furthermore, have seen either you or your brother talking to him at the prison. However, my visit to you was to aid your client, and of no immediate value to me, and I have no desire to force the recognition of your client upon you, and will therefore bid you good day." Upon my withdrawing to the door, he followed me, and said, "Wait a moment; I

will go down to the prison and see what my client
means; you come here again, shortly."

I replied that I should be in Judge Harvey's
office, and upon his return he could call there if
he wished to talk further with me. I would then
accompany him to his office. He did call for me,
and upon reaching his private office was willing
and ready to talk. Our conversation resulted in
my placing in his hands for collection nearly $500
worth of good accounts, authorizing him to apply
$300 of the proceeds to the robber's use. I
also gave him my Chicago address, in case he
wished to write me.

As I was leaving his office he said, " My client
wished me to ask you, if he succeeds in gaining
his liberty, if you will aid him in a certain piece
of bank work he wishes to do." I replied that it
was wholly out of my line, and I should be of no
more service to him in such work than a dead
man; moreover, my recent imprisonment had
shown me the necessity of being even more careful to avoid laying myself liable to arrest in the
future, but that I would furnish the chloroform
and nitroglycerine he needed upon my arrival in

Chicago, and have it placed in a safe place with a suit of clothes and other articles we had planned during our interview, and possibly might aid him later in disposing of certain bonds and stocks he expected to gain possession of; but that there would be ample time to plan for that after he had gained his liberty, for which I would watch the papers closely.

Upon this I left his office, and started for Chicago the same evening, where I had previously sent Pitezel to commence arrangements among the lumber men whom he knew for the formation of the stock company before mentioned. I reached Chicago August 1, 1894, and upon calling upon my attorney there and also my agent, both assured me that it was dangerous for me to stay in Chicago, as there were then Fort Worth parties there looking for me, and forming an alliance with some persons whom I was owing to cause my arrest, and thereby force me to procure the money due them.

My attorney instructed me to go elsewhere if I thought sufficient money could be made to satisfy these debts and organize my company, and upon my asking him where I should go, he told me that either New York or New Jersey were favorable States in which to organize companies to do business elsewhere. Having other business in New York I decided to go there, though under a different name, lest the granting of a charter to a company of which I was an officer should, by being published, be noticed by the Fort Worth parties.

I suggested to Pitezel that he should finish some patents, one of which I wished to use in this company, and it was later decided that he should go with me to New York to act as one of the incorporators and to work upon his patents in some small shop he was to hire for the purpose. Before leaving Chicago he reminded me that his insurance premium would be due before our return, and wished me to give him the money to pay it before he went away, remarking that he still thought I would be glad to fall back upon this plan of getting money after my company had failed me. I told him that, owing to the stringency of our money matters, I had allowed my own insurance to lapse and wished he would do the same. He was not willing to do this, advancing, besides the reason already given, that while it was safe for me to allow my insurance to lapse, as I had other things with which to protect those dependent upon me in case of my death, he had little or nothing. He also knew that I had collected a considerable sum of money since coming to Chicago, and could, if necessary, give him what was needed. I finally settled the matter to his satisfaction in the following manner: Upon the day his insurance expired I was to give him sufficient money to take out a three months' accident policy for $5,000 ; it was supposed he at that time carried $1,000 of the same kind of insurance, and I agreed to be personally responsible to his family to the extent of $4,000 in case he died, this aggregating the sum of $10,000. He was satisfied with this, it being agreed that at the end of three months, when our money matters were in a more flourishing condition, his regular insurance should be renewed. During our trip to New York, in my talk with him, not having had much opportunity to plan and hold genial conversation together since he left Fort Worth months before,

I noticed that he was not as pleasant as usual,
was more inclined to sit by himself and smoke
and think and frown and worry.   I spoke to him
of it, and asked him if he had encountered any
new trouble at home, to which he answered that
he had not.

We reached New York about August 5th, I
think. I went to the Astor House and he secured
a boarding place near Thirty-third street. I at
once commenced to look about for some small
space in a shop where he could carry on his
work.

Up to this time, since I had sent Miss Williams
the various sums aggregating $1,500 from Texas,
during the preceding winter, I had received only
two letters from her, both forwarded to me from
New York through a friend in Denver, who had
acted as my agent in the matter. About the
time I left Fort Worth, I had written her asking
that she send me $600. I found this amount
awaiting me at New York in Bank of England
notes, which I later converted into United States
currency at Drexel & Co., in Philadelphia and in
New York.

For the first few days of my stay in New York, I was busy visiting several large machinery stores and in doing some other work pertaining to my company's business of years before. Upon the morning of the 9th of August, Pitezel reminded me that his insurance expired that day, and requested that I aid him in placing his temporary insurance.

I had been waiting for him to make this announcement. He had a very valuable, undeveloped patent, nearly finished, a machine for testing eggs, which I wished to use at once. I therefore said to him, suppose I pay you $500 cash for your share of the new patent (I by previous contract already owned one-half of it), then you can use the money as you choose, both for insurance and other matters. He answered that he ought not to take less than a $1,000. I finally gave him $600 for it, and upon his asking me which he should do, retain his old insurance or take out the new, I at once advised him to retain the old, for two reasons: *First*, it would help my old friend again. *Second*, if he took the third insurance, long before the expiration of that time his money would have been blown away, and I should feel obliged to give him more.

He then said, "I will go and telegraph to the company in Chicago, and see if they will keep my insurance in force until the money can reach them." I said, wire them the money instead. This was apparently a new idea to him, for after understanding it he not only wired them what was due, but also a small amount to St. Louis to his wife. I, as usual, cautioned him to be careful of the rest of the money, and make it last as long as he could. Besides this I had done all I could to cheer him up, and get him out of the morbid condition he had been in, and he voluntarily promised that for the following thirty days he would not drink liquor.

He told me afterwards that so hard did he try to keep his promise after I left him in New York that he went to the post-office there, and sent by registered letter to B. F. Perry* in Philadelphia, nearly all the money he had, so as to place himself beyond temptation for the first hard days of his struggle. At this time I had come to

* The name he had assumed for the purpose of aiding me to organize our company.

Philadelphia to meet my wife, to do some business
with the Link Belt Engineering Company, with
some stationers and with the Pennsylvania Railroad, all of whom were using a patent in which I
was interested. Upon reaching Philadelphia I
found that this and other work would detain me
some time, and not knowing of Pitezel's precau-
tion already taken, and fearing lest he should
become drunk in New York, I wrote to him to
come here. This he did, and, deciding to make
our headquarters here, I hired some rooms for
my wife and myself.

He immediately commenced to look about for
a part of a shop in which to do his work. My wife
was taken seriously ill about this time, and continued so during the remainder of our stay in
Philadelphia. I was not able to be away from
the house more than a few hours at a time, and
therefore did not see as much of Pitezel as I
otherwise should. About the middle of August
he told me he had hired an entire house at 1316
Callowhill street, it being but little more expen-
sive than a shop. That he had met another
patent man who had promised to pay a part of

the rent, remarking at the same time that when I
got ready to help him in what he wished to do,
he would buy out the other man's business or
move elsewhere, and if I perfected my company
and went South to unload it, he, if he could make
any money in his patent exchange, would have
his family come to Philadelphia for the winter,
as under the name of Perry he did not fear
trouble.

I did not have anything to do with the leasing
of the house, nor was I in it to exceed four times
prior to the day before his death.

Upon Saturday, September 1st, I called on
him to execute some patent papers to send to
Washington, and at this time he certainly was
doing a good business. During the time I was
there no less than twenty customers called, some
of them being agents he was supplying with certain washing and cleaning compounds that he
manufactured. He had also surrounded himself
with a great number of models of patents he was
trying to sell for other parties on commission.
So busy was he, that after waiting patiently for a
long time, I told him I would go to my house and

would return next day to execute the work he wished to do. Just before leaving he asked me to lend him $30 or $35, saying he wished to use it to pay his rent that was then due and to place some advertisements in the next day's papers, explaining to me that all his money was in two large bills, which he did not wish to change until necessary, as, if once broken, he feared he would spend them faster.

I laughingly said to him, "Ben, you are sure they are not spent already?" He answered, "Oh, no! I have them placed away safely up-stairs; I can go up and get them if you want me to;" and then started as if to do so. I gave him the money, saying that I did not require him to verify his statement.

That evening he came to my place of residence at about 8.30. I noticed at once that he had been drinking, and spoke to him of it, though not in anger, as it had always been my custom to wait until he became sober before chiding him. He told me that he had received word that one of his children was sick, and it might become necessary for him to go home. I asked him which child it

was, and also told him he had better telegraph
and instruct his wife to wire him if she thought it
was necessary for him to go. He then spoke of
leaving his business, and asked me what he should
do about it if the man he was expecting to take
an interest with him did not come on at once. I
told him I thought it best for him to select the
most trustworthy of his agents to leave in the
office for a few days, reminding him that I had to
go to St. Louis upon some legal business early in
the week, and therefore could not aid him. I then
bade him good night, telling him I had to go to
the market near by before it should be closed.
He said he would go with me. He waited at the
market while I made my purchases, and returned
with me almost without speaking. I then again
said "good night."

He said, "Can't you come out again? I want to
see you." I told him as my wife was not well, I
could not very well be absent longer. attributing
his unusual request to his having been drinking;
I also reminded him that I was to see him early
the next day. He said in reply, "Then come
out a moment now, and I will go home." I did

so, and he said, "You will have to let me have
some money in case I have to go to St. Louis."
I said, "that will hardly be necessary; use what
you have, and if the child dies or other unforeseen
expense arises, I shall be in St. Louis during the
week, and can then see to it." He replied,
"Well, I will have to tell you; I have not got any
money save what you gave me to-day, and I have
used part of that for liquor instead of paying my
rent with it." I said, "Ben, this makes over
$1,600 you have wasted in debauchery and drink
within the last seven months while your family
have needed it. I am done. I told you in Fort
Worth if it occurred again I should settle our
business affairs, and thereafter you would have to
care for yourself. I don't want to talk with you
to-night, but to-morrow I will go to your house,
and I want to settle up not only the patent work,
as we had intended, but all our other affairs, and
in the future if I can spare any money it will be
given to your family instead of to you, but I will
go to see them upon my arrival in St. Louis, and
will, if the child is dangerously sick, send you
money to go home with."

He said they had no money then to live on. I said, "If I find this to be so, I will give them some. It will not be the first time I have done so, and far in excess of what would have come to them had you been working elsewhere. For your own part, you will have to keep sober here in Philadelphia in order to make a.living, which I know you can do if you try." He was crying at the time. He then asked me if I would not help him to carry out the insurance work, having it appear he had been robbed there in the Callowhill street house. I replied, that inasmuch as he was persisting in drinking, it would not be a month after it was carried out before he told some one of it. He said, "You are in earnest; you will not help me any more; I can do nothing alone."

I replied, "I am in earnest, and will talk it all over with you to-morrow, and plan as best we can for the family," and again bade him good night, and as he reluctantly started away I asked him to promise me not to drink again that evening, and to go at once to his home and to bed.

He promised to do this after first going again to the telegraph office to see if there were any

messages for him. He then left me, and that is
the last time I ever saw him alive.

I wish to say, however, that while I thought it
wise and for his advantage for him to suppose he
had got to care for himself in the future, I had
no intention of abandoning him, if for no other
reason than that he was too valuable a man, even
with his failings taken into consideration, for me
to dispense with. I should have gone through a
form of settlement with him next day, and upon
my return from St. Louis, if I found him sober,
have gone on as before.

The next morning I went to the Callowhill
street house, reaching there about 11 o'clock,
entering with a key he had given me some weeks
before to use if I came there in his absence. I
found no one in the front portion of the house,
and passed back into the kitchen; finding that
also deserted, I went to the stairway and called
him by name; receiving no answer, I went up the
stairs so that I could look into the room where
he slept.

He was not there, and I was much worried,
thinking that, instead of coming home as he had

promised, he had gone about the city and perhaps had been arrested. Upon returning to the kitchen, however, I noticed that there were evidences of a fire having recently been built in the stove, and, therefore, did not think more of the matter, concluding that he had gone to the post-office or telegraph office.

I then left the house, but before doing so I placed a chair in a narrow passageway at the end of a counter, to denote to him, if he returned before I did, that I had been there. I went to the Mercantile Library and read the foreign papers for about an hour, went to a place on Eleventh street where I had a box for my private mail, and then, buying a Philadelphia Sunday paper, I returned to the Callowhill street house, entering as before.

The chair was as I had left it. I sat down for a few minutes to read, then went into the kitchen and rekindled the fire, so that he could prepare us a light lunch as soon as he returned, while I was making up the necessary papers.

The fire soon making the lower rooms uncomfortably warm, I went up stairs and lay down upon

HOLMES BURNING PITEZEL'S CLOTHING IN CALLOWHILL STREET HOUSE.

his bed and resumed the reading of the paper. While there I noticed an unusual odor and finally got up. Upon going into the adjoining room I found perhaps two dozen small bottles containing a certain cleaning fluid upon the mantel, some of which were uncorked. This fluid contained some chloroform, ammonia and benzine among other ingredients, all being of a volatile nature.

I don't know how long I stayed there, nor what time it was when I finally thought it best to go home, and I then went down stairs to his desk to write him a note. There among the paper I found a note written in 'a cipher we sometimes used, which read, "Get letter in bottle in cupboard." or words to that effect. (This note being one that no one could read without my aid, I carried it in the small watch pocket of my pantaloons, until in Toronto, having a new suit of clothing made, from which my tailor had omitted such a pocket, I placed the note in a tin box of papers that later was taken by the authorities. The note is now, or should be, in their hands.)

I went to the kitchen cupboard, which was the only one I had noticed in the house, and there I found a whiskey flask, within which I could see some paper.

To get at it I quickly broke the bottle, and upon opening the letter I read, "I am going to kill myself, if I can do it. You will find me up stairs. I am worth more dead than alive." I did not wait to finish the letter at that time, but went hurriedly up stairs. The only place on the second floor I had not had occasion to visit that morning was a small room under the stairway, and looking into it I found it empty.

I then ran up this stairway to the third story, a portion of the house I had never before been in.

It consisted of two low, small rooms, each having one small window. The door to one of these rooms was open. I instinctively turned to the room that was closed. Thrusting open the door and stepping within, I saw Pitezel lying upon the floor. I rushed to him, but before I had remained longer than to remove a large towel that was wrapped around his head, and not having time to find if he were alive, I was forced, owing to the overpowering odor of chloroform, together with the shock of coming upon him so suddenly and in such a condition, to leave the room, falling upon my knees and crawling a portion of the way until I finally reached the window in the adjoining room, which I opened, and in a few minutes had recovered myself sufficiently to return to the room where Pitezel lay, but again was forced to leave before I could make a satisfactory examination.

This time I had opened the window in this room as well, and presently was able to ascertain that he was dead. I then went to the hallway and sat down upon the stairs. I do not know how long I sat there, nor what I thought in the meantime. I had not yet wholly recovered from the effects of the chloroform, and was dazed. This was not due to having come suddenly upon a dead body, for my medical experience of years before had rendered me accustomed to disagreeable sights and scenes—but the man had been to me far more than an ordinary employee ; one whom, although most of our tastes were dissimilar, I had always liked and had had fewer disagreements with than would likely have been the case had he been my own brother. And to come upon him thus had unmanned me.

I know the thought never came to me while sitting there that it might be dangerous for my own safety, the street door being then unlocked. After a time I returned to the room and made a careful examination.

He lay upon his back, his lower limbs fully extended, one arm folded upon his chest, the other thrown out at his side.

His head was slightly raised by means of a coarse colored blanket, closely folded. He was fully dressed, except his coat and vest which hung on a chair beside him. The pockets of his trousers were turned inside out, and in the waistband was a letter within an envelope addressed " C. A. P."*

If asked to express an absolutely true opinion as to how long he had been dead, I should say not more than six hours.

Upon the chair was a large gallon bottle laying upon its side, so arranged that it would nearly empty itself, it being held in position upon one side by a hammer and upon the other by a small block of wood ; from the bottle, and connected thereto by a perforated cork in which an ordinary

* Mrs. Pitezel's initials.

quill toothpick had been inserted, there trailed a
long piece of small rubber tubing, terminating at
its free end in the towel I had removed upon first
entering the room. This tube was constricted
midway by a piece of cord tied about it. so that
the flow of liquid would be slow.

Owing to the time that had elapsed after his
death all the chloroform that could escape from
the bottle, in the position in which it lay, had
passed through the tube, filling his mouth and, as
I later learned from the Coroner's physician, his
stomach as well; this one fact alone being sufficient to prove to any scientific person, or physician
at least, that any one having a medical training
would not, if obliged to use chloroform for such a
purpose, carry it to such an extent if he wished
it to appear later that the man died as the result
of inhaling the vaporous fumes of chloroform and
benzine, that had exploded in a bottle held in the
victim's hands.

The excess of the liquid had then run out upon
the floor and on the blanket underneath his head.
The only other articles in the room besides those
already enumerated were some small pocket

belongings, a knife, memoranda book, match box, containing some of our patent stamps, and perhaps twenty small coins; all these were placed on the chair beside the bottle. Upon the window-sill was a small handful of tacks with which he had fastened some newspapers upon the sash in lieu of a curtain.

By this time, owing to the excoriating effect of the chloroform his face had become somewhat discolored, and I went to the rooms below and procured a wet towel, and after covering the face with it I started down the stairs fully intending to call in some of the neighbors. Then came the thought that, instead of filling the house with a crowd of curious people, it would be better to go direct to the Coroner.

I know this thought was in my mind as I passed down the stairway, for I distinctly remember wondering in what part of the city the Coroner's office was located, whether at the City Hall or elsewhere, and if it would be open on Sunday.

Reaching the kitchen I picked up the letter which, in my haste, I had let fall before going up stairs in search of him. The substance of the

letter, beside that already given, was that he had
tried to take his life in Mississippi during the
previous June, and now with his drinking habit
growing so much stronger day by day, he could
not hope to make a living without my aid. He
wished me to so arrange his body in one of two
ways that it would appear that his death had been
either accidental or that he had been attacked by
burglars and killed, giving the details of how I
was to carry out either course:—

First, that his family should not at present know
of his death ; * second, that the children should
never know he had committed suicide (this he
also repeated in the letter left for his wife); that
the insurance money should be used to place the
Fort Worth building in an earning condition,
and that I should exchange some Chicago property we owned for some house in a city with good
school advantages ; that none of the money should
be so placed that relatives could borrow it away
from his wife. He spoke of our close connection
for years, and that he could depend upon my

* Before going to Denver when he had felt so sure of carrying out the plan, I afterwards learned that he had spoken to one of his family about his sudden disappearance
at any time not necessitating them to worry.

aiding him now and in the future, ending his directions with the words :—

"Do enough with me so there won't be any slip-up on the insurance ; I shan't feel it." The letter was poorly written, and it took me some minutes to decipher it, and upon finishing it, I sat down for a time and re-read parts of it. This gave me time to consider my own position, and as soon as it came into my mind, but before I had decided to carry out his instructions, I went into the front office and locked the street door.

The thought that troubled me most at that time was, that under no conditions, whether the insurance part was carried out or not, was I the one to discover his dead body. I was here in Philadelphia under an assumed name. A few years earlier I had stopped at some hotels and met people under the name of Holmes. Some years before that I had done businsss here under still another name, and at another time, earlier yet, I had visited relatives here under my true name.

And now at this time, to be called as a witness before a Coroner's jury, would almost certainly cause me to be identified by some one; and if

under the name of Holmes, it was more than
likely to be seen in the papers by some Fort
Worth people, and would probably result in my
arrest upon the charges there, and my arrest at
this time I was satisfied would mean death to my
wife.

Again, I had an engagement in St. Louis for
the following Thursday morning, to fail to keep
which would result in the loss of a considerable sum
of money, and also prove a source of great annoyance to my attorney, who was personally responsible for my appearance there. Besides this,
Pitezel was dead; nothing I could do here would
aid him, while in St. Louis I could be of the
utmost benefit to his family, by forestalling the
announcement of his death reaching them through
the newspapers, by seeing them personally, and
also caring for the child that was sick, if need be.
This portion of the matter was settled in my mind
at once, then came the question whether I should
do anything to aid in the deception of the insurance matter or simply remove the letter he had
written to his wife, lest it contain matters that
should not be made public and go away. One of

his plans I did not entertain for a moment, the one involving striking him upon the head severely enough to crush his skull. Had my own life depended upon it, I could not have forced myself to strike his dead body even had I been sure there was no suicide clause in his insurance policy. I should have preferred to have told his family at once of his death, contrary to his wishes, in preference to doing anything to mislead the authorities, involving, as it necessarily must, some mutilation of the body.

I had never seen the policy, but from my friend the insurance agent's statement that it was similar to mine, I judged it contained such a clause. Nor did I know whether or not the suicide clause was inoperative in Pennsylvania as it is in many other States. (All these things I most certainly should have found out previously if I had been intending to immediately carry out the fraud.) After considerable deliberation, I went to the room in the second story that he had partially prepared, uncorked the small bottles I had previously found there, and also found the pipe he had filled with tobacco, the top of which was slightly burned as

CALLOWHILL ST. HOUSE WHERE B. F. PITEZEL'S BODY WAS FOUND.

though he had just lighted it before his accident occurred.

He did this part of the work previous to his death, knowing that I did not smoke or knew little of filling pipes intelligently enough to deceive any one. Having placed the room in the condition necessary (breaking the large bottle, placing pipe upon the floor, etc.), I moved his body as carefully as possible to this second-story room. I found that the chloroform had given the side of the face and neck and part of the chest quite the appearance of having been burned, and this made my task the easier, although it seemed terrible enough in any event.

At last I forced myself to burn the clothing upon one side of the body, smothering the flames when they reached the flesh, and in this way produced partially successful results; then hastily gathering together several small articles that I wished to take away with me, I placed the room somewhat in order, and after going again to the room where he lay to see him, as I then supposed for the last time, I at once left the house, disguising myself to some extent by wearing one of his hats, for I had been fully alive to the necessity of care after I had first had time to think of the matter. Among the things taken from the house was a bottle of chloroform, which he had previously bought in Philadelphia, and prepared to send to Chicago to be placed with the clothing and other things for Hedgpeth's use.

In going out of the house I was careful to leave the door both unlocked and open, in order to call attention to the condition of affairs within as soon as possible. Upon reaching the more pure air of the street I was seized with a feeling of nausea and dizziness, resulting probably as an after-effect of the chloroform-laden air within.

I knew my general appearance must have been that of an intoxicated person. To become relieved of this feeling somewhat if possible, I decided to walk a portion of the distance to my residence, and while doing so decided that it was best, my wife being well enough, to leave Philadelphia at once, thinking that Pitezel had no doubt spoken of me to some of his newly-made friends, and perhaps told them where I lived. I, therefore, went to the Broad Street Station

and ascertained that a train would leave in half
an hour (so I know now that I left the Callowhill
street house. at about 3.45 o'clock, as the train
referred to was the regular 4.30 Western train);
I found that another train left for the West at
10.25 P. M.; and although my wife was not able
to do so, I took her as carefully as I could to this
train and left at that hour.

I have often since that day tried to analyze
the feelings which I had at the time of Pitezel's
death. I felt it to be a terrible matter, and certainly could not have deplored it more had he
been a relative, but I did not then, nor have I
since felt the great horror concerning it that I
experienced at the time of Nannie Williams' death
in Chicago, which was wholly unprovoked and for
which I felt that I was the indirect cause; while in
this case, his death occurred as the result of his
own premeditation, in consequence of his having
allowed himself to slowly drift into pernicious
habits for which he was more than any one else to
blame. Upon reaching Indianapolis, I was occupied
until Wednesday noon, September 5th, in arranging comfortable quarters for my wife, at which

time I started for St. Louis, reaching that city
about 7 P. M., having bought upon the train a St.
Louis *Globe-Democrat*, giving in a Philadelphia
dispatch an account of the finding of Pitezel's
(Perry's) body in the Callowhill street house
upon the previous day.

After a short delay I went at once to Mrs.
Pitezel's place of residence, about an hour's ride
from the centre of the city, hoping to be in time
to tell them of the matter myself. Upon reaching
the house, however, I found all in a state of
commotion.

The neighbors were there, a physician had
been summoned, and it was some time before I
could obtain a suitable opportunity to talk with
Mrs. Pitezel. I found her in a very nervous
and over-wrought condition, and I thought it best
to palliate her fears for a time, and, therefore,
said to her, "Perhaps Ben is not dead. There
may be a mistake in the person, as I saw him
alive last week."

To which she answered, "Oh, no! I am sure
it is he, for I have been writing to him under that
name and at that address." Just at this moment

HOLMES' "CASTLE" CHICAGO.

Dessie, the oldest daughter, called me to one side and said, "Do you think papa is really dead?" I replied that I feared so, but that her mother should not be told until we were certain of it. She said, "I don't think he is. Last spring, when I was sick and he was leaving me, he told me that if I ever heard that he was dead not to believe it, as some work he was going to do might require him to have people think so for a time." I asked her if he had told her mother of this, and she said, "No; her father had told her not to tell any one." As soon as a favorable opportunity occurred, I said to Mrs. Pitezel, "Did Ben ever say anything to you about not worrying if you heard of his death?" She replied, "Yes;" and, after stopping a moment, added, "If he has gone and done that without letting us know, leaving us to worry ourselves to death, I could almost wish he was dead. Is it the insurance matter?" "I guess it is," I replied, in such a tone that she would think that I knew it to be so. She then asked if he would get the money all right, and I told her that it would be paid to her, if any-one. She asked, "Where is Ben now?" I replied that it was his plan to go South at once. She said, "Well, I do not want him writing to me ; all his letters for me must go to you ; and the children need not know but that he is really dead, for they would certainly tell of it ; they are young, and will soon get over the worry." I asked if the insurance policy was there in the house, and she said, "I do not know ; I will see ; he ought to have given it to you if he was going through with it so soon ; it may be in Chicago among some things stored in a warehouse there."

I did not allow her to look for it at that time, as she was too ill yet from her shock to do so, but instructed her to look for it next morning, and if well enough, to bring all the papers she had to my attorney's office. Some question then arose as to whether she could find this office, and she remembered that at the time of my arrest her husband had called there and had brought home one of their cards, which she said was still among some of his papers, and with this she could find her way.*

*At the time referred to a daily paper had stated that these lawyers were to act as my attorneys, and upon Pitezel's calling upon them, they had given him this card, and also directed him to the attorney they had recommended to me in the same street.

At about 9 o'clock, the family being more quiet
at the time, I returned to the hotel for the night,
and I feel sure that Mrs. Pitezel at the time of
this visit, which was the first confidential talk I
had ever had with her, had no previous knowledge of an intention to perpetrate a fraud upon
this company other than a vague idea that under
certain conditions and at a more remote time it
might have been carried out, which was the exact
condition of affairs as they had existed upon the
day of Pitezel's death.

She is not a woman of extraordinary gifts, and
any simulation on her part at this time would not
have deceived me. The next morning I went to
Judge Harvey's office and found that owing to
his absence my case had been postponed. I left
word there for Mrs. Pitezel, if she called during
the day, to wait for me, and I went to the offices
of another attorney and spoke of the insurance
claim and told him if it was promptly paid I could
use some of that money. He said insurance
companies are slow and it will probably be some
time before it is settled. He asked how large an
amount it was, and upon my stating it was

$10,000, he said, "You will need an attorney in fixing the papers; can't I do it for you?" I re-replied that I was about to consult Judge Harvey. He said, "Let me have it; I have just settled a fire insurance loss and had first-rate success, besides you are really my client, as we sent you to Judge Harvey because my partner was away at the time." After returning to Judge Harvey's office and not finding him there, I saw him again and told him that the claim was a false one, that the man was, in reality, not dead. He made a number of inquiries as to the details of the fraud and finally said, "Well, if you have any one to attend to it here it had better be me, for neither Judge Harvey or my partner would dare to take hold of it. I do not belong to this firm, although I have an office here with them. You will notice my letter-heads appear with my own name alone; still I can avail myself of their judgment in important cases, and on account of this supposed death occurring under a fictitious name, you will find you need help."

I then explained that Mrs. Pitezel was to come into the city that morning, if she was able, with the papers, and he remarked, "Well, she must not know that I have any knowledge that the claim is not a legitimate one."

It was then arranged that he should write some letters to the company's office in Chicago, to ascertain if Pitezel had, in reality, paid the premium as he had stated, there being no receipts showing this had been done, and also to write to the authorities in Philadelphia.

I asked him in regard to his fee, and he stated that it would depend upon how much work had to be done, but that being a young attorney he would make it a reasonable sum. Later, in going out of the building, I met Mrs. Pitezel and explained to her that this lawyer would take care of the case for her, and that she should not have him know that she was aware of his knowing the true state of the case. In other words, she, while in his presence, was to appear and speak as though it were a genuine loss.

So, at this stage of the case, I knew Pitezel was dead; Mrs. Pitezel and the attorney each supposed him to be alive, but, by a separate agreement each had voluntarily made with me, both were to deceive each other in this respect, making a most unique case of conspiracy, if conspiracy it was.

I was not present during all of the attorney's first interview with Mrs. Pitezel, but she authorized him to write the necessary letters, and I told her that he had made satisfactory arrangements with me in regard to his fee, which I would be responsible to him for.

I then gave Mrs. Pitezel some money for her immediate wants and left the city, intending to return again in ten days, at which time my case was to be called in Court. Before going away I told the attorney he could address me at Indianapolis at any time. About five days thereafter I received a letter from him, stating that he had received an answer to his letter of inquiry sent to the Philadelphia authorities, in which they stated that the man referred to was only known to them under the name of Perry, and would be buried as that person unless some one identified him at once as Pitezel. He also stated that Mrs. Pitezel instructed him to ask me to return to St. Louis and aid her if I could do so.

This I did at once, and upon meeting him he told me it would be necessary for some one to go to Philadelphia at once, and wished me to furnish the money for him and one of the family to make the trip. I told him that until the first of the following month I could not well do this, but suggested a person with whom Pitezel had formerly dealt that I thought would advance the necessary sum, if it was agreed that it should be returned to him with interest as soon as the insurance was collected. The attorney later negotiated such a loan, receiving $300.

At this time I saw Mrs. Pitezel, and she not being strong enough to take the trip, it was decided that the daughter, Alice, should go. This choice of the children being principally due to arrangements previously made by Pitezel, that if Miss Williams came to this country, and returned to her old occupation as a teacher, that Alice should live with her for a year to go to school. I had received a letter from Miss Williams that she had decided to do this, and at the time of Pitezel's death had asked her to come to settle in Cincinnati, thinking thus she would break away from her old life, making it safer for me to be also where she could help in regard to some Texas papers, which I had found must at any hazard, be duplicated. Therefore, a few days later, when Alice left St. Louis, it was with the full understanding that she was to stay East with Miss Williams, or go with her to Cincinnati, if all located there.

At the time I was about to leave, having made these arrangements, I received a letter that had been forwarded to me from Chicago, asking for my assistance in identifying Pitezel, it being known to the Chicago office that he had been in my employ. To intelligently answer this letter, I went to the attorney's office, at which time I first closely examined the insurance policy. I then wrote to the company as accurate a description as I could give of him.

At this time the attorney said, "Why don't you go to Philadelphia, also?"

I replied that it would be an unnecessary expense, and I wished to go to Cincinnati at that time to arrange for a house for the family. He said, "I had better wait until the money was paid," and I replied that the family would have to have a house whether the money was paid or not. Finally it was decided I should go to Philadelphia via Cincinnati, which I did, writing to the company from the latter place that I had business calling me toward Philadelphia, and I would call upon them in a few days, and if possible aid them in identifying the body. Later in the same day I met Alice *en route*. The next day, early in the afternoon, I called upon the Insurance Company in Philadelphia.

I was introduced, after a little delay, to Colonel Bosbyshell, one of the officers. He talked with me for some time regarding the case, and finally, having asked me a good many questions as to Pitezel's general appearance, said, "Well, I think that it is either a case of mistaken identity or a fraud. The man found here, and who has been buried under the name of B. F. Perry, was a man who weighed forty pounds more than Mr. Pitezel, both according to your judgment and according to his application for insurance; and moreover, this man had red hair while Pitezel's was black. An attorney and some of Mr. Pitezel's relations are expected here at any time, and I wish you could stay and aid us in clearing up the matter.

He then left the office, and in a few minutes returned with some money, which he tendered me, saying they would be glad to have me stay at their expense. I replied that I would not take the money, but having other work to attend to, I would call from day to day, and if I was put to much expense or loss of time, I would ask them to pay me, otherwise no charge would be made, explaining further that Pitezel was indebted to me, and if the claim was a genuine one I would be willing to devote some time to it in order that I could collect my money, which I had no doubt his wife would pay.

That afternoon I saw our attorney, he and Alice having arrived in the interim. I told him of my interview, and he at once said, "We shan't collect a dollar. They have either substituted a body for the one you used, or your choice was so poor it had not deceived them." He was in favor of abandoning the case and returning to St. Louis.

ALICE PITEZEL.

Finally it was decided that he should see the
company the next day, but he insisted, as he
said, for his own safety, that if we met at the
company's office he should not have it appear he
had ever seen me before. The next day, about
half an hour after I called at the insurance office,
the president of the company, who I had met the
day before, and our attorney entered the room
where I was seated, and the following conversation took place:—

Mr. ——, the president, then introduced me to
our attorney, saying:—

"This is Mr. Holmes, of Chicago, who carries
insurance in our company, and who formerly was
well acquainted with Mr. Pitezel."

Upon our shaking hands, he said, "I am glad to
know you, sir."

After some general conversation, I said, "The
officers of the company inform me that you
have certain letters and other papers in Mr. Pitezel's handwriting, and I think, if agreeable to you,
I can identify them if belonging to him."

Our attorney then turned to the president, saying, "Who is this man? Before I show any

papers or have anything more to do with one who is apparently an outsider, I wish to know more about him."

The president then said in a conciliatory manner, "Oh! I think you can depend upon Mr. Holmes acting independently and for the interest of all in the case. He is a man formerly in business in Chicago, and for whom Mr. Pitezel worked for a long time, and if any one is able to give an accurate description of him, Mr. Holmes should be able to do so."

"My inquiry was a precautionary one," said our attorney, "I am willing under those circumstances that Mr. Holmes should examine the papers and aid us if he can."

During that afternoon our attorney entered into an agreement in writing with the company, stipulating, that in order to establish his claim, certain marks of identification should be found upon the body, which it had been arranged to have disinterred the next day. Among those marks should appear a large wart, or mole, upon the back of the neck, jet black hair, a cowlick upon the forhead, a peculiarly decayed condition of the teeth, a bruised thumb nail and a scar upon one of the lower extremities.

That evening, quite late, our attorney came to me freshly terrified, and again ready to abandon the case. He had met a man named Smith, who, in conversation with him, had stated that while in Pitczel's place of business he had seen a man come in and hold some conversation with him, who he had understood was a friend then living in the city. Smith had stated that the friend had not come forward at the time of his death and he thought it strange, and also remarked that if he ever saw the man again he would know him.

Mr. Smith was to be at the Coroner's office next day, and was also to be present at the time the body was viewed. I told him that from what I remembered of the man Smith, I did not think he was a very close observer or overburdened with general intelligence, and I would take the chances of his recognizing me, rather than give up the case at that stage of it. Next morning we all met at the Coroner's office. My judgment had been correct in regard to Smith. He noticed me only as he would have done any stranger, and upon being introduced to him, and being in his company and holding a general conversation with him, I met with the same result.

It was decided at the meeting at the Coroner's office that later in the day those interested should go to the cemetery where the body would be exhumed for identification. This was done, there being in the party the president and two others, representing the insurance company, a physician and a Deputy Coroner representing the city ; our attorney, Alice Pitezel and myself, besides Mr. Smith before referred to.

Upon reaching the cemetery we were told that the body had already been placed in a small house and was ready to be seen.

I felt, that there being two other physicians present, it was not necessary for me to take part in the identification, unless called upon to do so ; and had, upon first arriving together with Mr. Perry, taken the daughter to a distant quarter of the enclosure. The physician made the examination of the body, which lay in a well-lighted room ; and, after taking abundant time for this purpose, came out of the building and announced

that all marks of identification were wanting.
After some further conversation, the president said
to our attorney that they were satisfied before
they came there that such would be the case, and
a general movement was made preparatory to
leaving the place.

The attorney asked me what I thought should
be done, and upon my answering him, he told
the president that he would like to have me examine the body as well. I asked the doctor if he
would object, and he said "No," but that I would
not find it a pleasant task.

I entered the building, and hardly had passed
the door before I was positive that the doctor had
been mistaken in the color of the hair. Upon a
close examination, all the marks were easily
found: the wart upon the neck, equal in diameter
to that of a lead pencil, and projecting fully a
quarter of an inch from the surface; the cowlick,
the bruised nail, the teeth decayed exactly as had
been described; and lastly, the scar an inch and
a half in length upon the foot.

I could do no less than call the doctor in, and
one by one he grudgingly admitted their presence;

and that there should be no further question as to the identity of the man, I asked him to remove the wart for microscopical examination, some of the hair, the nail and the scar. He said he had no implement with him that he cared to use for this purpose. I had only a very small lancet, but I removed the necessary portions, and later turned them over to the Coroner's representative.

I then endeavored to have a decision reached at once in order to save the necessity of the daughter seeing the body, feeling it to be cruel to have her do so, and if possible to prevent it. The president would not agree to this, but it was finally arranged that she should see only the teeth. All other portions of the body were therefore excluded from view, and I led the child into the building.

It was a terribly hard thing that I had to do, for she was but a delicate child of perhaps fourteen or fifteen years, yet she was courageous and very willing to do what she could.

Upon reaching the body she said, "Yes, those are papa's teeth, I am sure of it." I at once led her away. but I found the impression left upon her tender mind would remain as long as she lived, and have always felt it to have been a wholly unnecessary requirement upon the part of the company.

Without regard to what the reasons were, the doctor's report was destined to cost me dearly, as will later be seen in this history. This ended the examination at the grave-yard, and we all returned to the city.

Even at that time the officers of the company would not express themselves as willing to allow the claim, but later in the day they reluctantly admitted that they were satisfied with the identification. Upon reaching the Coroner's office again, the Coroner very kindly offered to take my testimony the next morning, which was Sunday, in order that I could leave the city without further loss of time. After making this arrangement, I went to the insurance company's office where I was reweighed, remeasured and in other ways readjusted my own insurance, and later went to an undertaker's office, and made every arrangement to have the body properly buried in a good

locality, well satisfied to be able to perform this
final act for my friend.

The next day at 4.30 P. M., having previously
gone to the Coroner's office, I left Philadelphia,
taking Alice Pitezel with me. I had not heard from
Miss Williams as I felt sure I should do, informing
me of her expected arrival in New York, and thus
not hearing, I addressed her there, asking both
she and Hatch to come to Cincinnati as soon as
they conveniently could, stating my reasons for
asking them to do so.

Alice did not like to return to St. Louis on
account of having told every one she knew before
leaving that she was going away for the winter,
although she would have been very glad to have
seen her mother; and upon reaching Indianapolis
I told her she could choose between returning to
St. Louis or remaining there for the few intervening days while I went to St. Louis and returned
with some of the rest of the family upon our way
to Cincinnati, it having previously been arranged
with Mrs. Pitezel that this move should be made
at once to save commencing another month in
St. Louis, where she was paying rent.

Alice having decided to remain in Indianapolis, I took her to Stubbin's Hotel and left her there in charge of those whom I had become acquainted with during my previous stay in that city. The next day I received a telegram from the attorney, stating that the company had paid him the insurance, after deducting several hundred dollars for expenses, which, I think, was wholly unjust towards Mrs. Pitezel, the whole amount, if any, being due her.

I then returned to St. Louis, where, owing to my absence, my own case had again been postponed, and I therefore decided to return to Cincinnati.

Taking the two children, Nellie and Howard, I started for that city via Indianapolis, telegraphing to the hotel to have some one accompany Alice to the train in the morning to join us. This was done, and at about 8 A. M. we reached the Cincinnati station where Hatch met us. It was the first I had seen of him since early in December of the previous year.

Miss Williams had remained in New York, being unwilling to go to Cincinnati where she had previously played, and therefore was known to some people.

Being in haste to commence my work among the real estate men, I gave the children into Hatch's charge, and he took them to a small hotel near the station. But not liking the surroundings, I returned to the Hotel Bristol. I spent a very busy day, but was not successful in finding property to exchange for Chicago property, and at last I thought it safer to rent a house for a time, and then, by advertising my property, find something more suitable for the children's wants. I therefore hired a house, paying one month's rent and six months' water tax. I also made arrangements for its being comfortably furnished.

Miss Williams not having come, I looked around for some trustworthy person to care for the children until their mother could reach them. Mrs. Pitezel having a desire to visit her parents before going elsewhere, did so.

Not finding such a person as I wished, and not liking to leave the children without proper attention, I decided to take them with me to Indianapolis, where I expected to be engaged in some

real estate work for the following two weeks.
This I did, Hatch accompanying us, and then
going on to Chicago from whence he returned in
a few days.

We reached Indianapolis about October 1st;
the children stayed one day at English's Hotel,
and then I engaged permanent board for them at
the Circle House, my wife and myself being at
another hotel near by, so that I could visit the
children each day and know they were properly
cared for. This form of life was new to the
children, and they thoroughly enjoyed it, going
about the city either by themselves, Hatch's or
my own company.

I shortly afterwards returned to St. Louis, and
upon entering the attorney's office, he said,
"Well, I am glad you have come; my partner
had been wishing that you would return." I
said, "Why?" He replied, "Because he wants
to get this matter settled up and get our fee out
of it. You know how close work it was to get
the company to believe the claim was straight,
and something may occur to make them change
their minds. But, I said; "Why has he to be

considered, even in that event?" He replied,
"Because, in a case as big as this, he will have to
be considered; besides, if it had not been for his
letter of introduction to Superintendent Linden
in Philadelphia, the money would not have been
paid." I then told him that I had not yet seen
Mrs. Pitezel, but we would arrange the settlement
when I did so, and I would have her come in and
sign the necessary papers later. "Well," said
he, "what do you think we should receive?" I
said, "I have no idea; you must set your price,
not I."

He then said, "Well, usually in these insurance cases the attorneys get fifty per cent. of
the claim. I have asked three disinterested
lawyers about it, and they say I ought to have
that much, they not knowing it as a fraudulent
claim, which makes it all the worse."

My answer was, "Well, if it comes to taking
$5,000, which, from your own statement to me, is
more money than you ever before earned in your
life, you will have the opportunity to keep the
balance as well." After some further conversation, he offered to choose an attorney if I would

choose one, and leave the fee to their decision, and with this understanding I went away to return the next morning. When I returned he met me with the announcement that his partner would not agree to his proposition. I then said, "I wish to see him if he is the principal." At that time I had never been introduced to him. He left his office in a few minutes and returned and conducted me into his partner's private office. He was seated at his desk, apparently much too busy to leave his work for so small a matter as the settlement of a $5,000 fee.

Finally he turned upon me and, in an an overbearing, bull-dozing manner, said, "What is all this trouble about? Don't you expect to pay your attorney after you have hired him?" I was angry at his insolent manner, and at once told him that I would have no words with him. If they wished to receive $500 for their services (reminding him that had it not been for my presence in Philadelphia they would not have collected the claim, as he had shown so very little tact in treating with the company—so much so that they had been twice upon the point of ordering him from their offices) then that amount could be deducted, but no more.

He then said, "I will allow no man to come into my office and dictate to me in regard to a fee after the work has been done for him, and as for $500 it is an insult to offer it." I then reminded him that I was not making it as an offer to him, one of the most prominent lawyers of St. Louis, but to his partner, a recent law graduate, to whom a $500 fee would be a large one, inasmuch as his expenses upon the trip had been elaborately pro vided for.

He said, "Well, we will take $3,000 for this work and nothing less." I replied, "It cannot be paid."

He said, "Then there is no further use for us to discuss the matter." Turning to his part-ner, he then said, "Go to the bank and get a New York draft for what you have left; I am going to return the money." I said, "Very well, sir, noth-ing could be more to my advantage than this, and upon Mrs. Pitezel receiving the money direct from the company I shall tender to you your fee of $500."

He replied, " You will never have a chance to do this ; when the money is sent back I shall at the same time write a letter to my old friend, Captain Linden of the Philadelphia Police Department, stating that since my return we have found out that the claim is crooked and cannot handle such money, and that we think it our duty to aid him by placing him in immediate possession of all the facts pertaining to the matter ; moreover, you are wanted in Fort Worth, Texas, and I shall at once cause your arrest before you can leave the city."

I replied, "You could only cause me trouble in regard to the insurance matter at the cost of your partner's disgrace." He said, "It is not so; it would be the word of our firm, which is well known throughout the country, against your single statement, and you a man that has already been under arrest once and will be again inside of an hour." This so angered me that I said, "You can send back the money, you can arrest me, but you cannot intimidate or browbeat me. I will spend ten years in the penitentiary before giving in to you now."

Upon this I left the office. Mrs. Pitezel was
seated in the outer room, having come in in the
meantime. I asked her to come at once to Judge
Harvey's office, and upon her hesitating to do so,
when he asked her to remain a moment, I told her
to make no settlement that involved a greater re-
duction than $500 from the amount the company
had paid. Upon my doing this I left the office, and
waited a long time for Mrs. Pitezel; and when she
met me she was in tears and said that they would
not let her leave the office until she allowed them to
deduct $2,500 from the insurance money, and that
she had also signed a long typewritten agreement of some kind. She then had the remainder
of the money, about $6,000, with her, the lawyers
having previously paid some bills upon her giving
them a written order to do so.

Some days previous to this I had made arrangements that the amount of money to be
used at Fort Worth should be paid at a bank at
St. Louis in exchange for a note her husband
had executed while there.[*] Mrs. Pitezel went to

* The claim so persistently advanced that this note was a forgery is untrue; it was
still in existence a short time ago, and if the prosecution will produce it the signature
can speak for itself.

the bank and lifted this note, and of the balance
gave me $225 for my expenses, as she supposed.
As a matter of fact, the $5,000 thus paid upon
the note came to me, I having months before
had to satisfy the claim by the use of other property. That afternoon, some time later, I left St.
Louis, intending to return to Cincinnati and complete the arrangements there for the home of the
Pitezel family. Before leaving St. Louis, however, I arranged that Mrs. Pitezel and the two
other children should go to Galva, Ill., upon their
intended visit to Mrs. Pitezel's mother, and also
made private arrangements to be informed of
any movements that should be made by the attorneys detrimental to my interests.

Upon my returning to Indianapolis I found
that both the children were apparently enjoying
themselves. Hatch had received a letter from
Miss Williams (to whom he claimed he was married) asking that we both meet her in Detroit.
This meeting was delayed, as I had some more
real estate work to do in Indianapolis which had
been neglected, owing to the insurance work.
While attending to this work I received word that

the attorneys were intending to make trouble for
me, and almost at the same time word came from
Chicago that some Fort Worth detectives were
again there, and had heard of my being in Cincinnati, Indianapolis and St. Louis.

After consulting with Hatch, who was very
much worried lest if I were arrested it would
implicate him as being with me, and perhaps Miss
Williams as well, we concluded that we should
go away at once. Finally I decided to abandon
the Cincinnati house, and have the Pitezel family
locate elsewhere, as the attorneys knew of my
former trips to that city. I therefore wrote Mrs.
Pitezel at Galva, advising her to change her plans
and go to Detroit.

Up to this time, all that I had done for Mrs.
Pitezel she had been aware of, but I did not now
think it prudent that she should know of the probability of trouble arising from the insurance company. I preferred having her locate in some large
city at that time, and explain to her afterwards
about her husband's death as he had requested me
to do, and also of the necessity of remaining quiet
until I could ascertain if any real danger existed.

Quite early upon the morning of October 10th, I went to the children's hotel, and found them eating their breakfast. I told them we were going away that day, and went with them to their rooms and instructed them to divide their belongings into three separate packages, they having previously been contained in a very old trunk, which was not in a condition to be taken further. There was left in this trunk some old clothing, among which was a suit of heavy clothes which had belonged to Pitezel.

I then asked the children whether they would go with me to Chicago, and then to Detroit, or go with Hatch. Howard Pitezel chose to go with Hatch, while the girls desired to go to Chicago, hoping, while there, to have time to visit some of their former acquaintances. Having some purchases to make before leaving, I therefore, after telling the girls at what time to meet me at the station, left the hotel, having instructed Howard not to leave until Hatch should come, in order that he could direct him to come to the station before my train left. I met Hatch and Howard later upon the street. This was the last time I ever saw the

HOWARD PITEZEL.

boy Howard, at which time he was both well and
contented. The first few days after his leaving
home he had been homesick.

While I was in the barber shop at the station
upon this same morning, I asked Hatch to go
to the hotel and have the nearly empty trunk
taken to the station and have it checked to any
destination he might choose, there being nothing
of value in it, and it not being desirable to have
it left at the hotel. Upon reaching Chicago, I
took the two girls to a hotel, as I had business
in a distant part of the city. I stayed during the
one night I remained there at a new hotel upon
the west side of North Clark street, less than a
block north of the Lincoln avenue car junction.*

Not deeming it prudent, owing to the late news
I had heard at Indianapolis, to go to my attorney's
office, I had both him and my agent meet me
elsewhere, and arranging my work as quickly as
possible, I left Chicago upon Friday, October 12th,
going directly to Detroit, taking the girls with me.
During the latter part of this trip my wife was

* In any instance, when not registering under my own name, my handwriting will
substantiate my statements.

upon the same train, she having left Indiana that morning in response to a request from me to do so.

Anticipating this. I had made arrangements with Hatch before leaving Indianapolis to be at the Detroit Station to take charge of the children. Upon our reaching Detroit I at once took my wife to a hotel about one mile from the station, and as I was leaving the train I saw Hatch helping the girls from the car in which they had traveled. About a half hour later Hatch met me at the Western Union telegraph office in response to a note I had given to Alice for him.

It was very late at night, and I returned with him to the hotel, where he had taken the girls, to see that they were all right, and while going there he told me that he had been delayed twenty-four hours at some junction between Indianapolis and Detroit, so that he had only reached Detroit that afternoon, and Miss Williams not wishing by any accident to meet my wife had gone to Buffalo to visit some theatrical friends, taking Howard with her. I did not think strange of this, for I knew Howard had known and liked

Miss Williams the year before, when she was in my office in Chicago. The next day I engaged permanent board for both myself and wife, and also for the children, in two separate portions of the city, as I expected to remain there for some time, and enlisting Hatch's services, we proceeded to look for a house that, if possible, could be bought in exchange for Chicago property, and by so doing save money.

If this could not be accomplished, then a house that should be rented for a few months, until such a trade could be made. A small house was found so favorably located, with school advantages for the children, that I thought it best to pay the small deposit required, five dollars, to hold it for a few days.

On Sunday morning Mrs. Pitezel came to Detroit, and I did not think it wise to tell her positively that she was to settle there until I should have heard again from both St. Louis and Chicago. During the interval, I had her board at a hotel; nor did I think it wise to tell her the other children were in the city, until I knew that no further move was to be made, lest she not understanding the danger of arrest—if such danger I should find still existing—she would be unwilling to go elsewhere, unless she supposed the children and her husband, or both, had already gone.

I had brought with me a package of papers from Chicago, which I did not care to carry in my own trunks, and it was arranged to conceal them in the house lately rented in Detroit. I took them there in company with Hatch, and proceeded to place them above the ceiling of the upper story, when he suggested that in case of fire they would be lost, and volunteered to prepare a place next day in the basement for their safe-keeping. And this he did by first buying a new shovel, and then making a small excavation in the earth, not using this shovel, as it afterward appeared, but another found in the basement.

Upon the morning of October 17th I received startling intelligence from both St. Louis and Chicago, and, upon holding a consultation, it was with reluctance that we decided to leave Detroit and go either to Canada or Europe; for I felt that any move, without regard to expenses, was better than to have Mrs. Pitezel arrested and myself as well. This day was a very busy one. Before Mrs. Pitezel left St. Louis I had bought a large trunk, which I loaned to her to carry part of her personal effects to her new house. When it was decided to make a move into other lands, I arranged with Hatch that, while I was busy about other matters, he should take the trunk to his room and repack it, and exclude a multitude of worthless articles, after having told Mrs. Pitezel that this was to be done.

It also became necessary to go to a city called Ypsilanti upon that same day to get a package of valuable papers I had ordered forwarded to me there, and, being so busy about other matters, I requested Hatch to make the trip for me. He hesitated considerably about doing it, saying he must see to repacking this trunk. I told him that I could better take the time to do this than to go to Ypsilanti. He replied that I could not well take it to his room, as I was not known to the people of whom he rented. I told him I would arrange it otherwise, and he then started for Ypsilanti.

At about one o'clock I found an expressman, and accompanying him to a feed store near by

bought a flour barrel with the address of a party
in Hartford, Conn., upon one end of it. We then
drove to Mrs. Pitezel's hotel and had the trunk
taken to the depot. There, upon the platform, I
took such worthless articles as Mrs. Pitezel had
placed in a separate part of the trunk and put
them in the barrel, and leaving the trunk at the
depot had the expressman take the barrel to either
the United States or American Express Company's office, and ship it to Hartford, Conn. At
about 2 P. M. I went to a livery stable on ———
street, and hiring a horse and buggy drove to
the house that had been rented and took the two
girls with me for a drive. I entered the house
and procured the papers I had previously left
there. I also left a note instructing Hatch to the
effect that if he came there from Ypsilanti with
the other papers, not to bury them. I then drove
to Hatch's room and left a small note, and this
accounts for the note being later found in the
house where I directed the authorities to search.

Earlier in the same day Hatch and I visited
several large stores, and at one obtained a $500
and two $200 bills, which, together with other

small bills, making in all $1,000, which sum he took to Miss Williams to pay upon what was due her on the Fort Worth transaction. Before leaving Detroit, Hatch brought to the depot the new shovel wrapped in a paper, and wished to put it in the trunk, but upon my remarking that it seemed more useless than things I had just taken out to make more room, he said he had paid for it and did not care to throw it away.

The next morning my wife and I left Detroit for Toronto at 10 o'clock. Mrs. Pitezel and the two children started two hours later. The next morning Hatch took the two girls, Alice and Nellie, to the train and they made the journey to the same city alone twenty-four hours later, and over the same road I had come, while Hatch came to Toronto by the way of Buffalo, where he stopped to see Miss Williams.

I reached Toronto early Thursday evening, October 18th, and went at once to the Walker House. After taking dinner, I went to the station and met Mrs. Pitezel, taking her to a hotel near by, and returned to the Walker House for the night. Next morning we breakfasted at about

NELLIE PITEZEL

8.30. I visited Mrs. Pitezel at her hotel about a
half hour, and then with my wife visited several
fur stores, purchasing a fur cape and returned
with her to the Walker House for the mid-day
meal. Immediately thereafter we went for a long
country drive, and did not return until about 6
P. M. I ate dinner and then, as upon the preceding
evening, went to the station. This time I met
the two girls, Alice and Nellie, with whom Hatch
had started from Detroit that morning, as stated.

Upon their arrival I placed them in an omnibus
running to the Albion Hotel, in care of the run-
ner for that house, and returning to the Walker
House had hardly time to prepare for the theatre,
which I attended that evening with my wife. The
next morning, after eating a late breakfast,* my
first occupation upon this day was to go to the
Hotel Albion and visit the children. I found
them in their room, greatly interested in watching
the immense open market across the street. I
remained with them until almost, if not quite, 10
A. M. I then went to the post-office, making a

* At the risk of being tedious, I have entered into a minute description of events
while in Toronto, especially as it applies to Saturday, the 19th, and Thursday, the 19th
of October, as they seem vital dates in the case.

few calls at some haberdashers on the way. I reached the post-office not later than 10.30, when I met Hatch, in accordance with an arrangement made before leaving Detroit. He had visited Miss Williams at Buffalo, upon the trip to Toronto; and, in answer to my inquiry, stated that the boy Howard was well, and that he had wanted to come to Toronto with him, but he had thought it best for him to wait and accompany Miss Williams if she came.

He then left me, as he stated, to find for himself a private room, agreeing to meet me at the same place at 2 P. M.

Now, in this short time between 10.30 A. M. and 2 P. M., it appears from the testimony recently taken in Toronto at an inquest, that a visit was made to a real estate agent then in a distant part of the city; a call was made upon the owner of the house at Vincent street of sufficient length to arrange for renting the property, and to enter into a detailed description of the family supposed to be the future tenants, and become well acquainted with the owner; then to take possession of the house, to call upon a neighbor and make their acqaintance as well, and, presumably, to eat a lunch at some restaurant, and buy a small amount of furniture for the house just hired. Add to this the almost certain probability that the lessee had visited other houses as well, it being hardly possible that he could have found a house at once so well adapted to the purpose as this seems to have been, and there is little time left for other work before 2 P. M. of the same day.

My movements during these same hours were as follows: Leaving Hatch at the post-office, I went to Mrs. Pitezel's hotel, fully one mile away, stopping upon my way at the telegraph office for fully fifteen minutes, while a search was instituted in a different part of the building for undelivered telegrams. After making a short call at the hotel, I returned to the Walker House, went again to the fur store where our purchase of the day previous had been made (one of two stores located very near each other about two blocks west of the post-office and north of K street). Here fully one-half hour was taken up in the work done there, which included the purchase of two storm garments. We then went to King street, made

several calls at furnishing stores and one large
dry goods store, and then, after spending some
time in selecting a good pocket compass, returned
to the Walker House for lunch; to do which, and
to write two letters, certainly occupied fully an
hour, probably more.

I then went again to the Albion Hotel, stopping
to buy the children some fruit and toys upon the
way. At the appointed hour, I went to meet
Hatch at the post-office. He was late in keeping
his appointment, and I made several purchases in
that neighborhood, and I think at this time
selected the material and was measured for a
suit of clothes at a custom tailor shop, upon the
west side of Young street, near junction of the
street leading to the post-office.

Upon meeting Hatch, I told him I was to be
absent from the city on Sunday, and asked if he
could see to the children while I was away, and
if they wished to go for a street car ride, he would
accompany them. This he agreed to do, and after
making some further plans with him for the following week, I went to the Hotel Albion again and
told the children of the arrangement made for

their ride, then went to the furnishing store on King street kept by a man named Dickson, I think.

When I found the grade of goods I had been in search of, and after purchasing some, I returned to the Walker House with hardly time left to be shaved and go to Mrs. Pitezel's hotel, to let her know I was to be out of the city the next day, and to catch the 4 or 4.30 train for Niagara Falls.

At this time my wife's trunk and the large trunk from Detroit, were both at the Toronto Depot, and I asked that they be checked to Niagara. I remarked to the baggage agent that I had no need to take the large one, save to avoid storage. He asked how long I desired to leave it there, and I replied that was uncertain, but perhaps a week. He asked for a half dollar and said that there are no further charges if it was taken away in a week's time. The trunk never left the Toronto Depot during my stay there. Sunday, October 21st, was passed by us at the Falls, returning to Toronto by the way of Hamilton in the early evening, at which time I went to the Palmer House.

During Monday I was busy about the city, returning to my hotel often during the day. Part of the time I was with Hatch searching for a suitable location in which he and Miss Williams could open a respectable massage establishment, if they all settled there, which was the real object of the Toronto trip, as I have reason to believe.

During the day he asked me if I would not spend Tuesday night with him in and about the city. I gave him to understand that I might do so. Tuesday morning we met, as had become our custom, at the post-office between 10 and 11 o'clock.

I received additional and disquieting messages from the West, and by noon-time we had made up our minds that the conditions favorable to the business we had hoped to find did not exist in Toronto, and had decided to go to England instead. Hatch particularly favored this plan, as they had had a prosperous business there during the foregoing year, and he at once wrote Miss Williams to that effect, and for her to meet the two girls at Niagara at as early a day as possible, which she was to appoint by letter.

She was to take the three children to London, while Mrs. Pitezel took the others there a little later on, or as soon as we could become settled again.

When Hatch again urged me to stay with him during the night, I finally told him that since my terrible experience of the year before, which the indirect results of my loose living had been Nannie Williams' death, and more particularly since my marriage, I had endeavored to live a clean life, and thought best not to deviate in this instance. I returned to the Palmer House not later than 4.30 P. M. Later, in thinking the matter over, I thought, inasmuch as he had helped me so much during the preceding weeks, it seemed like ill-treatment towards him, and decided that if he brought the matter up next day I would spend a part of the evening with him.

Acting upon this decision, I told my wife next morning, Wednesday, that I might not return until late, but later in the day I reconsidered my former plan and returned to the Palmer House at about 2.30 P. M., and my wife being absent and the room locked at the time, I threw some flowers

I had just bought into the room through the open transom, my wife finding them upon her return a short time later.

During the day I had been buying a quantity of small articles to send to my relatives in New Hampshire, and had gotten them together temporarily at the furnishing store previously mentioned. At noon-time I had eaten lunch with the children and in the afternoon Hatch had taken them for a drive. In the evening I accompanied my wife to the theatre, enjoying myself far more than the case would be had I been going about the city together with Hatch and a guilty conscience.

On Thursday, October 24th, the day when it is reasonable to suppose the two girls were killed, I was busy about the city during the forenoon. The girls came to the post-office at about 10.30, and either went with Hatch for a drive or a street-car ride, they having been in Hatch's care more than with me while in Toronto, for the reason that their hotel was so distant it encroached upon my time to ride to visit both them and Mrs. Pitezel and do what work I wished. That morning

we heard that Miss Williams would meet the girls
at Niagara upon the arrival of the afternoon
train. They ate lunch with me between 1 and 2
o'clock, Hatch being elsewhere at the time. The
girls returned to their hotel afterwards for a few
minutes to change part of their attire for some
that was warmer, which I had bought for them
in anticipation of their sea voyage. Later they
joined me again and I bought them a number of
presents. I also bought Miss Williams a small
brooch, which I gave to Alice, together with a
note, which she was to deliver personally to Miss
Williams.

My object in sending it in this way was
that Hatch knew of our former relations, and I
had avoided sending by him as he then claimed
she was his wife. About half an hour before
train time, which I think was 4.30 P. M., we were
upon Young street. I sent the girls to a restaurant or bakery near by to get some lunch prepared to take with them upon the train, instructing
them to then come to a large store which I pointed
out to them, where I would await their arrival. I
then entered this store and bought some small

articles for the children, having in my hands at the time some underwear I had previously purchased to send to Howard, the boy, when I heard a familiar voice, and turning, saw Mrs. Pitezel and the other two children.

I quote from her recent statement, made in Toronto, as to what took place between us then, and state that it could only have been on this day, for while there I asked her if she could get ready to leave Toronto that evening :—

"I am convinced that my two children were right here in Toronto while I was here," said Mrs. Pitezel. "One day while I was shopping in a large store here, I suddenly saw Holmes. He said you wait here a little while until I return. I believe my children were right there in that store at the time, and Holmes took them out some other way so I should not see them."

As a matter of fact, they were at the bakery before spoken of, and I can only wish now that they had been with me, and met their mother, though at the time I should have considered it an unfortunate circumstance for the same reasons that obtained in Detroit.

I at once left the store and took the children to
the depot, where Hatch met me with some
bundles of goods he had bought. I took the children to the ladies' waiting room and giving Alice
$400, directed her to go into the private waiting
room and fasten it securely within her dress, and
later give it to Miss Williams. I also gave each
of the girls a small amount of spending money. I
I wrote a telegram, directing it to myself at the
hotel opposite the Palmer House, for Alice to
send me early next morning from Niagara, if anything happened to prevent Miss Williams meeting
them as had been agreed upon.

I also gave them explicit directions as to where
to stay, and told them that I would surely go to
them at once if any trouble arose. I then asked
if they were afraid to go alone. Alice answered,
"Oh, no; I wish you or Mr. Hatch were going
along, though." The train came so quickly that
I had little time to bid them good-bye, and therefore got upon the train and accompanied them
perhaps a mile to a station where the train
slowed up ; Hatch going still farther, at his suggestion, to see that the conductor took their

tickets and agreed to transfer them at Hamilton to the right train.

I sat in the seat with Nellie during this time, Alice being in the seat in front. They spoke of their prospective voyage, gave me messages for their mother and the baby, and asked how long it would be before we all came to London. I told them to help Miss Williams all they could, and especially cautioned Nellie about quarreling with Howard, which she was apt to do when they were together, finally telling them that upon my arrival there the three who had not quarreled would receive a present of considerable value.

My opportunity to leave the train having now arrived, I hastily bade them good-bye, and started to leave the car. Little Nellie followed me to the door, and said, " Don't forget about baby," and reaching up kissed me good-bye, and ran back to the seat again. With all truthfulness, I most earnestly state that under the circumstances, and at this time, about 4.30 P. M., Thursday, October 25th, I last saw these children.

I immediately returned to the Palmer House, telling my wife we should leave the city next morning, and said to her that if she had any more purchases to make, she should attend to it at once, as certain of the stores closed early. For the next hour I was busy collecting my various purchases about the city, and taking them to the depot to place in the large trunk, and at not later than 6.30 Hatch was again at the depot, and stated that the conductor had taken the children in charge before he left the train. He then left me, agreeing to meet me early next morning at the hotel to learn if the children arrived all right. I then returned at once to the Palmer House and ate dinner.

Without delay I went to Mrs. Pitezel's hotel, and assisted her in packing her trunk and having it taken to the train before 8 o'clock, the larger trunk going upon the same train; but Mrs. Pitezel and Dessie remarked to me later that they saw that trunk upon their arrival at Prescott early next morning, and a day later the Custom's officer at Ogdensburg, during his inspection, came across the shovel Hatch had insisted in placing in it at Detroit, remarking that he did not know but that it was dutiable on account of being new.

If this trunk had been at the Vincent street house there would have been no necessity of one's going to the neighbors to borrow a spade with which to conceal the evidence of the terrible crime committed there. I returned to the Palmer House before Mrs. Pitezel had started—not later than 8.15 P. M.—and during the evening aided my wife in her preparations for the next day's journey; and only left the hotel before taking the train next morning at 8 o'clock, for about two minutes, to step across the street and ascertain if the girls had met Miss Williams, as was reasonable to suppose as no telegram was there. Hatch was waiting for me at the hotel, and said he should wait one or two days in Toronto to get his mail and to buy some dutiable goods to take across the border.

I did no smuggling while upon this trip, nor was I even absent from my hotel any evening or night, save when accompanied by my wife to some place of amusement; nor did I ever leave my hotel before 8.30 A. M., save upon this last morning.

Thus it will be seen that this is not an unimportant statement, for according to a witness named Rodgers, if his testimony at the inquest at Toronto is correctly reported, he saw the two children at 1 P. M., Thursday, and that early next morning a spade that had been previously borrowed had been returned to him.

In an informal talk upon this subject, Mr. Rodgers has several times stated that this occurred quite early before working hours.

The hackneyed expression that "a spade is a spade" may be true, but I feel that it but poorly expresses the full value and significance of this particular article. Again, Mr. Rogers states that "Some time—in one published account some days later—the keys were left with me ; I fully believe that the children met their death and were buried during the night, Thursday, October 25th ; the spade returned before 8 o'clock—for Hatch was at that time at the hotel—that during the day their clothes were slowly burned"—and this, while I was journeying towards Prescott, Canada, a railroad trip of about eight hours, and where I registered at the Imperial Hotel not later than 4.30 P. M. that day.

It may be asked how at this late date I can fully remember what occurred upon one certain

Saturday, nearly a year previous to the writing of
these pages, to distinguish it from the preceding
day or any other day that is less important?
Upon first hearing of the children's death, I was
no more in a position to be positive in regard to
this particular day than any other, until after
thinking of the matter for hours and days together, as I believe only a man can force himself
to think when he feels that perhaps his life depends
upon such exertion, I arranged the facts in my
mind in something like the following order:—

Being first sure, from some written memoranda,
that I arrived in Toronto upon Thursday, October 18th, upon the next day, which was Friday,
I was sure that no purchases had been made, save
the fur garment referred to, because this took up
the entire morning, and our ride occurred the
same day, which fact was firmly impressed upon
my mind by remembering that the livery conveyance came to the Walker House. This could
not have occurred on any other day, as next afternoon we were going to Niagara, and at all later
dates we were at the Palmer House. I also remember that the second purchases at the fur store,

that of the storm coats, were made upon the day
following our previous purchase ; this being further strengthened and impressed upon my mind
by remembering that upon my return from
Niagara the day following these purchases, a delay
had occurred of several hours at Hamilton. The
weather being such as to require it, I went to the
baggage car, and after considerable conversation
with the baggage man, was allowed to open our
trunk for this garment.

This date brought to my mind that the compass
had been used while at Niagara, showing that that,
too, was bought upon the day previous. This in
its turn made me think that the purchase of the
compass had occurred while passing from one
furnishing store to another, looking for the special grade of underwear I wished, and which was
bought later in the day, showing me clearly that
at least a dozen other calls had been made at
different other establishments for a like purpose,
and which must of necessity have occurred prior
to the purchase which ended my search.

My suit of clothes was promised to be delivered
to me upon the following Tuesday, if possible,

and upon Wednesday at the latest, and I was required to call once in the meantime to have them fitted. If instead of Saturday I had been measured Monday, and told to call the next day to be fitted, they could not have been promised to me upon Tuesday, and so on in regard to the other visits made after this day, until I became so thoroughly convinced that I have not yet verified them by tracing the several stores, not knowing their names; but I fully believe that the order books and delivery slips of at least three responsible establishments will show that I must have been transacting business in their stores at the very hours when it had been sworn I was in remote parts of the city paying friendly visits to the owner and neighbor of the Vincent street house.

From there the remainder of my journey was by private conveyance, hired for that purpose, and through a blinding snow storm. My pen cannot adequately portray the meeting with my aged parents, nor, were it possible, would I allow it to do so for publication. Suffice it to say that I came to them as one from the dead, they for years having considered me as such, until I had written them a few days before.

That after embracing them, as I looked into their dear faces once more, my eyes grew dim with the tears kindly sent to shut out for the moment the signs of added years I knew my uncalled-for silence of the past seven years had done much to unnecessarily increase.

For the next two days I tried to feel that I was a boy again, and when I could go away by myself for a few minutes, I would wander from room to room, taking up or passing my hands lovingly over each familiar object, opening each cupboard and drawer with the same freedom I would have used twenty years before.

Here I found some letters written to my mother when I was a boy, and later as a young man; then as a physician, giving her careful directions regarding her health; then the letter written the day before my supposed death, all bearing evidence of the many times she had sorrowfully read them. There also I found toys that years before had seemed so precious to me, and old garments carefully laid away, principally those which I had worn, and which I felt sure mother had purposely caused to be placed separately, thinking me dead, for if such had been the case it would have been the first death in our family.

And, moreover, I had always been looked upon by the others as " mother's boy." When I went to the room where, times without number, I had been given such faithful teachings, and prayed with so earnestly, and had I been the earnest Christian my mother had then entreated me to become, I could have prayed for guidance beside the same dear old chair in which she had so often sat with me. I could not stay here, I felt it was too sacred a place to be entered now, and with tears in my eyes, that come again as I write, I reluctantly closed the door and went away.

Later, I visited what had been my own room, finding it much as I had left it twenty years before. Many of my old school books were here, but my most precious though worthless possessions I had carefully placed elsewhere ; and now I took them, dust laden, from their places of concealment. First, a complicated contrivance that when finished was to have solved the problem of

perpetual motion, then a piece of a wind-mill so
arranged as to make a noise when in operation
sufficient to scare the crows from the corn field;
going further I came to some small boxes containing almost everything from a tooth, the first I
remember of having extracted, to a small bunch
of very tenderly-worded notes and a picture of
my little twelve-year-old sweetheart. These experiences were repeated next day when I drove
to the old farm my grandfather had owned during
his life-time. Here mother had lived as a child, a
girl, and a young woman, and accompanying me
she no doubt saw many things as dear to her.
I, too, had lived here for a time, and could not leave
the place until I had found my "marks" denoting
my height at various times—the first of which
was less than three feet. I also explored the
yards and barns. Here many changes had taken
place ; even my initials that had been deeply cut
in one of the large elm trees that grow so slowly
had become obliterated. This touched me deeply,
seeming so much in keeping with what had in
reality occurred to the name itself; and feeling
that I must find one unchanging remembrance, I

went to a huge boulder upon a hill near by, having to cross the brook with much difficulty that in earlier years had offered no impediment to the progress of my unclad feet.

Reaching the rock I raised my voice, uttering the same words I had used as a child, and listened for the echoing answer. It did not come; it, too, was dead, owing, no doubt, to the woods upon the surrounding hills having disappeared meantime. Returning I found my brother had come in answer to my request that he should visit me. He was accompanied by several sturdy boys whom I had never seen, and in whose faces I could see my brother and myself of years ago; but when, in conversation, they spoke to and of their father as "Arthur," his given name, I could but wonder if he thought of what would have been our portion had we ever addressed our parents in like manner. The day before I came away father told me of what disposition he had made, when he thought me dead, of the portion of his property that would have belonged to me if I had lived, and told me that he would rearrange it. This I begged him not to do, and a good occasion

having thus been brought about, I had him bring
from his trunk of private papers the several
promissory notes that he had guaranteed for me
years previous, and later had paid, and after
adding the interest, I insisted upon his taking the
money so represented. The next day, after a
leave-taking nearly as pathetic and hard to bear
as my meeting had been, I left them. I have seen
neither of them since, nor do I ever expect to do
so. Each prison mail delivery I receive with
trembling hands, expecting it to be an announcement of their death, caused by this great sorrow
and shame so cruelly forced upon them.

The morning following my return to Burlington I visited the post-office and received my mail.
It had been handed to me and I had stepped to a
small desk to open some of it when, glancing
toward the delivery window, I saw what seemed
to me to be the entire office force staring with all
wonder at me. I knew instantly that I was in
danger, and this was made more sure to me by
the manner in which they at once sought to dispel
this feeling by dispersing from the window. I at
once resumed my reading, for I felt that it would

be hazardous to have them know I was aware of
their acts. As soon as I could do so safely I
went to Mrs. Pitezel's house and told her I
had been hastily called to Boston and New
York ; that she should remain in Burlington until
I should return or send for her prior to her going
to the children. At this time (when I knew that
momentarily there was a possibility of officers
coming to the house for me) she reminded me
that the supply of coal was nearly exhausted and,
not wishing to go upon the street to order more,
I accompanied her to the basement and, after removing some of the decayed boards from the
floor of the coal bin, I shoveled together a considerable quantity of coal that had accumulated
there It was this circumstance that later, when
she was suffering so acutely in Toronto,.she distorted into the statement that she believed I was
then preparing to take her life. The dispatches
I had received in my Burlington mail left no doubt
in my mind that detectives were following my
movements, although I could not determine then
how they had undermined my apparently safe
plans. Later I found that, by making absolutely

erroneous statements to the Post-Office Department at Washington, they had been given the
right to examine all of a certain line of mail matter, thus accomplishing their purpose.

Having made these arrangements with Mrs.
Pitezel, I left Burlington Tuesday morning, November 13th, and reached Boston the same evening at the Adams House. The next day I secured some rooms in a quiet street for my wife
and myself, and proceeded at once to arrange for
Mrs. Pitezel's departure for Europe. But that
evening while writing some letters at the Parker
House, a careless shadower, in his earnestness to
learn their address, allowed me to know that I was
being watched. As in Burlington, I tried not to
have it known that I had observed it, but from
that moment I knew I was in their hands. After
leaving the hotel and entering several crowded
stores to ascertain the number and vigilance of
my followers, I adopted the only feasible plan I
considered was left open to me. I wrote Mrs.
Pitezel a letter, asking her to meet me upon a
certain day at Lowell, Mass., intending to see her
and instruct her as to taking the trip alone. After

throwing off my followers, I sent this letter to
Burlington by express, including tickets and full
directions for their journey. I then returned to
my rooms, intending to tell my wife of my threatened trouble and the causes that had led up to it.
I could not do it.

We had been married less than a year, and
during that time I had endeavored to shield her
from all annoying influences, and to cause her
such great unhappiness now, until I absolutely
knew it was upon me, was impossible. The next
day I was continually shadowed, and finally returned to my room, and while my wife was absent made a small opening in the now famous
trunk.*

I then went to a relative, living in a suburb, intending to ask him to aid me in making my
escape, by means of the trunk, if absolutely necessary. Here again my courage failed me, when I
had visited him, lest it should involve him in some
difficulty, and I returned to my room resolved to
meet whatever was in store for me.

* The tacks used later to replace the portion removed were taken from the carpet in
the room, and have been compared with those still there to make good my statement
that here was where the mutilation of the trunk occurred.

Saturday P. M., November 17th, I left the house
intending to send two letters, if possible. I had
proceeded hardly a block when I was surrounded
by four greatly excited men, two of whom said,
"We want you, you are under arrest, and it will
be useless for you to try to escape, as there are
four of us." I said, "I shall make no effort to
escape." We were near the police headquarters,
where I was at once taken into Inspector Watts'
private office. I knew that no time would be lost
in sending to my room to search my belongings,
and I therefore asked that my wife be called to
me, preferring to tell her myself of what was in
store for her. The request was granted, and in a
few minutes she was ushered into the room.

Of this scene I also cannot write. No one was
present save Inspector Watts, and I can never
forget or fail to appreciate his efforts to make it
as easy for her—for us both, for that matter—as
was possible. Before she had left me I told her
what had brought about my arrest and also my
right name. Only true-hearted, loving wives, who
have been made to suffer in the same way, can
know what the blow meant to her. They also

alone can understand her feelings expressed to
me in a letter months afterwards, from which,
sacred though it is to me, I quote these words,
"Our idols once shattered, though cherishing the
broken fragments as best we may, can never be
the same." After she had returned to our rooms
I had a long conversation with Inspector Watts,
a representative of the Insurance Company and a
Pinkerton detective. I found I had been arrested
upon the charge of stealing horses in Texas; that
I was to be held upon this charge until requisition
and other papers could be obtained from Pennsylvania in order to have me tried in that State
upon the charge of conspiring to defraud the
Insurance Company in Philadelphia. I at once
waived the necessity of requisition papers, and
told them I was ready to go with them.

I was then closely questioned regarding the
whereabouts of the Pitezel family, and knowing
that Mrs. Pitezel would in a few days be in
Lowell with no one to plan and care for her, and
fearing lest she should see an account of my
arrest and become alarmed thereby, I thought it
best to tell them where she was, asking them to

meet her upon her arrival. They thought it best
to go to Burlington, and it was there arranged
that they should escort her to Boston, but it was
agreed not to place her under arrest. I told them
that Pitezel and the other children were in the
South, not wishing to deviate from Mrs. Pitezel's
understanding of his condition until I could see
her. In my interview with Mr. Perry, the company's representative, it was agreed that in consideration of my aiding them in clearing up the
case, that I could depend upon the company's influence and aid in selecting a suitable location for
a home for my wife in Philadelphia. That my
name, then only known to a few persons, should
be withheld, allowing me to appear before the
public as H. H. Holmes, thus shielding my relatives from disgrace. That I should, upon reaching Philadelphia, see and talk with Mrs. Pitezel,
and plan for her future, and that my wife should
visit me upon my arrival there. No one of these
promises was kept save to obtain a boarding
place for my wife, and that principally that they
could use their best endeavors to so prejudice her
against me that she would not care to visit me.

Upon the following Monday evening I started for Philadelphia in company with Detective Crawford, being chained to him, in fact. Upon this trip my wife came into the car in which I was traveling to visit me for a few minutes, and while there saw Mrs. Pitezel and her two children for the first time in her life—they being then in the same car. Nor had she even known of the existence of such a family until my arrest in Boston. She had known of Pitezel in Fort Worth as a man working for me by the name of Lyman.

Upon reaching Philadelphia I was placed in a darkened cell in the City Hall, and here, figuratively speaking, the thumb-screws were applied. I was not allowed to see or hear from my wife, save that she was seriously ill. Mrs. Pitezel and the two children I knew were in the same place of confinement, but only by hearing their voices or the cries of the child, as I was not allowed to speak to them. After a time I was taken to the photograph department and weighed and measured, a process which has been too often described for publication to be of interest, save to say that so scientifically is it done that a person once placed under the ban in this way has little chance of ever escaping recognition. Later my photograph was also taken with what must have been a magical camera, judging from the thousand and one different reproductions from time to time appearing in print. Returning to my cell, Superintendent Linden visited me and advised me to see no attorney, and wishing to retain his good-will, if possible, I for a time gave heed to this. He also urged me strongly to tell him Pitezel's exact location. Upon Friday, October 23d, I was committed to prison upon the conspiracy charge, but before I went I made a detailed statement of our attorney's connection with the case, for I had found that he had been the cause of my trouble, and was then standing back, as he had said he should do, relying upon his reputation as a member of an influential firm of lawyers, to escape trouble himself. What followed during the next weary months of my life I feel that I can best express by copying from my prison diary, kept during this time, which now lies before me. I give such portions as relate more particularly to my case, stating first, however, that during all my

life I had always been active and had taken much
out-of-door exercise, and that on this account, together with worrying about my wife's safety, and
financial affairs, it seemed for a time after
my imprisonment commenced that I should die
from the effect thereof.

MOYAMENSING PRISON DIARY.

Saturday Evening, November 24, 1894.—A
week ago to-day I was placed under arrest in
Boston, and after a preliminary hearing was
brought here to Philadelphia, where I was confined at City Hall police headquarters. Yesterday P. M. I was placed in a crowded conveyance
filled with a filthy lot of humanity, and after what
seemed to me an endless drive reached the county
prison, located at Tenth and Reed streets, which is
known as Moyamensing. I was assigned to a
thoroughly clean, whitewashed room, about 9 x 14
feet in size, lighted by one very narrow grated
window. The entrance to the room is closed by
a small latticed iron door, beyond which is still
another solid door of wood, which, when closed,
excludes nearly all sound, and thus renders the

room practically a place of solitary confinement. A register furnishes furnace heat, and one sixteen candle power electric burner gives light during a part of the evening, it being turned off promptly at 9 P. M. The superintendent of the prison came to my door for a few moments this morning, and spoke to me of some of the prison rules and regulations. My attorney, Mr. Shoemaker, also called on me, also assured me that my wife should see me on Monday, and that she was no longer seriously ill, to hear which makes my heavy load seem lighter. I have now had three meals served to me since coming here, and can judge something of what my food will be if I have to stay here any length of time. For breakfast a plentiful supply of plain coffee and a quantity of coarse white bread ; at the noon hour a small pail well filled with soup, thickened with barley and a few beans, and containing a large piece of beef; at 5 P. M. I was agreeably surprised at receiving a liberal quantity of cocoa, made, I judge, from cocoa shells—a most healthful drink for one in such close confinement. This was accompanied by another piece of bread, which completed the day's rations. One thing is certain, even if not a great variety, the quantity is sufficient, and is cleanly cooked and served.

Sunday, November 25, 1894.—A long, still day, doubly hard to bear, inasmuch as since my marriage it has, owing to our long talks, reading and driving, grown to be a day of delight to me. At 3 P. M. the outer door to my room was opened about four inches in order to admit the sound of the religious services held at that hour and lasting until 4 o'clock, which consists principally of singing, some of which is quite good.

November 26, 1894.—My wife came to see me at 9.30 this morning. I had not been allowed to see her since my arrival in Philadelphia, and it required all the courage I could command to go to her under such humiliating circumstances. Our meeting took place in the presence of one of the prison officials. She has suffered, and though she tried heroically to keep me from seeing it, it was of no avail ; and in a few minutes to again bid her good-bye and know she was going out into the world with so heavy a load to bear, caused me more suffering than any death struggles

can ever do. Each day until I know she is
safe from harm and annoyance will be a living
death to me. I am promised that for the present
she shall visit me two times a week, each week,
not to exceed fifteen minutes in duration. If she
can bear the humiliation of coming here it will be
a Godsend to me, but I shall not urge her to do
so against her will.

Tuesday, November 27, 1894.—My attorney
called to see me to-day. He only is allowed to
visit my room and converse with me alone. Our
time was principally occupied in planning to furnish bail for Mrs. Pitezel, who must be set at liberty at all hazards. I am threatened with arrest
upon the charge of murder, if I give bail myself,
which is only another form of saying that I must
stay here until it is their pleasure to call my case
for trial; for if charged with murder, bail would
not be accepted. Had letters sent to Miss
Williams. The other two children are here in
Philadelphia, and I am assured are well cared for.
Was agreeably surprised to-day to find that un-
sentenced prisoners are allowed to receive eat-
ables, at their own expense, from outside the

prison, and I shall make arrangements to have this brought about. I also can have all newspapers and periodicals I wish. Money here in the prison, aside from these uses, is absolutely without value.

November 30, 1894.—My wife came, looking brighter and stronger. This time a seat was given her outside my door, though a keeper was present during the entire interview. I can see only too plainly what an effort it is for her to come into this terrible place, for she sees more of the prison in passing in and out than I do myself, and to one of her sensitive nature it is a most trying experience. Was instructed to-day that, after I have completed several important business letters I am writing, I must restrict all of my correspondence to one letter a week. All mail is inspected in the prison office. I think my weight is twenty pounds less than at time of my arrest; but I am getting more used to my unnatural surroundings and to my bed of straw, and am sleeping better. The great humiliation of feeling that I am a prisoner is killing me far more than any other discomforts I have to endure.

I notice quite a difference, however, between my wooden stool and a comfortable office or rocking-chair, but still feel that I have much to be thankful for, as thus far I have been allowed to wear my own clothing and to keep my watch and other small belongings. The escape from wearing the convict garb I greatly appreciate.

December 3, 1894.—I have commenced to write a careful and truthful account of all matters pertaining to my case, including the fact that Pitezel is dead and that the children are with Miss Williams, and as soon as I have completed it I shall ask my attorney to place it in the hands of the authorities that they may verify what I have written.

I feel that I could very easily have carried out the statements I made relative to his being alive and the substitution of a body if there was anything to be gained by it, but Mrs. Pitezel, at all events, should know of it before the children return, lest the question arise as to where he was, and give occasion for the prosecution to feel that other motives than this had caused me to conceal the true state of affairs.

December 25, 1894—Christmas. I shall receive no presents, and caused only a few flowers
to be sent to ———, as I feel that any reminder
of a year ago to-day would make it harder for
her to bear. Nor will I trust myself to write at
length to-night. I did not have a dinner sent in
to-day. To-morrow will also be another sad an-
niversary, and a day hard to bear.

January 1, 1895.—The New Year. I have been
busy nearly all day in prison formulating a
methodical plan for my daily life while in prison,
to which I shall hereafter rigidly adhere, for the
terrible solitude of these dark winter days will
otherwise soon break me down. I shall rise at
6.30, and after taking my usual sponge bath shall
clean my room and arrange it for the day. My
meal hours shall be 7.30 A. M., 12, and 5 and 9
P. M. I shall eat no more meat of any kind
while I am so closely confined. Until 10 A. M.
all the time not otherwise disposed of shall be
devoted to exercise and reading the morning
papers. From 10 to 12 and 2 to 4, six days in
the week, I shall confine myself to my old medical works and other college studies, including

stenography, French and German, the balance of my day shall be taken up with reading the periodicals and library books with which ———— keeps me well supplied. I shall retire at 9 P. M. and shall as soon as possible force myself into the habit of sleeping throughout the entire night. Received a most kind and tender letter from my wife, filled with encouraging words. But each day seems to make it harder to bear.

January 9th.—We have abandoned for the time being all hopes of procuring Mrs. Pitezel her liberty. The insurance company, misconstruing our motives, are determined to keep her under their control. Efforts are being made to keep me from making satisfactory settlements of my business matters, as well as trying to induce my wife to abandon me. Came across these two lines in my reading to-day:—

> " I only know the sky has lost its blue,
> The days are weary and the night is drear."

They so thoroughly described my own condition that I cannot refrain from copying them to-night.

January 25th.—Had a long, quiet talk with my wife at City Hall to-day, where I had been taken to be interviewed by the authorities. I feel better and stronger to-night than for many days. Caused advertisement to be sent to Miss Williams, and also sent out a large number of business letters, there being no restriction against doing so while there.

In February Mr. Shoemaker started West and South to settle up my business matters for me; I expect him to be absent fully two weeks. Owing to the interference of the insurance company, property that I would have refused $50,000 for three months ago, some of which I would not have sold at all, will have to be sacrificed, so that not more than one-half that sum will be realized for it.

March 1st.—Commenced to-day to arrange for my trial. Mr. S. P. Rotan is to act with Mr. Shoemaker as associate counsel. Thus far I have devoted but little time to this work, but shall now give my 10 to 12 study hour to it each day.

March 11th.—Read Trilby, and was much pleased with parts of it. My wife also brought me some very nice flowers, speaking so strongly to me of our former life that I have had to put them from my sight.

March 23d.—The days are fast lengthening; the sun shone into my room for a few minutes to-day for the first time since I came here.

May 16th.—My birthday. Am 34 years old. I wonder if, as in former years, mother will write me. Was at the City Hall and pleaded with the Assistant District Attorney again that my present case be abandoned and that I be at once tried upon the charge of killing Pitezel, as I feel that I cannot too soon have this matter settled, inasmuch as they so boldly accuse me of it. This they flatly refused to do, saying I only wished to avoid serving a sentence upon the minor charge. Then the only satisfaction I could obtain when I urged that the conspiracy charge be tried at once in order that Mrs. Pitezel may be set at liberty was, "Don't you worry yourself about Mrs. Pitezel; we will care for her and will also give you all you want to do before we are through with you. Have retained Mr. R. O. Moon as special counsel.

May 21st.—My case was called in Court to-day, and I entered a formal plea of " not guilty."

The trial was postponed until a later date. On
Monday, May 27th, my case was called for trial.
I went to the City Hall, where the Court was
held, in the same kind of conveyance that had
brought me here over six months before, and was
conducted by two officers into the Court room,
and placed in a small enclosure in the centre of
the room. After a little delay, the Court was
called to order, Judge Hare presiding. Little
time was lost in securing a jury, as those first
called, almost without exception, appeared to be
both intelligent and honest. After administering
the oaths, the District Attorney arose and addressed the Court. Theretofore I had not looked
upon my case as serious, for after I had placed
before the authorities my written statement, some
months earlier, stating that Pitezel was actually
dead, some of the prosecution and the insurance
company had openly stated that they believed it
to be true, and knowing myself that his death
had actually occurred, it left little, save the charge
of conspiracy, to be disposed of; but when the
prosecution drew into the case matters altogether
foreign to the conspiracy charges, I felt that it

could not help but influence the jury. The authorities had also brought Mrs. Pitezel into Court, and had seated her in a prominent portion of the room, and later, while giving his testimony, one of the witnesses led the Court to understand that with a knife I had proceeded, in a cold-blooded manner, to mutilate the body of Pitezel at the time of examination for the purpose of identification. I saw that the prosecution were determined to magnify and dilate each point that could be turned in their favor.

During the afternoon session I learned that a subpœna had been issued requiring my wife to appear in Court, contrary to a distinct arrangement that I had previously made with the insurance company that she should not be used as a witness or annoyed in regard to the case, and I felt that I would rather serve a longer term of imprisonment than thus humiliate her. At the close of the Court for the day I learned that the prosecution were prepared to place upon the witness stand the doctors before referred to, who had seen the body at Callowhill street, both of whom would swear the body found there could not have

been Pitezel, a matter I could not disprove, and
that evening, after considering all the proceedings
of the day, I resolved to ask my counsel to allow
me to change my plea, relying upon them to show
the Court when I should, at a later date, be
brought before the Judge to be sentenced, that
while there had existed an agreement to perpetrate a fraud under certain circumstances, there was
no active conspiracy at the time when Pitezel's
death had occurred, and that the death being
genuine, the insurance company had not been defrauded. This, together with the fact that I should
save at least a week's valuable time to the Court
by ending my trial as I did, I hoped would cause
the Judge to reduce my sentence to one-half the
fullest extent, thus allowing me to go to Texas in
October, 1895, which would be in season to attend to my business matters there before they
would seriously suffer from the delay. Before
leaving the Court the Judge stated that I should
be allowed the six months I had already been in
prison, which I could not but appreciate, as it was
wholly discretionary with him. Later during the
day I was called before the District Attorney, in

his private office, and there made a statement as
to the probable whereabouts of the children, telling them as truthfully as I knew all the facts I
could think of that would aid them in the search,
and later gave them the cipher I had formerly
used in communicating with Miss Williams. I
then returned to my prison room at Moyamensing.

Upon the 18th of June I was taken to the Court
House as a witness in the case against Howe;
but a long continuance being taken, I was not
called upon to testify. Shortly thereafter one of
my attorneys, after careful preparation, went to
London, and did considerable hard work for me
in endeavoring to locate the missing children by
searching for the old addresses given me by
Hatch; and the assertion made by the Assistant
District Attorney that I had deceived my counsel
and sent him upon a search I knew to be useless,
is simply one of many statements he has made
both to me and for publication that are painful
evidence of the want of discernment and good
judgment one had a right to expect from the
occupant of so important a position.

Later in June Detective Guyer called on me, and, in a long conversation with him, I made a most honest endeavor to place him in possession of all the facts I could think of that would be instrumental in facilitating the proposed search, which I looked upon and welcomed as one of corroboration of the same statements I had previously made, feeling that upon his following my movements from place to place, and finding that I had not misled him in any way, he would return more free to believe other statements that were not so easily verified; and I do not think I need to state to any intelligent reader that had I known of the death and burial of the little ones in the Toronto cellar, and wished to conceal the same, I should have avoided all mention of other houses where furniture had been brought and, in one instance, an excavation made, and I feel that if Mr. Guyer were called upon for a truthful statement, he could not fail to say that but for my aid, freely given him at this time, together with detailed statements and drawings previously made relating to those places where I had forgotten the exact location, his search would have been a failure, inasmuch as he would have had no incentive to prosecute a similar investigation in Toronto.

On the morning of the 16th of July, my newspaper was delivered to me at about 8.30 A. M., and I had hardly opened it before I saw in large headlines the announcement of the finding of the children in Toronto. For the moment it seemed so impossible, that I was inclined to think it one of the frequent newspaper excitements that had attended the earlier part of the case, but, in attempting to quickly gain some accurate comprehension of what was stated in the article, I became convinced that at least certain bodies had been found there, and upon comparing the date when the house was hired I knew it to be the same as when the children had been in Toronto; and thus being forced to realize the awfulness of what had probably happened, I gave up trying to read the article, and saw instead the two little faces as they had looked when I hurriedly left them—felt the innocent child's kiss so timidly given and heard again their earnest words of farewell, and I realized that I had received another burden to carry to

my grave with me, equal, if not worse, than the
horrors of Nannie Williams' death.

I think at this time I should have lost my
senses utterly had I not been hurriedly called to
prepare to be taken to the District Attorney's
office. I went there securely handcuffed and accompanied by two officers for further safety, and
not until these extra precautions were taken did
I realize the new and terrible change that had occurred affecting the entire aspect of my case.
Upon reaching the City Hall the Assistant District
Attorney met me. I was in no condition to bear
his accusations, nor disposed to answer many of
his questions. I felt it right that he should know
that I had already seen the morning papers, and
upon his demanding that I tell him where the
body of the boy could be found, I answered, that
in the light of the Toronto development, I had
reason to think he would be found buried in or
about the house that had been hired in Detroit.
He then accused me of killing him in Detroit and
destroying his body by burning it in a furnace
that was in the cellar. This I denied, and moreover felt sure and told him that the body could

not have been destroyed there in that way by any
one else, as I had been in the house upon two
occasions and knew that if human remains had
been cremated there even at a considerably
earlier date the odor would have been noticeable.
I did not see the District Attorney at this interview and was very soon taken to the prison again.

For the next forty-eight hours I reasoned and
thought, studying minutely each step of our journey from the time Hatch had joined us; but what
seemed utterly incomprehensible to me then, and
even now, was how any sane man would take such
awful chances, even if he had no other scruples to
restrain him, yet I well knew it could have been
no one else that committed the crime, for in that
event the non-arrival of the children would have
been known to us. I knew also that the small
sum of $400, that was given to the girls just pre-
vious to their death, could have been no incentive
for the commission of the act, and was forced to
look further for the motive. I could only think
that it had been done at Miss Williams' suggestion and in furtherance of her threat of the previous year, which, owing to friendliness at a later

date, I had believed wholly abandoned, probably
also intending to give color to a theory (if later
for her safety such had to be advanced) that I,
and not she, had killed her sister, pointing to
these disappearances that had occurred at a time
when I was known to have had the children in my
charge as corroborative of the same, though I felt
sure that her hellish wish for vengeance for the
imagined desertion of the previous year was much
the more potent of the two motives.

Finally I commenced at the time I had first
asked them to come here, and following carefully
each step and conversation we had held, I became
certain that when Hatch had first met me in
Cincinnati he could have had no matured plans.
Then going over our route I could see no change
until after reaching Indiana. He had gone away
for a few days to Chicago, as he then said, but, as
I now believe, to Detroit, to consult with Miss
Williams, as it occurred directly after he had first
known I was liable to be arrested. He then commenced taking more interest in the children,
taking them about with him and buying them
presents. It was at this time, also, that he took a

private room, saying that inasmuch as I was liable to be watched, it was unsafe for any of us to be at a hotel. It was then that he had his beard removed from his chin* in the barber shop at the Indianapolis depot, each act being a trifle in itself, yet taken together showed to me that then was when the change had commenced. Following still further, I had at first wished to go to Chicago alone, thinking it safer to do so than to be accompanied by the children. I had asked him to take them all to Detroit with him, to which he replied that if this was done it would keep him from looking about for a house there for Mrs. Pitezel, which we were anxious to obtain as quickly as possible ; that he could take the boy with him easily, for he could accompany him about the city in his search. This, together with the girls' desire to go to Chicago, led me to carry out the arrangement in this way. Then came our arrival in Detroit, two days later, when Hatch stated that the boy had gone with Miss Williams to Buffalo, and that he had been delayed

* In answer to a recent question from the authorities, if, after Hatch had thus changed his appearance, he looked like myself, I answer, No, at least not to a sufficient extent to be mistaken for me by one who knew us both.

twenty-four hours *en route* to Detroit at some junction where a wreck had occurred, thus accounting for his having made no search for a house.

Then of another circumstance, which ordinarily I should not have considered more than a coincidence. While in Cincinnati, Alice and the boy had disputed as to which should wear an old watch that had belonged to their father. Alice advancing her claim of superior years, Howard, that he was the boy of the family, accompanied by the remembrance that his father had promised it to him when he grew older. I settled the matter by taking the watch in charge and buying each of them a small nickel open-faced watch and chain. This left little Nellie with a broken heart, and as soon as I noticed her trouble, I told her that before our journey was ended I would also buy one for her, or something else equally pleasing to her, if she preferred. The day after our arrival in Detroit she came to me much elated, saying Mr. Hatch had bought her a watch. Upon looking at it, it proved to be of the same make and design as the one Alice had, and I now believe it was the same watch I had given Howard some days before. Then in Detroit occurred the buying of the spade and his insisting upon taking it to Toronto, giving the weak excuse that he had paid for it and did not wish to throw it away, when he could have sold it at a second-hand store much easier than to have taken it so far to the depot to place it in the trunk. Then, the letter from Miss Williams, asking that I pay the $1,000 due upon the Fort Worth property then, instead of later, as she wished to use a part of it ; it seeming hardly probable, if this had been the real reason of requiring the money at that time, that so much trouble would have been taken in trying to convert the money I gave into a $1,000 bill.

The only other circumstance I could then think of was his almost querulous objection to my buying a jacket in Detroit for one of the girls, and later heavier clothing in Toronto, he saying that Miss Williams could better understand their needs, and his efforts to borrow $500 from me in Burlington, and also that Alice had told me in Toronto that Mr. Hatch had given her a letter or a postal card to write for him, as he had no writing materials at his room. I asked her what it was about, and she answered, as near as I can remember, that it was to a Mr. Cooke about a house that he did not need longer and about a sale of furniture or that it had been sold. If I thought sufficiently of the matter at the time, I supposed it referred to the Detroit house, as this was the only one I had reason to think he had engaged, and I think it will be later found that at Logansport or Peru, or some other junction town in Indiana, a house was hired upon October 10th or 11th, while I was in Chicago, and the body of the boy shipped from the hotel in Indianapolis in accordance with the report that a large trunk was that day shipped to an unknown destination, and the remains buried similarly to the Toronto case, and that this was the true cause of his delay in reaching Detroit.

Some days later I told the authorities that such was my belief, giving them my reasons for thinking so, and for my pains I was severely taken to task for having previously stated that I thought he would be found in or about the

Detroit house. From this I have been charac-
terized by them as a supreme falsifier.

With the one exception of the statements made
at the time of my arrest, and adhered to until I
knew Mrs. Pitezel could be no longer saved from
worriment by so doing, I know of no material
misstatements made, save that the children were
in England, which I most honestly believed to
be true.

The next day I saw an account in the papers
of my wife's coming here in answer to a telegram from the District Attorney's office. This
said to me far more than was printed in the
paper. I knew she must have been intimidated
to have come at this time and in answer to a
summons from them. My fears were confirmed
a few days later when I learned from a trusted
source that such was the case, and that the threat
had been made that if she made any effort to see
or communicate with me she would be arrested and
held as a witness. (It will here be remembered
that our prison interviews were invariably held in
the presence of a keeper.) And upon the other
hand if she remained away from me and aided

them, all her expenses would be paid by the prosecution or the insurance company.

I knew that the latter would have no weight with her, but I feared that the threats they made would cause her to worry until she became ill, and I therefore felt justified in resorting to almost any means to see her and try and quiet her fears. With this in view I wrote the District Attorney that if I could have an interview with him, my wife being present, I would endeavor to make it plain to him where they could expect to find the remains of the boy. This interview was promptly accorded me and, upon being taken into his private office, I met my wife, and it needed but one glance to know what she had been and was then suffering, which caused a feeling of almost uncontrollable anger to take possession of me, both towards the authorities for unjustly causing her hard lot to be made worse, and towards myself that for the sake of business gains I had ever allowed myself to enter into the petty transactions that had been the cause of all her troubles. My first inquiry, as could naturally be expected, was as to her physical condition and if she was

in comfortable quarters and free from actual restraint. I also told her that until the world at
large ceased to look upon me as a murderer I
should not in the presence of others greet her as
was my usual custom. If at this time my wife
shrank from me as though in fear, as was given
out from the District Attorney's office for publication, I, in my blindness, did not see it, and in
the days and nights that followed until I again
heard of her welfare almost my only source of
comfort was the remembrance of the few kind
words she had said, and, what was even more to
me, that she had worn both her engagement and
her wedding rings, and as many of the gifts I had
presented to her during our happier days as she
could without exciting undue notice, choosing
those that would convey to me from their associations the kind thoughts she knew she would
have no opportunity to say in words.

This was particularly plain to me, inasmuch as
it was wholly contrary to her usual custom to
appear thus attired at that early hour of the day,
and in so public a place, and until she tells me
that such is not the case I shall hold to the belief

that she is yet loyal to me. There were present at this meeting, beside the District Attorney, Mr. Shoemaker and Supt. Linden, and for a part of the time Mr. Fouse and the Assistant District Attorney. I endeavored to state to them, in as few words as possible, the circumstances of Hatch's delay of twenty-four hours, and the letters sent from either Detroit or Toronto about a house. They at once branded my statements concerning Hatch as untrue, and said that he was a mythical person, asking me to name any one who had ever seen him. In reply I said, "I do not consider that you have any more grounds for doubting the fact that he was at these places than to doubt that Mrs. Pitezel or these children were there, because they did not happen to meet. However, you need not rely upon my statements."

Last November or December Mr. Perry, a representative of the insurance company, came to the prison, in company with another witness, to question me about some other matters pertaining to the case, and while there said to me, "Who was the man you met at the Burlington depot you seemed so surprised to see, and immediately went

to the telegraph office and took up a message
you had previously written?"

I told him it was a man named Hatch, a friend
of Miss Williams, who was not connected with
my case in any important way. I also stated in
further answer to the District Attorney's question
that I felt sure that the barber in the Indianapolis
depot would remember his coming there with me,
it being so unusual an occurence for me to be
accompanied by any one; that the proprietor or
clerk of the small hotel where he had taken the
children upon their arrival in Detroit would
remember him, and probably the woman where
they boarded during most of their stay in that
city, as he accompanied them to the train the day
following my departure for Toronto. That Mrs.
Pitezel will remember his calling at her house at
Burlington, and upon her going to the door he
made some trivial excuse and went away, having
expected to meet me there. And that my wife
will remember my leaving her upon the steam-
boat landing at B. for a moment to step across to
the depot to speak to him, and upon two subsequent occasions while in that city of recognizing

him upon the street, she remarking upon my
knowing any one there, and parties who have
lately testified that they knew of my visiting Miss
Williams in New York in 1888, and later in
Denver, will know that it was Hatch and not myself, as I never was in Denver until January, 1894,
and never saw Miss Williams prior to January,
1893.

"Call him Hatch, Jones, or Smith, if you will,
but you have known for months that there was
such a person at certain places during the trip
with whom I communicated, and with whom I
was seen, and whose existence you cannot now
ignore."

I then tried to explain to them that for want of
time alone, even if I were the bloodthirsty villain
they were inclined to make me appear, I could
not be guilty of the Toronto murders, and begged
them to allow me to go there before by any
chance evidence that could now be obtained
should become unavailable to me. To this the
District Attorney replied, "I shall not do it;
I shall try you here." What more could be
said? If a man as broad-minded as I knew the

District Attorney to be, both from common
report and from my own observation, would not
consider so important a statement, what could I
expect from others having a less thorough knowledge of the case? I was much disappointed, both
at not being allowed to go there, and at the harsh
and unjust way he looked upon the matter, and
the feeling was increased a few minutes later
when I asked to be allowed to provide for my
wife's support while here, by having him tell me
that he did not consider it any part of my business at the present time to either know of or care
for her welfare; and some weeks later by his re-
fusing to allow my relatives and business agent
to visit me at the prison, and by a number of
trivial matters like withholding my newspaper and
intercepting and keeping letters that, after reading, he could see did not pertain to, and could
not influence my case in any way, saying that if
I, were given hardships enough and kept long
enough away from others, I would confess these
crimes. Feeling it was useless to prolong the
interview, and noticing that my wife was suffering
intensely, I brought it to a close as quickly as

possible. I bade her good-bye and was again handcuffed and taken to prison.

During the previous days the part of the Toronto matters that had seemed the most unaccountable to me was how Hatch could have returned to the depot so soon after I had left both him and the children upon the train, and what excuse he could have given to them to forego their journey. This information my interview had supplied. In questioning me, Superintendent Linden had said, " Who was that light young man standing upon the corner of the street near the house where the children were killed, that you spoke with at some length and then went away to hire an expressman ? " I hesitated in my answer to him, and finally told him that I had not met any one there, but if he knew that such a meeting had taken place it was of the most vital importance to my case. There had instantly come into my mind when he had asked this question a remembrance of two years previous, but owing to their scoffs at the possibility of Hatch's existence, I felt it wise to refrain from speaking of it to him until I could hear from those by whom I could prove the statement I would have liked to have made at the time.

One day in the spring of '93, soon after Miss Williams' trunks, containing her theatrical costumes, had been brought to our rooms in the block in Chicago, returning from the city one afternoon, I met upon the stairway leading to my office a jauntily dressed young man, whom, as I passed, I asked to cease smoking his cigarette within the building, and a few minutes later was being saucily laughed at in my office by Miss Williams. So clever had the deception been, both in clothing and change in facial expression by aid of her color box, that upon her wishing to do so, I allowed her to accompany me upon a trip to Aurora, Ill., and later to St. Joseph, Mich., costumed in this manner. That both of these trips, made under these circumstances, actually occurred, I am able to prove by competent and disinterested persons, and I feel sure that Miss Williams was in Toronto, probably meeting the children at Hamilton, and returning with them, and keeping one with her while the other was killed; and next day, while I must necessarily have been hundreds of miles away, inasmuch as I registered at Prescott at 4 P. M., she, if any one, met Hatch near this house, disguised in this manner. On August 15th, Mr. Cops, a Fort Worth attorney, obtained permission of the District Attorney to interview me, and, after questioning me for a time, said he would like to tell me his theory of how I had killed my Chicago victims, which was that while they were in my office I had in some way induced them to step inside the vault and then caused their death by suffocation. He said, "Why, Holmes, it is the plainest case I ever heard of, even the footprints of one of them are to be seen upon the door, where in their desperation they had tried to make their escape."

I asked him when he believed the last of these deaths had occurred there. He replied, "Probably in July, 1893. In fact, if you could show me that Minnie Williams was alive after that date, I would be much inclined to believe that she was alive now and that she killed her sister, as you say, for, if alive, only that could have been a sufficient motive to induce her to conceal her whereabouts for so long from her Texas friends." I said, "Will you grant me that I am not guilty of taking life there since I left Chicago about January 1, 1894, for Texas." He replied, "Yes, I think that would be safe from the evidence I have gathered in Chicago." I said, "In August, 1893, a fire occurred in the building, causing the destruction of many valuable letters and papers, and upon the building being repaired I bought this vault, in October or November, 1893, from a safe and vault company whose offices were one block west of La Salle street, between Madison and Adams, in Chicago. The purchase was made in the name of the Campbell-Yates Company, and in December, 1893, it was put in place and plastered by a workman named Kriss.

"A very few days thereafter I left Chicago and have never been in the rooms since. There was never any other vault in the building, save one upon the first floor that for years had been under the entire control of tenants occupying the drug and jewelry store in which it is located. I cannot give you the name or exact address of this company, but it is plainly printed upon the door of the vault, and upon your return to Chicago, if you care to do so, you can satisfy yourself of the truthfulness of my statement regarding it." He said, " Until I can do this I cannot believe it to be true, but if I do find that such is the case I shall be inclined to return to Fort Worth and abandon my case, and upon the strength of what you have told me, I will say to you that I have lately learned that there has been found at Fort Worth among mail that was sent to you after you left that city, a London letter from Miss Williams, but being so sure in my own mind that she died nearly a year previous to that time, I have supposed it to be a clever forgery sent there by you to mislead those who found it." I told him that Miss Williams had sent me three letters there which were forwarded by Mr. John L. Judd, my Denver agent, 1609 Lawrence street, that city, to whom he could write to or visit to corroborate my statement. That two of these letters I had received and had supposed the other had been sent to the Dead Letter Office and destroyed ; that if he would take the letter to Mr. ———— and others in Fort Worth, who knew her writing, they would at once tell him it was not a forgery. A

few days later I heard of the explosion and fire
at the block in Chicago, and felt, as has lately
been the case whenever I hear of any loss of life,
strange disappearances or other misdemeanors
not easily accounted for, throughout the United
States—anywhere in the world in fact—almost
thankful that the strong doors of my prison room
make it impossible for such acts to now be
ascribed to me.

OTHER DISAPPEARANCES.

A Miss Van Tassand to the best of my knowledge I never saw. Certain it is that I hired no
fruit store in Chicago, nor did I have a person of
that name in my employ at any time.

A Mrs. Lee, said to have disappeared some
time in 1893, I do not know of ever having
seen.

Cora Quinlin is said by the newspapers to be
alive. No insurance of any kind was ever caused
to be placed upon the life of this child by me nor
did I know that such had been placed by others.

A Miss Cigrand was sent to me by the National
Typewriter Exchange in Chicago in May, 1892.

She worked faithfully in my interests until November, 1892, when, much against my wishes, she left my employ to be married, as I understood at the time. Some days after going away she returned for her mail, and at this time gave me one of her wedding cards, and also two or three others for tenants in the building who were not then in their rooms; and in reponse to inquiries lately made I have learned that at least five persons in and about Lafayette, Ind., received such cards, the post mark and her handwriting upon the envelope in which they were enclosed showing that she must have sent them herself after leaving my employ. While working for me she had also acted as the secretary of the Campbell–Yates Co., a corporation in which I was interested; and in 1893 certain papers relating to the business of this company that had been overlooked required her signature, and after considerable delay she came to the office in November, which was about one year after she left my employ. She accompanied me to lunch at Thompson's restaurant, where I had eaten regularly for years, and where during the previous year she had often eaten with me. Here the man known as Henry, who for a long time has been head usher in this establment and knew us both well, remarked to her, as he gave us our seats, "It is a long time since you were here." She replied, "About one year." A few days later she met me elsewhere in Chicago, at which time Arthur S. Kirk, a member of the well-known soap manufacturers, Kirk & Co., and two employees were present, and upon my recalling to Mr. Kirk's memory certain business transactions I had with him at about this time, he, as well as his employees, will remember the circumstances, and be able to fix the exact date and give an accurate description of Miss Cigrand.

Before leaving Chicago, she expressed a desire to re-enter my employ, stating that unless more kindly treated she should not longer live with her husband, but should either return to office work or re-enter the convent, where she had been educated, or some other similar institution.

She also told me that she had written her people, but should not visit them until she could give them financial aid, as she had been in the habit of doing before her marriage, and I think she will let

me know her location and present name before I
am made to suffer for her disappearance.

Miss Mary and Miss Kate Dunkee are both
acknowledged by the Philadelphia authorities to
be alive. Charles Cole is also known to be
alive.

The Redman family, the child or its abductress,
I never saw, and know nothing of the case save
from the accounts published at the time.

Robert Latimer, a former janitor, a Mr. Brum-
mager, one in my employ as a stenographer, also
a Miss Mary Horacamp, from Hamilton, Canada,
are alive, as shown by letters recently received
from friends or relatives of each.

Miss Anna Betz, formerly of Englewood, Ill.,
whose death I have been so persistently charged
with during the past year, the claims being made
that it had been caused by a criminal operation
performed by me at the instigation of ———, of
Chicago, for which I received a release of the sum
of $2,500 that I owed him, I was but little ac-
quainted with, and if her death was occasioned in
such a manner I certainly am not the cause of it,
and checks given upon my order by F. W. Devoe

& Co., of New York, will show when and how my indebtedness to Mr. ———— was canceled.

The same charge concerning a domestic named Lizzie is untrue, although I have no means of verifying it save that it has been proven that she was alive and in Chicago some months after I left that city, early in 1894.

PHOTOGRAPHIC IDENTIFICATIONS.

In 1883 there were conducted within my knowledge a series of experiments illustrative of the unreliability of photographic identifications, and other similar experiments have often been made. These consisted in calling upon ten students who had witnessed two skillful sign writers executing some work upon a street window to later identify them from photographs. An open album was first handed to the student who was told to choose which one of two pictures before him was the party in question, they all made a prompt decision as to one or the other being the person they had seen, the fact being that neither of the pictures were of these men. To another group of ten that had also seen the painters under like circumstances was given a frame containing forty photographs, they being instructed that the picture of one of the men they had seen was among the number. Only one chose the right picture, and none looked for or found more than one, although without their knowledge pictures of both were plainly before them in the group. The result of the entire number of experiments was that over 95 per cent. failed in their efforts at identification. In my own case by means of pictures, a man in Milwaukee is or was ready to make oath that I was in that city, accompanied by the two children, at a time when the Philadelphia authorities know we were else-where. A woman in Chicago is equally positive that I was several days at her boarding house with Miss Williams and the two children, at a time when the authorities know I was in Cincinnati, Ohio. In the same manner two Detroit parties are ready to swear that Miss Williams was in that city, accompanied by a man answering my description of Hatch, at a time when I know he was with me in Indianapolis. In all these instances, and in the Toronto identifications, I believe that the parties have been honest in the statements made, but it must be remembered that they have been led to understand that no other decision was possible. A good example of the methods employed was furnished some months ago when at police headquarters here. I was taken before some twenty or thirty people by a detective who, when near enough for them to hear, said, "Mr. Holmes, these people are witnesses in the case for which you are to be tried here, and I wish to see if they can identify you."

MOTIVES.

Had my early life and associations been such as to predispose me towards such criminal proceedings, still the want of motive remains. I can show that no motive did exist. Those who knew me personally can see that it could not have been avarice, for whenever I possessed even a small surplus of ready money, those whom I was owing or friends in need of same could always receive the most or all I possessed. Any ungovernable temper is excluded, for I do not possess it. Appetence cannot be ascribed as a motive, age and other

circumstances to a great extent excluding same.
The principal motive thus far ascribed, namely,
that I had first involved my alleged victims in, or
made them parties to, dishonest transactions can
be excluded, from the fact that all such transactions are matters of recent date, and almost
without exception they are found to have done
nothing criminal. Either one of the foregoing I
should prefer having my supposed shortcomings
attributed to than the only remaining motive I
can think of, namely, insanity, to which, either
hereditary or acquired, I can plead not guilty,
and be substantiated in so doing by a sufficient
number of medical experts, whose testimony
cannot be lightly overlooked.

Of the three more important cases, first that
of the Williams sisters. Nannie Williams was
wholly without means. The following account
will show that had I given Hatch the $500 he
wished to borrow of me in Burlington, there
would have been little due Nannie Williams;
nothing in fact, if I had included various small
sums paid her from time to time, of which no
account was kept. It should also be borne in

mind that she still holds the title to the $10,000 Wilmette property, which, on this account, is valueless to me.

RECEIVED OF M. R. WILLIAMS.

April, 1893, Cash, ...	$2,500	
April, 1893, Real Estate, . .	7,000	
August, 1894, Cash, ...	600	
		$10,100

PAID M. R. WILLIAMS.

May, 1893, Cash, ...	$2,500	
July, 1893, Cash, . . .	1,000	
December, 1893, Cash, . . .	750	
January, 1894, Fort Worth Incumbrance, ...	1,725	
February, 1894, Cash, .	1,750	
October, 1894, Cash, . . .	1,000	
October, 1894, Cash, . . .	412	
		$9,137
		$963

Shown by cashed drafts and checks endorsed by M. Williams, and other forms of evidence.

In the case of Benj. F. Pitezel, the motive is said to have been the money to be derived from his insurance, and more than this from his Texas real-estate holdings. In regard to the former, I can only reiterate that he was worth more to me each year he lived than the amount he was insured for, and each year he was becoming more valuable to me ; therefore, why should I take his life? His real estate was not of one dollar's value to him, and could only be of value to me after he had signed certain papers, the want of which I felt within thirty days after his death. This is also true of his patents and other belongings. The claim that I designed to kill the six other members of the Pitezel family to avoid being held accountable for the small sum of $5,200, seems too unlikely a motive to call for a denial, and, excluding this, it will be hard to find another, when the care and attention I have given them for years is considered.

In conclusion, I wish to say that I am but a very ordinary man, even below the average in physical strength and mental ability, and to have planned and executed the stupendous amount of wrong-doing that has been attributed to me would have been wholly beyond my power, and even had I been able to have performed it, a still greater

task would have been the successful elaboration
of a story at the time of my arrest that, if untrue,
would have provided for the many exigencies
that at that time I could not have known would
have occurred later in the case ; and I feel justified in asking from the general public a suspension of judgment as to my guilt or innocence, not
while the various charges can be proven against
me, but while I can disprove them, a task which I
feel able to satisfactorily and expeditiously accomplish.   And here I cannot say finis—it is not the
end—for besides doing this there is also the work
of bringing to justice those for whose wrong-doings I am to-day suffering, and this not to prolong
or save my own life, for since the day I heard of
the Toronto horror I have not cared to live; but
that to those who have looked up to and honored
me in the past it shall not in the future be said that
I suffered the ignominious death of a murderer.

MINNIE R. WILLIAMS

HE WAS MARKED BY H. H. HOLMES

A Weird Coincidence Related by a Neighbor of Mr. Biles.

TALE OF THE FATAL "LIVE" WIRES

They Blazed On the Day the Murderer Was First Taken Into Custody.

THE MALIGNANT INFLUENCE AT WORK

The Curious Fact Developed That Many Who Were Concerned In the Trial Have Since Met With Fatality or Misfortune.

"I now believe fully that Holmes not only looks like a devil, but is one in reality," said a neighbor yesterday, in speaking of the strange and awful death of Linford L. Biles, the foreman of the jury that convicted the murderer of Benjamin F. Pitezel; and then he told a story which, if true, proves beyond the shadow of a doubt that the man now

awaiting death at Moyamensing Prison
is possessed of an influence malignant
in the extreme, and which not only per-
vades the very atmosphere about him,
but, so it would seem, has actually the
telepathic property of transmission, and
played a wonderfully weird part in the
tragedy of the man who passed away
yesterday.

Mr. Biles, according to his statement,
was a marked man the very day Holmes
was arrested in Boston, for on
that day the same wires that electrocuted the man who was then to
be foreman of the jury that would convict the murderer flashed out for the
first time, in the same manner that
they did yesterday, and, as then, threatened to set the house afire.

The impressed narrator of the strange
story is of the opinion that the malignant influence of Holmes was even at
that moment at work, and that Biles,
who was to be the foreman of the jury
that would convict the murderer, became a "marked man."

The simple fact that misfortune or fa-
tality has attended those who were in
any way concerned in the murderer's
trial would seem to corroborate the
story and prove that there is, after all, a
baleful influence attending Holmes.

The violent death of Mr. Biles, the
sudden taking off of Dr. William K.
Mattern, who, as Coroner's Physician,
was an important witness against
Holmes, the accidents that befell
Judges Arnold and Yerkes, who were in
the case, and finally the misfortune that
followed Lawyer Shoemaker are facts
that cannot well be explained away.

If nothing else, these occurrences are
strange, and would prove interesting
data for psychologists.

WAS IT THE "ASTRAL" HOLMES.

A Story of Dark Presentiment Which
Reads More Like a Ghostly Ro-
mance, and Is Woven Strangely
About the Death of Linford Biles,
Who Was on the Murderer's Jury.

The death of Linford L. Bile, the

foreman of the jury which convicted H. H. Holmes, and above all the peculiar manner of the death, recalls a strange coincidence that occurred on the very day when the murderer was arrested in Boston, two years ago, and which wonderful to relate, concerned in a manner the lives of both men.

Strange, almost weird, and, in fact, startling as it now seems, after the lapse of time, the recollection of this incident only serves to add to the conviction already aroused in the minds of the superstitious, that there is something magnetically evil about the man whose murders have shocked the world, and that, indeed, there is after all something in the statement made but recently that legacies in the shape of misfortune would fall upon those who had any hand, act or part in his "taking off."

The story of this incident, as told by one who was an eye-witness of the strange spectacle, reads more like a ghost story than anything else, and were it not for the fact that it can at the moment be backed up by the strongest kind of proof, its narration might go down to history as one of the many fabrications that have already arisen regarding the wonderful criminal now awaiting death at Moyamensing Prison.

That it is not a ghost story, but, on the other hand, the most solemn truth, may be averred by any of the old neighbors living in the vicinity of Eleventh and Tasker streets, and who from time to time have had their attention called to the two interlacing and crossing wires that overlapped the roof of the house 1031 Tasker street, where Mr. Biles, the victim of yesterday's strange tragedy, lived.

The house is one of a row that stands in the vicinity of a cemetery, and the surroundings are fully in accord with the weird details.

The date of the strange occurrence coincides exactly with that of the arrest of H. H. Holmes two years ago by the Boston police. The same two wires played the same kind of a part, and attracted attention from passers-by on that day as they did yesterday, when Mr. Biles was virtually electrocuted on his own roof.

The two wires, it seems, had from time to time given trouble to the occupants of the house, and more than once it had been pointed out that they crossed dangerously and overlapped the roof in a manner that was not condusive to safety. Previous to this particular time, however, they had not seriously interfered with the peace of the family, and nothing was thought of the occasional sparks that shot up from the wires whenever they chanced to become entangled during an occasional storm.

On Saturday afternoon, however, just as a number of workmen were on their way home from the oil works at Point Breeze, their attention was called to a single fork of flame that shot up, from one of the houses in the row, between Teuth and Eleventh streets, on Tasker street. Stopping to investigate, the gang, for there were six or seven of them, found that two wires had crossed and set fire to a vine trailing the side of the wall, and the flame thus communicated had shot up to the roof, and was already at that moment threatening the eaves.

In a moment there was excitement in the neighborhood, a policeman was called, the family was notified, and before a crowd that, in the recollection of the narrator, numbered almost a hundred, the two wires were separated.

That same afternoon the news reached town that "an alleged insurance swindler" had been arrested at Boston on charges preferred by the Fidelity Mutual Life Association, and was to be brought later, in the custody of detectives, to answer at the bar of justice in this city, and that possibly "one of the biggest and most barefaced schemes to defraud and rob by wholesale" would then be exposed.

That man was H. H. Holmes, who afterward proved to be not only an insurance swindler, but a forger and everything else included in the calendar of crime, including the cardinal crime of murder itself. and one of the most notorious law-breakers that ever managed to elude for years the strong arm of the law.

It was that moment, when he was

possibly being led back to a felon's cell in the Boston prison, that the two wires which were to play a strange part in the death of one of the men who afterward convicted him were spitting out bluish tongues of flames, immediately over the Tasker street house, and attracting a crowd of men, women and children in just the same way that it attracted them yesterday.

Those who noticed the wires that memorable afternoon, and saw the bluish flames shoot up; who followed the trend of events even as far as the empanelling of Mr. Biles on the jury; who remembered the prediction made in the horoscope, that there was a malignant influence about Holmes, and who saw what seemed a verification of the prediction in the death of Mr. Biles by the very same wires that flashed out in the very same way the day of the arrest, cannot but believe that there was some dark warning conveyed that day by the mystic signs.

One old woman, who has lived in the neighborhood quite a while, said last night she remembered the incident well.

"Those two wires were always spitting about like real devils," said she, "and it kept my nerves jarred, fearing every night that there would be a fire."

"Coming to think of it," she continued, "it looks to me more and more as if the blaze that afternoon was nothing more nor less than an evil warning to Mr. Biles. It was strange, but nevertheless true, that he was picked out on the jury that convicted Holmes, and it was, nevertheless, true that he died, by those very same wires that seemed to have conveyed the dark message."

Another neighbor, a working man, corroborated the story, and remembered well how the two wires almost set fire to the place about two years ago.

"I now believe," said he, "what I saw in the papers, that Holmes was beginning to look like the devil. I believe he is one already."

The curious part is that quite a number of "down-towners" living in the vicinity believe that Mr. Biles was a marked man the day that the wires first blazed, and the same day that Holmes was arrested in Boston two years ago.

THE DEATH OF MR. BILES.

The Foreman of the Jury That Convicted Holmes, Is Virtually Electrocuted by Live Wires On the Roof of His Home.

The death of Linford L. Biles, who had been foreman of the jury which convicted H. H. Holmes of the murder of Benjamin F. Pitezel, and who met a fearful death by coming in contact with a live telephone wire on the roof of his house at 1031 Tasker street, yesterday morning, recalls a curious and at the same time wierd story that was told by the notorious murderer during his trial.

At that time it was stated that a horoscope of the murderer would show that any one connected with the murderer, and especially concerned in the consummation of his conviction and death, would meet with misfortune and possibly death. The combinations of the planets at his birth denoted many changes in life, much mystery, extraordinary conduct, a fanciful, emotional temperament and a most fickle character. The next succeeding signs showed infallible tokens of disaster, foreshadowing failure in business enterprise, the casting of misfortune on others and finally signs which could not be mistaken as meaning other than death, by Judge and jury.

The intimation contained in the horoscope that misfortune would visit all those who had any hand in the murderer's trial was not thought of seriously until yesterday, when the sudden and untimely death of Coroner's Physician Mattern, who played an important part in the case, was remembered, and following it came the sudden and awful death of Biles, the foreman of the jury.

Biles was awakened at an early hour yesterday morning by a commotion in the street, and, getting up and going to the window, he saw a crowd standing in front of the house and pointing to the roof. He donned his clothes, and, going down to the crowd, saw that their attention was attracted to a bluish flame which shot out from the edge of the roof, and which was caused by the contact of a live telephone wire with a telegraph wire, and which, running through a vine on the side of the house, had caused a slight blaze.

Becoming alarmed at the mere supposition that the blaze might communicate with the house, Biles ran upstairs and in a few moments was out on the roof attempting to hack away the wire and if possible sever its connection with the roof. His daughter, fearing he would meet with some disaster, called to her brother to follow her father out on the roof and, if possible, dissuade him from fooling with the dangerous wire.

The son had no sooner gotten on the roof, when the listeners below heard a heavy thud, like the fall of a heavy body, and then there was silence.

Neighbors were called in, and finally the police took a hand and went on the roof. There the two—father and son—were laid side by side, and at first it was believed both were dead. An inspection showed that the son still retained feeble signs of life.

The father had evidently received a shock that was sufficient to kill a dozen men. His left hand was scorched, the forehead was discolored, and there was a scar on the foot.

The body was removed to the rooms beneath, and the son was conveyed to St. Agnes' Hospital, where he now lies in a critical condition.

The dead man, it is thought, met death by walking on an end of the wire before he was aware. The roof being wet also acted as a conductor to the charge which killed him.

Mr. Biles was 64 years of age, occupied the position of paymaster for the Atlantic Oil Refining Company, and was a well-known Mason and Odd Fellow.

., 1896.—COPYRIGHT, 1896, BY THE PHILADELPHIA INQUIRER CO.

ES 27 MURDERS

ERN TIMES TOLD BY THE FIEND
N SHAPE.

ld by the Man Who Admits He Is Turn-
pe of the Devil.

ST CRIMINAL IN HISTORY

[handwritten note:]

Pamphlet was written
[in] Philadelphia County Prison
in Inquirer as a
confession for all
the other confession

e Progress of the Bear's Diplomacy in the East Watched With Envious Eyes—News and Gossip of the Greater World in London.

LONDON, April 11.—The reassembling Parliament has been the feature of a week for London, and the daily sessions regarding foreign affairs that showered upon the Secretary of State for the Colonies, Joseph Chamberlain, and the Under Secretary of State for Foreign Affairs, George N. Curzon, have served to again draw attention to the unsettled state of affairs in all directions. Well-informed persons think that Africa is going to blaze with war, from Cairo to the Cape of Good Hope, and there is said to be a strong possibility of Great Britain having to conquer the Transvaal, a task which alone would require at least 100,000 troops, consequently, it is likely that the British army will soon be largely increased. It strength, as it is considered extremely doubtful if it is capable of grappling with the work seemingly cut out for it in Africa alone.

In the meanwhile, Great Britain's European enemies are on the qui vive. The attitude of Russia is especially disquieting. Even a newspaper like the St. James Gazette expresses disgust with the supineness of the government, which allows Russia to pursue her advance unchecked in the direction of Port Arthur, and says:

"To-day Russia has got all, and more than she dreamt of in Crimean days. France is her maid-of-all-work; Germany is her friend; Turkey is her vassal, and half of the powers of the world are dancing to Russia's time."

The situation in Gloucester, where virulent small-pox is raging, is so serious that the government is likely to take charge. Up to March 28 there were

lege faculty of the
sylvania yesterday, a
ception, which was held
1876. She was 224 feet long, had about
33 feet beam, was about 21 feet dee
and was owned by Hughes & Co.

ADAMS STILL HELD

The Alleged American Embezzler Awaiting Extradition.

LONDON, April 11.—Matt Adams of Denver, Cal., who is in custody pending extradition proceedings on the charge of having embezzled $41,000 in Denver, was again remanded at the Bow Street Police Court to-day, pending the arrival of papers in the case from the United States.

The sum of $170 was taken from the money found upon Adams when he was arrested at Southampton, on his way to Cape Town, the money to be used to send his wife and servant home.

CECIL RHODES BETTER

He Will Accompany the Troops to Buluwayo.

SALISBURY, Matabeleland, April 11.—Cecil Rhodes, formerly Premier of Cape Colony, who has been suffering from fever here for some days past, is now much better.

He proposes to march to Buluwayo with the column of troops intended for the relief of that place.

COLONEL MARTIN NAME

St. Louis Democrat for Sergeant-Arms at Chicago.

CHICAGO, April 11.—Colonel J. Martin, of St. Louis, will be the sergeant-at-arms of the Democratic National Convention. His selection was made this morning by Chairman Harrity and his committee of the Democratic National Committee.

Colonel Martin is a well-known politician and very popular in St. Louis Democratic circles.

The other candidates for the position were John J. Curley, of Philadelphia, ex-Congressman Elijah J. Yorkshire

700 cases
an incr
age of
a sta[t]

lec
ters i
of W
card
and n
tury,"
so, "o
bish,
ed by

The
import[s]

The c
train vi
will be
stored s
will con
walls of
with arti
of rare

In the

of my fearful e'
...ee make. I
crating all the
...how it condemns
Signed
April 9th 1896

"PAGE"

HOLMES CONFESS

THE MOST AWFUL STORY OF MOD
IN HUMAI

Every Detail of His Fearful Crimes Tc
ing Into the Sha

THE TALE OF THE GREAT

The following sta
by me in Philade
for the Philadelp
true + accurate
......

During the past few months the desire has been repeatedly expressed
that I make a detailed confession of all the graver crimes that
have with such marvelous skill been
traced out and brought home to me
I have been tried for murder, convicted, sentenced, and the first step of
my execution upon May seventh,
namely, the reading of my death warrant, has been carried out, and it now
seems a fitting time, if ever, to make
known the details of the twenty-sev-
en murders, of which it would be useless to longer say I am not guilty, in
the face of the overwhelming amount
of proof that has been brought together, not only in one but in each and
every case; and because in this confession I speak only of cases that have
been thus investigated and of no others, I trust it will not give rise to a
supposition that I am still guilty of
other murders which I am withholding.

To those inclined to think thus, I will
say that the detectives have gone over
my entire life, hardly a day or an
act has escaped their closest scrutiny,
and to judge that I am guilty of
more than these cases which they
have traced out is to cast discredit upon their work. So marvelous has been
the success of these men into whose
hands the proving of my guilt was
given, that as I look back upon their
year's work it seems almost impossible that men gifted with only
human intelligence could have been
so skillful, and I feel that I can here
call attention to what the prosecution
at the close of my trial was denied the

pleasure of stating, concerning their ability, though no words of mine can fittingly express what the world at large owes to these impartial and untiring representatives, and more especially to Assistant District Attorney Barlow and Detective Frank Geyer and to O. La Forrest Perry, of the Fidelity Mutual Life Association of Philadelphia; for it is principally owing to their unerring judgment, skill and perseverence that in a few days I am to be forever placed beyond the power of committing other, and, perhaps, if possible, more horrid wrongs. Surely justice, if attended by such servants as these could no longer, in the sense of making mistakes, be appropriately portrayed as being blind.

I am moved to make this confession for a variety of reasons, but among them are not those of bravado or a desire to parade my wrongdoings before the public gaze, and he who reads the following lines will, I beg, make a distinction between such motives and a determination upon my part to enter plainly and minutely into the details of each case without favor towards myself. And having done so I have chosen to make it public by publishing it in THE PHILADELPHIA INQUIRER.

A word as to the motives or causes that have led to the commission of these many crimes and I will proceed to the most difficult and distasteful task of my life, the setting forth in all its horrid nakedness the recital of the premeditated killing of twenty-seven human beings and the unsuccessful attempts to take the lives of six others, thus branding myself as the most detestable criminal of modern times—a task so hard and dis-

tasteful that beside it the certainty
that in a few days I am to be hanged
by the neck until I am dead seems but
a pastime.

Acquired homicidal mania, all other
causes, save the occasional opportunity for pecuniary gain having by others been excluded for me, is the only
constant cause, and in advancing it
at this time I do not do so with the
expectation of a mitigation of public
condemnation, or that it will in any
way react in my favor. Had this been
my intention I should have considered
it at the time of my trial, and had it
used as my defense.

All criminologists who have examined me here seem to be unanimous in
the opinions they have formed, although one inexplicable condition presents itself, viz.: that while committing the crimes these symptoms were
not present, but commenced to develop after my arrest.

Ten years ago I was thoroughly examined by four men of marked ability
and by them pronounced as being
both mentally and physically a normal and healthy man. To-day I have
every attribute of a degenerate—a
moral idiot. Is it possible that the
crimes, instead of being the result of
these abnormal conditions, are in
themselves the occasion of the degeneracy?

Even at the time of my arrest in
1894 no defects were noticeable under
the searching Bertillon system of
measurements to which I was subject-
ed, but later, and more noticeably
within the past few months, these defects have increased with startling
rapidity, as is made known to me by
each succeeding examination until I
have become thankful that I am no

longer allowed a glass with which to note my rapidly deteriorating condition, though nature, ever kind, provides in this, as in the ordinary forms of insanity where the sufferer believes himself always sane, so that, unless called to my attention, I do not notice my infirmity nor suffer * therefrom. The principal defects that have thus far developed and which are all established signs of degeneracy, are a decided prominence upon one side of my head and a corresponding diminution upon the other side; a marked deficiency of one side of my nose and of one ear, together with an abnormal increase of each upon the opposite side; a difference of one and one-half inches in the length of my arms and an equal shortening of one leg from knee to heel; also a most malevolent distortion of one side of my face and of one eye— so marked and terrible that in writing of it for publication, Hall Caine, although I wore a beard at the time to conceal it as best I could, described that side of my face as marked by a deep line of crime and being that of a devil—so apparent that an expert criminologist in the employ of the United States Government who had never previously seen me said within thirty seconds after entering my cell: "I know you are guilty."

Would it not, then, be the height of folly for me to die without speaking, if only for the purpose of justifying these scientific deductions and accrediting what is due to those to whom society owes so much for bringing me to justice?

The first taking of human life that is attributed to me is in the case of Dr. Robert Leacock, of New Baltimore,

Mich., a friend and former school-
mate. I knew that his life was insured for a large sum and after enticing him to Chicago I killed him by
giving him an overwhelming dose of
laudanum. My subsequently taking
his dead body from place to place in
and about Grand Rapids, Mich., as has
been so often printed heretofore, and
the risk and excitement attendant
upon the collection of the forty thousand dollars of insurance, were very
insignificant matters compared with
the torturing thought that I had taken
human life. This, it will be understood, was before, by constant wrong-
doing, I had become wholly deaf to the
promptings of conscience, for prior to
this death, which occurred in 1886, I
beg to be believed in stating that I had
never sinned so heavily either by
thought or deed. Later, like the man-
eating tiger of the tropical jungle,
whose appetite for blood has once been
aroused, I roamed about the world
seeking whom I could destroy. Think
of the awful list that follows. Twenty-
seven lives, men and women, young
girls and innocent children, blotted
out by one monster's hand, and you,
my reader of a tender and delicate nature, will do well to read no further,
for I will in no way spare myself, and
he who reads to the end, if he be
charitable, will, in the words of the
District Attorney at my trial, when
the evidence of all these many crimes
had been collected and placed before
him by his trusty assistants, exclaim:
"God help such a man!" If unchari-
table or only just will he not rather
say: "May he be utterly damned,"
and that it is almost sufficient to
cause one to doubt the wisdom of
Providence that such a man should

have so long been allowed to live. If so I earnestly pray that this condemnation and censure may not extend to those whose only crime has been that they knew and trusted, aye in some instances, loved me, and who today are more deserving of the world's compassion than censure.

My second victim was Dr. Russell, a tenant in the Chicago building recently renamed "The Castle." During a controversy concerning the non-payment of rent due me, I struck him to the floor with a heavy chair, when he, with one cry for help, ending in a groan of anguish, ceased to breathe. This quarrel and death occurred in a small outer office, and as soon as I realized that my blow had been a fatal one and I had recovered somewhat from the horror of having still another victim's blood upon my hands, I was forced to look about for some safe means of concealing the crime. I locked the doors of the office, and my first intention was to dispose of the body to a Chicago medical college, from one of whose officers I had previously obtained dissecting material, as they believed, but in reality to be used in insurance work. I found it difficult, if not impossible, to thus dispose of it, and was directed to call upon a party to whom I sold the bodies and whose name I withhold, but I have confessed his name to parties in whom I have confidence.

To him I sold this man's body, as well as others at later dates. In short, in this writing, in each instance when the manner of the disposal of their remains is not otherwise specified, it will be understood that they were turned over to him, he paying me from $25 to $45 for each body, and

right easily could he, during the recent investigations, go from room to
room in the building when each was
more or less grewsomely familiar to
him. It is not necessary for me to
add that the efforts of his friends to
shield him when it became ovident
that he had talked too freely for his
own safety should not have saved
him from being compelled to turn
over the remains of these persons for
decent burial or to point out the various museums where they were
sold.

The third death was to a certain
extent due to a criminal operation. A
man and woman were cognizant of
and partially responsible for both the
operation and the death. The victim
is Mrs. Julia L. Connor. A refer-
ence to almost any newspaper of
August, 1893, will give the minute details of the horrors of this case, as they
were worked out by the detectives,
therefore making it unnecessary to
repeat it here, save to add that the
death of the child Pearl, her little
daughter, who is the fourth victim,
was caused by poison, and that the
man and woman above referred to
were equally responsible with myself
for its administration, although it was
at my instigation that it was done,
as I believed the child was old
enough to remember of her mother's
sickness and death. They wished, at
first, to place the child in the care
of their aged parents, who lived south
of the city, but were overruled by my
opposition. Owing to the suddenness
of the third death, a certain note of
considerable value, well secured by
property south of the Castle, was
uncollectible, and at tho time of my
death it will be sent to such of her

relatives as it may appear have the greater right to receive it.

The fifth murder, that of Rodgers, of West Morgantown, Va., occurred in 1888, at which time I was boarding there for a few weeks. Learning that the man had some money I induced him to go upon a fishing trip with me, and, being successful in allaying his suspicions, I finally ended his life by a sudden blow upon the head with an oar. The body was found about a month thereafter, but I was not suspected until after my trial here, and even then by a fortunate circumstance succeeded in having the report publicly denied, but did not succeed in changing the opinion of fifty or more persons living in the town who had recognized my picture in the daily papers.

The sixth case is that of Charles Cole, a Southern speculator. After considerable correspondence this man came to Chicago, and I enticed him into the Castle, where, while I was engaging him in conversation, a confederate struck him a most vicious blow upon the head with a piece of gas pipe. So heavy was the blow it not only caused his death without a groan and hardly a movement, but it crushed his skull to such an extent that his body was almost useless to the party who bought the body. This is the first instance in which I knew this confederate had committed murder, though in several other instances he was fully as guilty as myself, and, if possible, more heartless and bloodthirsty, and I have no doubt is still engaged in the same nefarious work, and if so is probably aided by a Chicago business man.

A domestic, named Lizzie, was the seventh victim. She, for a time, worked in the Castle restaurant and I soon learned that Quinlan was paying her too close attention and fearing lest it should progress so far that it would necessitate his leaving my employ I thought it wise to end the life of the girl. This I did by calling her to my office and suffocating her in the vault of which so much has since been printed, she being the first victim that died therein. Before her death I compelled her to write letters to her relations and to Quinlan, stating that she had left Chicago for a Western State and should not return. A few months ago the prosecution, believing from certain letters purporting to have been written by her that she was alive, at once showed me their willingness to give me a fair trial by having this publicly known, she being a witness that I could have used to great advantage in the Pitezel case, here.

The eighth, ninth and tenth cases are Mrs. Sarah Cook, her unborn child, and Miss Mary Haracamp, of Hamilton, Canada. In 1SSS Mr. Frank Cook became a tenant in the Castle. He was engaged to be married to a young lady living at some distance from Chicago who later came there and was married to him in my presence, by the Rev. Dr. Taylor, of Englewood, Ill. They kept house in the Castle, and for a time I boarded with them. Shortly Miss Mary Haracamp, of Hamilton, a niece of Mrs. Sarah Cook, came to Chicago and entered my employ as a stenographer. But Mrs. Cook and her niece had access to all the rooms by means of a master key and one evening while I was busily engaged preparing my last victim for shipment, the door sud-

HERMAN MUDGETT, ALIAS H. H. HOLMES

denly opened and they stood before me.
It was a time for quick action, rather
than for words of explanation upon my
part, and before they had recovered
from the horror of the sight, they
were within the fatal vault, so lately
tenanted by the dead body, and then,
after writing a letter at my dictation
to Mr. Cook that they had tired of
their life with him and had gone away
not expecting to return, their lives
were sacrificed instead of giving them
their liberty in exchange for their
promise to at once and forever leave
Chicago, which had been promised
them in return for writing the letter.
These were particularly sad deaths,
both on account of the victims being
exceptionally upright and virtuous women and because Mrs. Sarah Cook, had
she lived, would have soon become a
mother. Soon after this Miss Emmeline
Cigrand, of Dwight, Ill., was sent to
me by a Chicago typewriter firm to
fill the vacancy of stenographer. She
had formerly been employed at Dwight
where she had become acquainted with
a man who visited her from time to
time while she was in my employ.
She was finally engaged to him and the
day set for their wedding. This attachment was particularly obnoxious
to me, both because Miss Cigrand had
become almost indispensable in my office work, and because she had become
my mistress as well as stenographer.
I endeavored upon several occasions
to take the life of the young man and
failing in this I finally resolved that I
would kill her instead, and upon the
day of their wedding, even after cards
had been sent out announcing that it
had occurred, she came to my office to
bid me good bye. While there I asked
her to step inside the vault for some
papers for me. There I detained her,

telling her that if she would write her husband that at the last moment she had found that it would be impossible to live happily with him and consequently had left Chicago in such a way that search for her would be useless, I would take her to a distant city and live openly with her as my wife. She was very willing to do this and prepared to leave the vault upon completing the letter only to learn that the door would never be again opened until she had ceased to suffer the tortures of a slow and lingering death.

Then follows an unsuccessful attempt to commit a triple murder for the $90 that my agent for disposing of "stiffs" would have given me for the bodies of the intended victims, who were three young women working in my restaurant upon Milwaukee avenue, Chicago. That these women lived to tell of their experience to the police last summer is due to my foolishly trying to chloroform all of them at one and the same time. By their combined strength they overpowered me and ran screaming into the street, clad only in their night robes. I was arrested next day, but was not prosecuted. To this attempt to kill could very justly be added my attempt to take the lives of Mrs. Pitezel and two of her children at a later date, thus making the total number of my victims 33, instead of 27, as it was through no fault of mine that they escaped.

My next attempt was carried out with more caution. The victim was a very beautiful young woman named Rosine Van Jassand, whom I induced to come into my fruit and confectionery store, and, once within my power, I compelled her to live with me there

THE CALLOWHILL STREET HOUSE, WHERE PITEZEL WAS
MURDERED

for a time, threatening her with death if she appeared before any of my customers. A little later I killed her by administering ferro-cyanide of potassium. The location of this store was such that it would have been hazardous to have sent out a large box containing a body, and I therefore buried her remains in the store basement, and from day to day during the recent investigation at the Castle I expected to hear that excavations had been made there as well.

Robert Latimer, a man who had for some years been in my employ as janitor, was my next victim. Several years previous, before I had ever taken human life, he had known of certain insurance work I had engaged in, and when, in after years, he sought to extort money from me, his own death and the sale of his body was the recompense meted out to him. I confined him within the secret room and slowly starved him to death. Of this room and its secret gas supply and muffled windows and doors, sufficient has already been printed. Finally, needing its use for another purpose and because his pleadings had become almost unbearable, I ended his life. The partial excavation in the walls of this room found by the police was caused by Latimer's endeavoring to escape by tearing away the solid brick and mortar with his unaided fingers.

The fourteenth case is that of Miss Anna Betts, and was caused by my purposely substituting a poisonous drug in a prescription that had been sent to my drug store to be compounded, believing that it was known that I was a physician, I should be called in to witness her death, as she lived very near the store. This was not the case, however, as the regular physician was in attendance at the time. The prescription, still on file at the Castle drug store, should be considered by the authorities if they still are inclined to attribute this death to causes that reflect upon Miss Betts' moral character.

The death of Miss Gertrude Conner, of Muscatine, Iowa, though not the next in order of occurrence, is so similar to the last that a description of one suffices for both, save in this case Miss Conner left Chicago immediately, but did not die until she had reached her home at Muscatine. Perhaps these two cases show more plainly than any others the light regard I had for the lives of my fellow-beings.

The sixteenth murder is that of Miss Kate ——, of Omaha, a young woman owning much valuable real estate in Chicago, where I acted as her agent. This was at the time so graphically described by a local writer—as when I was allowed to hold property under one name, act as notary public under another and carry on a general business under still another title. I caused Miss Kate —— to believe that a favorable opportunity had come for her to convert her holdings into cash, and, having acomplished this for her, she came to Chicago and I paid her the money, taking a receipt in full for same, and thus protected myself in the event of an inquiry at a later date. I asked her to look about my offices and finally to look within the vault, and, having once passed that fatal door, she never came forth alive. She did not die at once, however, and her anger when first she realized that she was deprived of her liberty, then her offer of the entire forty thousand dollars in exchange for same and finally her prayers are something terrible to remember. It was stated that I had also killed a sister of Miss Kate ——, but I think this report has already been contradicted.

The next death was that of a man named Warner, the originator of the Warner Glass Bending Company, and here again a very large sum of money was realized, which prior to his death had been deposited in two Chicago banks, nearly all of which I secured by means of two checks, made out and properly signed by him for a small sum each. To these I later added the word thousand, and the necessary ciphers, and by passing them through the bank where I had a regular open account I promptly realized the money, save a small amount not covered by the checks in the Park National Bank, northwest corner Dearborn and Washington streets, in that city. It will be remembered that the remains of a large kiln made of fire brick was found in the Castle basement. It had been built under Mr. Warner's supervision for the purpose of exhibiting his patents. It was so arranged that in less than a minute after turning on a jet of crude oil atomized with steam the entire kiln would be filled with a colorless flame, so intensely hot iron would be melted therein. It was into this kiln that I induced Mr. Warner to go with me, under pretense of wishing certain minute explanations of the process, and then stepping outside, as he believed to get some tools, I closed the door and turned on both the oil and steam to their full extent. In a short time not even the bones of my victim remained. The coat found outside the kiln was the one he took off before going therein.

In 1891 I associated myself in business with a young Englishman, whose

name I am more than willing to pub-
lish to the world, but I am advised it
could not be published on my unsup-
ported statement, who by his own admission, had been guilty of all other
forms of wrongdoing, save murder,
and presumably of that as well. To
manipulate certain real estate securities we held so as to have them secure
us a good commercial rating was an
easy matter for him and he was equally able to interest certain English capitalists in patents so that for a time
it seemed that in the near future our
greatest concern would be how to dispose of the money that seemed about
to be showered upon us. By an unforeseen occurrence our rating was destroyed and it became necessary to at
once raise a large sum and this was
done by my partner enticing to Chicago a wealthy banker named Rodgers from a North Wisconsin town in
such a manner that he could have left
no intelligence with whom his business
was to be. To cause him to go to the
Castle and within the secret room under the pretense that our patents were
there was easily brought about, more
so than to force him to sign checks
and drafts for seventy thousand dollars, which we had prepared. At first
he refused to do so, stating that his liberty that we offered him in exchange
would be useless to him without his
money, that he was too old to again
hope to make another fortune; finally
by alternately starving him and nau-
seating him with the gas he was made
to sign the securities, all of which
were converted into money and by my
partner's skill as a forger in such a
manner as to leave no trace of their
having passed through our hands. I
waited with much curiosity to see what
propositions my partner would advance
for the disposal of our prisoner, as I
well knew he, no more than I, con-
templated giving him his liberty. My
partner evidently waited with equal,

expectancy for me to suggest what should be done, and I finally made preparation to allow him to leave the building, thus forcing him to suggest that he be killed. I would only consent to this upon the condition that he should administer the chloroform, and leave me to dispose of the body as my part of the work. In this way I was enabled to keep him in ignorance of my dealings with the medical college agent. That evening this large sum of money was equally divided between us, and my partner went to the Palmer House, where he was well known, and passed the night at cards with three other men, and at 10 o'clock the next morning came to the office to borrow $100 with which to redeem his overcoat, watch and rings that he had left to secure a final stroke.

So much has already been written of my own extravagancies and wrong methods of living that I can add little to what the detectives have already pointed out, save to say that during these years, reckoning only the amount of money which they have discovered that I defrauded others of, and as it is known to them that when I was arrested I had very little money, it is evident that my disbursements were over ten thousand dollars per month.

The nineteenth case is that of a woman, whose name has passed from my memory, who came to the Castle restaurant to board. A tenant of mine at the time immediately became very much infatuated with the woman, who he learned was a widow and wealthy. This tenant was married, and his wife occasionally came to the restaurant when this boarder was there, which did not tend to decrease a family quarrel that for quite a time had threatened this tenant's family with disruption. Finally he came to me for advice, and I was very willing to have him in my power in order that I could later use him in my work if need be. I suggested that he live with the woman in the Castle for a time, and later, if his life became unpleasant to him, we would kill her and divide her wealth. Soon, he suggested it was time to take his companion's life. This was done by my administering chloroform while he controlled her violent struggles. It was the body of this woman within the long coffin-shaped box that was taken from the Castle late in 1893, of which the police were notified.

The Williams sisters come next. In order that these deaths may be more fully understood it is necessary for me to state that what has been said by Miss Minnie R. Williams' Southern relatives regarding her pure and Christian life should be believed; also, that prior to her meeting me in 1893 she was a virtuous woman, thus rendering truthful the statements of Mr. Charles Goldthwaite, of Boston, that he had never known her other than as an intimate friend of his wife, and that in June, 1893, he did not wire her a considerable sum of money to Chicago in response to a demand for some from her; that she was not temporarily insane at a hotel opposite the Pullman Building, Chicago, May 20-23, 1893; was not a little later secluded within the Baptist Hospital at Chicago under the name of Mrs. Williams, and still later at a retreat in Milwaukee; and that she did not kill her sister and threaten to kill a nurse having her in charge at 1220 Wrightwood avenue, Chicago. All these statements it gives me a certain amount of satisfaction to retract, thereby undoing so far as I can these additional wrongs I have heaped upon her name.

I first met Miss Minnie R. Williams in New York in 1888, where she knew me as Edward Hatch and later under the same name in Denver, as has been testified by certain young women who recognized my photograph. Early in 1893 I was again introduced to her as H. H. Holmes in the office of Campbell & Dowd, of Chicago, to whom she had applied for them to secure her a position as a stenographer. Soon after entering my employ I induced her to give me $2,500 in

money and to transfer to me by deed
$50,000 worth of Southern real estate
and a little later to live with me as
my wife, all this being easily accomplished owing to her innocent and
child-like nature, she hardly knowing right from wrong in such matters. Thereafter I succeeded in securing two checks from her for
$2500 and $1000 each, and I also
learned that she had a sister Nannie
in Texas who was an heir to some
property and induced Miss Minnie
Williams to have her come to Chicago
upon a visit. Upon her arrival I met
her at the depot and took her to the
Castle, telling her Miss Minnie Williams was there. It was an easy matter to force her to assign to me all she
possessed. After that she was immediately killed in order that no one in
or about the Castle should know of
her having been there save the man
who burned her clothing. It was the
foot-print of Nannie Williams, as
later demonstrated by that most as-
tute lawyer and detective, Mr. Copps,
of Fort Worth, that was found upon
the painted surface of the vault door
made during her violent struggles
before her death. It was also easy
to give to Miss Minnie Williams a delayed letter, stating that her sister's
proposed visit had been given up and
also by intercepting later letters and
substituting others to keep her from

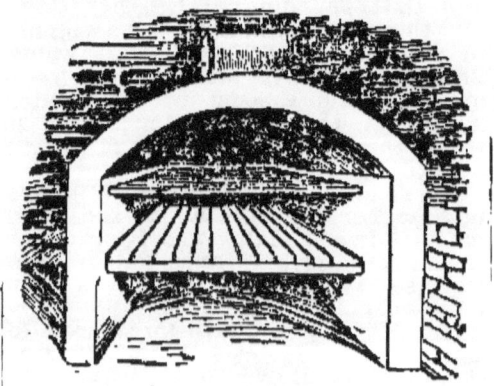

The Gas Oven.

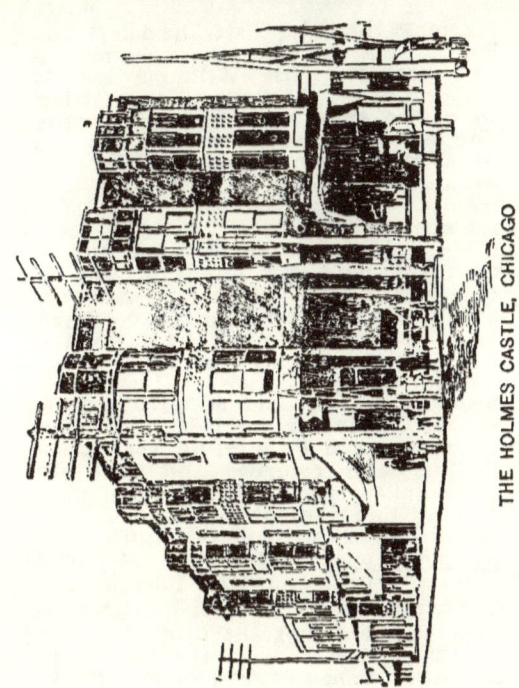

THE HOLMES CASTLE, CHICAGO

learning that the sister had left the
South. Having secured all the money
and property Miss Williams had it
was time that she were killed. Owing
to a fire that had occurred in the
Castle I was unable to resort to the
usual methods in taking her life, and,
after some delay, took her to Momence, Ill., about November 15, 1893,
registering at a hotel near the post-
office under an assumed name, but as
man and wife. My intention was to
quietly kill her in some sure manner,
but a freight wreck that occurred
upon the outskirts of the town the
day following my arrival there,
which, out of curiosity, I visited,
brought me in contact with a passenger conductor named Peck, who
knew me, and I therefore abandoned
it, but later returned and took her
eight miles east of Momence upon a
freight line that is little used, and
ended her life with poison and buried
her body in the basement of the house
spoken of at about the time of the
Irvington discovery in 1895. It was a
great wonder that the body was not
found at that time if the detectives
in reality went to that location. Nothing would at the present time give
me so much satisfaction as to know
that her body had been properly
buried, and I would be willing to give
up the few remaining days I have to
live if by so doing this could be accomplished, for, because of her spot-
less life before she knew me, because
of the large amount of money I defrauded her of, because I killed her
sister and brother, because not being
satisfied with all this, I endeavored
after my arrest to blacken her good
name by charging her with the death
of her sister, and later with the instigation of the murder of the three
Pitezel children, endeavoring to have
it believed that her motive for so doing was to afford an avenue of escape for herself if ever apprehended
for her sister's death, by pointing to
her as a wholesale murderess, and,
therefore, presumably guilty of the
sister's death as well; for all these
reasons this is without exception the
saddest and most heinous of all of
my crimes.

HOLMES MURDERING THE GLASS INVENTOR

A man who came to Chicago to attend the Chicago Exposition, but
whose name I cannot recall, was my
next victim. The Chicago authorities
can, if they choose, learn the name by
inquiries made of the Hartford Insurance Company, a Mr. Lasher, of the
Stock Exchange Building; D. T. Dun-
combe, Metropolitan Building, all of
Chicago; a sash and door manufactur-
ing company opposite the Deering, Illinois, Station, or F. L. Jones, a notary
public at Indianapolis, at some one of
which places I hope either his name or
handwriting may have been preserved,
thus affording a clue for identification
by his friends. I determined to use
this man in my various business dealings, and did so for a time, until I
found he had not the ability I had at
first thought he possessed, and I therefore decided to kill him. This was
done, but as I had not had any dealings with the "stiff" dealer for some
time previous to this murder, I decided
to bury the body in the basement
of the house that I formerly owned
near the corner of Seventy-fourth and
Honore streets, in Chicago, where, by
digging deeply in the sandy soil, the
body will be found. After Miss Williams' death I found among her papers an insurance policy made in her
favor by her brother, Baldwin Williams, of Leadville, Col. I therefore
went to that city early in 1894, and,
having found him, took his life by
shooting him, it being believed I had
done so in self-defense. A little later,
when the assignment of the policy to
which I had forged Miss Williams'
name was presented to John M. Maxwell, of Leadville, the administrator of
the Williams estate, it was honored
and the money paid. Both in this instance and that of a $1000 check given
by Dr. Tolman and checks aggregating $2500 by I. R. Hitt & Co., both of
Chicago, inasmuch as the indorse-
ments are forgeries, the Williams heirs
can now recover these amounts, al-

recently given considerable prominence in a local (issue there) regarding this case that there will be little for me to tell, save the actual manner in which his death was brought about. It will be understood that from the first hour of our acquaintance, even before I knew he had a family who would later afford me additional victims for the gratification of my bloodthirstiness, I intended to kill him, and all my subsequent care of him and his, as well as my apparent trust in him by placing in his name large amounts of property, were steps taken to gain his confidence and that of his family so when the time was ripe they would the more readily fall into my hands. It seems almost incredible now as I look back that I could have expected to have experienced sufficient satisfaction in witnessing their deaths to repay me for even the physical exertion that I had put forth in their behalf during those seven long years, to say nothing of the amount of money I had expended for their welfare, over and above what I could have expected to receive from his comparatively small life insurance. Yet, so it is, and it furnishes a very striking illustration of the vagaries in which the human mind will, under certain circumstances, indulge; in comparison with which the seeking of buried treasure at the rainbow's end, the delusions of the exponents of perpetual motion or the dreams of the haschisch fiend are sanity itself. Pitezel left his home for the last time late in July, 1894, a happy, light-hearted man, to whom trouble or discouragements of any kind were almost unknown. We then journeyed together to New York and later to Philadelphia, where the fatal house upon Callowhill street in which he met his death September 2, 1894, was hired. Then came my writing to him the discouraging letters, purporting to be from his wife, causing him to again resort to drink. Then the waiting from day to day until I should be sure of finding him in a drunken stupor at midday. This was an easy matter, as I was acquainted with his habits and so sure was I of finding him thus incapacitated that when the day came upon which it was convenient for me to kill him, even before I went to his house I packed my trunk and made other arrangements to leave Philadelphia in a hurried flight immediately after his death. After thus preparing I went to the house, quietly unlocked the door and stole noiselessly within and to the second story room, where I found him insensibly drunk, as I had expected. But even in this condition the question may be asked had I no fear that he might be only naturally asleep or partially insensible and therefore liable to at any moment come to his senses and defend himself? I answer no, and that even had he done so my great strength would have enabled me to have still overpowered him.

Only one difficulty presented itself. It was necessary for me to kill him in such a manner that no struggle or movement of his body should occur, otherwise his clothing being in any way displaced it would have been impossible to again put them in a normal condition. I overcame this difficulty by first binding him hand and foot and having done this I proceeded to burn him alive by saturating his clothing and his face with benzine and igniting it with a

Miss Yoke.

watch. So horrible was this torture that
in writing of it I have been tempted
to attribute his death to some more
humane means—not with a wish to spare
myself, but because I fear that it will
not be believed that one could be so
heartless and depraved, but such a
course would be useless, for by exclu-
sion, the authorities have determined
for me that his death could only have
occurred in this manner, no blows or
bruises upon his body and no drug administered, save chloroform, which was
not placed in his stomach until at least
30 minutes after his death, and to now
make a misstatement of the facts would
only serve to draw out additional criticism from them. The least I can do
is to spare my reader a recital of the
victim's cries for mercy, his prayers
and finally, his plea for a more speedy
termination of his sufferings, all of
which upon me had no effect. Finally,
when he was dead I removed the straps
and ropes that had bound him and ex-
tinguished the flames and a little later
poured into his stomach one and one-
half ounces of chloroform. It has been
asked why I did this after I knew that
he was dead, what possible use it could
have served? My answer to this is that
I placed it there so that at the time
of the post mortem examination, which
I knew would be held, the Coroner's
physician would be warranted in re-
porting that the death was accidental,
and due to an explosion of a cleaning
fluid, composed of benzine and chloroform, and that the chloroform had at
the time of the explosion separated from
the benzine and passed into his stomach, and upon receipt of such intelligence I believed the insurance company
would at once pay the full amount of
the claim. The chloroform did worse
than this, however, and developed a
condition of this body that in my lim-
ited medical experience I have never
seen or read of, and I mention it here
as a fact of scientific interest, that I
believe is not generally known. It drove

President Fouse, Fidelity Mutual Insurance Company.

they did not believe the man was
drunk at the time of his death, or
within twelve hours thereof. That they
were wrong in making such deductions
is proven by the well-known fact that
all other testimony and circumstances
at my trial tended to show that he
must have been insensible from liquor,
and that only in this condition could I
have killed him; a fact so strongly
brought out that the learned trial judge
in his arguments commented upon it
at some length. After his death I gathered together various assignments of patents and deeds to property he had
held for me that I had been careful
to have him sign some days before,
so I should not suffer pecuniary loss.
I also wrote the cipher message found
by the insurance company among my
papers after my arrest, imitating his
handwriting, and after placing the body

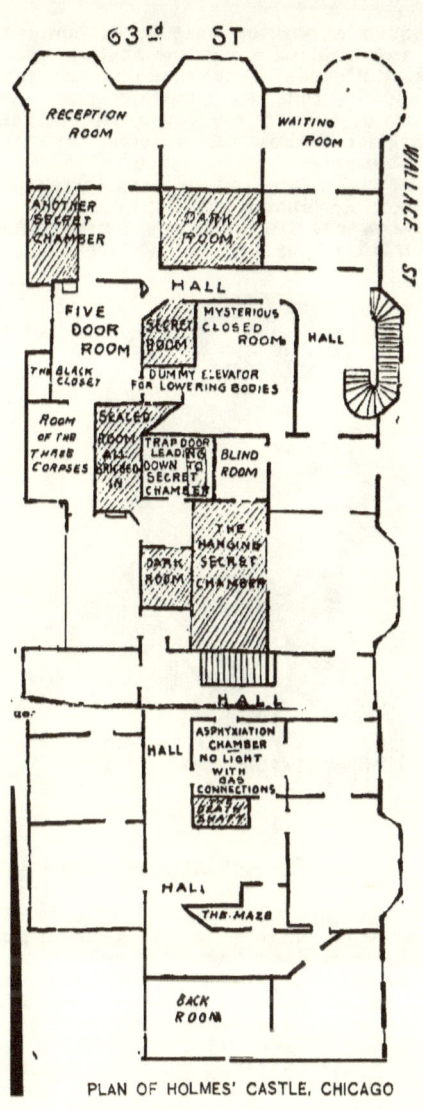

PLAN OF HOLMES' CASTLE, CHICAGO

in such a position that by a cunning
ar angement of a window shutter upon
the south side of the building the sun
would be reflected upon his face the
entire day. I left the house without the
slightest feeling of remorse for my
terrible acts.

For one month and six days thereafter
I took no human life, although about
three weeks after Pitezel's death I was
afforded an opportunity to gratify my

Assistant District Attorney Barlow.

feverish lust for blood by going to the
graveyard where he had been buried and
under pretense of securing certain portions of his body for microscopical examination removed the same with a knife.
And the heartless manner in which I did
this and the evident gratification it afforded me has been most forcibly told
by Mr. Smith upon the witness stand.
As an instance of the infallibility of justice, as a triumph of right over wrong,
and of the general safety of condemnation to death upon circumstantial evidence alone this case is destined to long

remain prominent as a warning to those viciously inclined that their only safe course is to avoid even the appearance of evil.

Two questions that have been often asked I would answer—why did I make no defense at my trial when by so doing I could lose nothing, and possibly could have gained? I answer that after Detective Geyer's Western investigation, which we could not at that time in any way refute, and in the face of Dr. Leffmann's learned statements to the effect that no one could or had ever been known to lose consciousness by chloroform self-administered, provided they had not first confined their movements. It would have been but a waste of my counsel's energies, and of my own, to have tried to convince the most impartial juries that it was a case of suicide and not a murder. Is it to be wondered at that I hesitated before placing the defense of suicide before a jury composed of men who had, with three exceptions, stated under oath, before being passed upon by the court as competent, that they had already formed opinions prejudiced to my interests? The second question is, did Pitezel during his eight years' acquaintance and almost constant association with me, know that I was a multi-murderer, and if he did know was he a party to such crime? I answer that he neither knew of nor was a party to the taking of any human life, and I earnestly beg that this statement may be believed, both in justice to his memory, and on account of the surviving members of his family. The worst acts he ever participated in were dishonesties regarding properties and unlawful acts of trade, in which he aided me freely. In support of my statement that he was not cognizant of any of the graver crimes which I have so freely confessed herein I will mention one of many instances already known to the authorities, viz.; that for six months previous to his death he had planned openly with his wife that their daughter Alice should spend a year at a school he believed Miss Williams intended to open near Boston, and these plans were of such a nature that Mrs. Pitezel knows he was not deceiving her. He would not have made these arrange-

dienta, and there would have been no
occasion for him to have deceived his
own family, if he believed Miss Williams
was not alive.

The Irvington, Indiana, tragedy is
next. Upon the 1st day of October,
1894, I took the three Pitezel children to
the Circle House in Indianapolis, where
I engaged permanent board for them until such a time as I could kill one or
more of them. Upon the evening of that
day I went to St. Louis, where I remained until October 4, busily engaged in
settling up the insurance matter with
McDonald and Howe, the attorneys. During this time I also called upon the
agent or owner of the Irvington House.
This was my first incautious step, and
was destined to fasten crime upon me,
for later when the detectives learned that
I made this call upon the date that
they knew the insurance settlement took
place, they no longer hesitated in stating that I, and I alone, could have
murdered the boy. Upon October 4,
I returned to Indianapolis, and later in
the same day went to Franklin, Indiana,
which is situated south of Indianapolis,
while Irvington is east thereof, Franklin
to Irvington representing the hypothe-
nuse of a triangle—Franklin to Indianapolis and Indianapolis to Irvington the
two shorter sides—so that one could
go from Franklin to Irvington direct
without making the longer journey via
Indianapolis. On October 5th the rent
of the house was paid and at about 9
A. M. October 6th I called upon Dr.
Thompson at Irvington for the keys,
he having been a former occupant. At
5 o'clock upon the same day I called
upon Mr. Brown at Irvington to engage
him to make some repairs upon the
house, and upon his appearing indifferent
I became very angry with him and my
only wonder is that I did not entice
him to the house and kill him also.
This small circumstance aided in bringing the crime home to me when it was
made known to the detectives and considered by them in connection with many
other complaints of my violent and ungovernable temper that had come to
their knowledge. On October 7 I called
at the Irvington drug store and purchased the drugs I needed to kill the
boy and the following evening I again

went to the same store and bought an
additional supply, as I feared I had not
obtained a sufficient quantity upon my
first visit. My next step was to secure
the furniture for the house. This was
done upon October 8, late in the afternoon, at such an hour that made it impossible for the store owner to deliver
them, and as I wished to stay at Irvington that night I hired a conveyance
and carted the goods to the house myself, keeping the horse there until the
next day. It was also upon the 8th,
early in the forenoon, that I went to
the repair shop for the long knives I
had previously left there to be sharpened.
Early in the afternoon of October 10th
I had the boy's trunk and a stove I
had bought taken to the depot, and they
arrived at the Irvington house at about
6 P. M., at which time Mr. Moreman
was the last person who saw the boy
alive, for almost immediately I called
him into the house and insisted that
he go to bed at once, first giving him
the fatal dose of medicine. As soon as
he had ceased to breathe I cut his body
into pieces that would pass through the
door of the stove and by the combined
use of gas and corncobs proceeded to
burn it with as little feeling as 'tho it had
been some inanimate object. If I could
now recall one circumstance, a dollar of
money to be gained, a disagreeable act
or word upon his part, in justification
of this horrid crime, it would be a satisfaction to me; but to think that I
committed this and other crimes for the
pleasure of killing my fellow beings, to
hear their cries for mercy and pleas
to be allowed even sufficient time to pray
and prepare for death—all this is now too
horrible for even me, hardened criminal that I am, to again live over without
a shudder. Is it to be wondered at
that since my arrest my days have been
those of self-reproaching torture, and my
nights of sleepless fear? Or that even
before my death, I have commenced to
assume the form and features of the
evil one himself.

After I had finished the cremation of
my victim I made the excavation in
which the few remaining portions were
found at the time the horror was brought
to light, which together with the stove

and other evidences of my wrong-doings, were brought here to Philadelphia at the time of my trial to mock me in my efforts to save my life. Then after I had removed the blood and other evidences of the crime, and had burned the contents of the trunk. I went to the office of Powell & Harter, at Indianapolis, for my mail; from there to the hotel for the other two children, whom I took at once to Chicago. I immediately returned to the Irvington House, and was seen there by Mr. Armstrong, a teamster, or such, in time as to have made it a foolish act for me to have persisted in saying that it was some other person whom he saw. My identification in Chicago by a women with whom the children boarded and by the station agent at Milwaukee, and later at Adrian, Mich., all show the uselessness of trying to escape from one's self or from the responsibility of one's wrong acts.

In Detroit I hired a house and made an excavation in the basement, where I left a note in my own handwriting, all of which I hastened to tell the detectives as soon as I was arrested, so that by their going to the house and finding both the excavation and the note they would not be inclined to prosecute a similar search in Toronto or other places.

I now, with much reluctance, come to the discussion of the twenty-sixth and twenty-seventh murders. The victims were Alice and Nellie Pitezel, whose deaths will seem to many to be the saddest of all, both on account of the terribly heartless manner in which it was accomplished, and because in one instance, that of Alice, the oldest of these children, her death was the least of the wrongs suffered at my hands. Here again I am tempted to either pass the matter by without speaking of it, or to altogether deny it, but to what purpose? It is publicly known and was freely commented upon at my trial, and to deny it now would only serve the double purpose of breaking my resolution to hold nothing in reserve, and of causing many who are somewhat familiar with the details of the different cases to disbelieve me in other matters; moreover, the testimony already given by Mrs. Aetlia Allcorn, and the opinion of Coroner Ashbridge and a Mr. Perry, who knew the mental condition of the child upon the following day, would, if called for, be sufficient to decide the matter. These children, after boarding in Detroit for about one week, reached Toronto, October 19, and were taken to the Albion Hotel, where they boarded until they were killed. Upon October 20 I hired the Vincent street house, having the lease made in the name of H. M. Howard, in order to avert suspicion as much as possible in case an investigation followed. Between 5 and 6 P. M, the same day I took a large empty trunk to the house and then passed the following day at Niagara Falls. On the 22d I bought and had taken to the house the furniture, stove and bedding, and on the 23d, the children went to the house for a few hours. The 24th was passed in other parts of the city, but upon the 25th, the fatal day of these deaths, they were seen at the house at 1 P. M., and a little later they accompanied me to several clothing stores and finally at 4 P. M., while they were in a restaurant near-by I entered a large store in which I believed I should meet Mrs. Pitezel, holding in my hands some heavy winter underwear I had bought for the little boy already dead. Of this meeting Mrs. Pitezel has said:

"I believe my children were at that time in that store with me."

I immediately took them to the Vincent street house and compelled them to both get within the large trunk, through the cover of which I made a small opening. Here I left them until I could return and at my leisure kill them. At 5 P. M. I borrowed a spade of a neighbor and at the same time called on Mrs. Pitezell at her hotel. I then returned to my hotel and ate my dinner, and at 7.00 P. M. went again to Mrs. Pitezel's hotel, and aided her in leaving Toronto for Ogdensburg, N. Y. Later than 8.00 P. M. I again returned to the house where the children were imprisoned, and ended their lives by connecting the gas with the trunk, then came the opening of the trunk and the viewing of

HOLMES CLOSING THE VAULT ON A VICTIM

THE VINCENT STREET HOUSE, TORONTO, WHERE ALICE AND
NELLIE PITEZEL WERE MURDERED

THE STOVE AND FALSE SAFE IN THE CASTLE

OLMES MURDERING ALICE AND NELLIE PITEZEL IN THE TRUN

A TRAP-DOOR IN THE CASTLE

THE IRVINGTON COTTAGE WHERE HOWARD PITEZEL WAS
MURDERED

Benjamin F. Pitezel.

Nellie Pitezel.

Minnie Williams.

Mrs. Julia Connor.

Alice Pitezel.

Mrs. Pitezel.

Pearl Connor.

Nannie Williams.

Detective Geyer.

To the Philadelphia Engineer —

I hereby respectfully deny the ac—
believing that any comparison has been made
by me except on & what is the only oculist
once be made this original comparison to
the one genus to the Philadelphia Engineer
to alone is genuine, all others an unknow—

August H. H. Holmes

April 11th 1846

their little blackened and distorted faces. Then the digging of their shallow graves in the basement of the house, the ruthless stripping off of their clothing, and the burial without a particle of covering save the cold earth, which I heaped upon them with fiendish delight. Consider what an awful act this was! These little innocent and helpless children, the oldest only being 13 years of age, a puny and sickly child, who to look at one would believe much younger; consider that for eight years before their death I had been almost as much a father as though they had been my own children, thus giving them a right to look to me for care and protection, and in your righteous judgment let your bitterest curses fall upon me, but again I pray upon me alone! There is little more to tell. The next day was passed in burning the children's clothing, and in resting from my terrible night's work, and upon the 27th I called an expressman and had the trunk removed from the house, and after giving the keys to a neighbor went away never to return.

From Toronto I went to Ogdensburg, from there to Burlington, Vermont, where I hired a furnished house for Mrs. Pitezel's use, and a few days prior to my arrest in Boston I wrote her a letter in which I directed her to carry a bottle of dynamite that I had previously left in the basement so arranged that in taking it to the third story of the house it would fall from her hands, and not only destroy her life, but that of her two remaining children, who I knew would be with her at the time. This was my last act, and happily did not have a fatal termination. The eighteen intervening months I have passed in solitary confinement, and in a few days am to be led forth to my death. It would now seem a very fitting time for me to express regret or remorse in this, which I intend to be my last public utterance for these irreparable shortcomings. To do so with the expectation of even one person who has read this confession to the end, believing that in my depraved nature there is room for such feelings, is I fear, to expect more than would be granted. I can at least, and do refrain, from calling forth such a criticism by openly inviting it.

Philadelphia County Prison,   Wednesday, Ap

HOLMES' BUSY DAY

The Murderer Realizes That His Time Is Growing Short.

Holmes is now using every second of time that is left to him to put his affairs in shape. All day yesterday he sat in his cell hard at work, with pencil and paper. Once in a while he would turn around to chat with a keeper or a prison official who passed down the corridor. He was at all times cheerful and good-humored. It was evident that his confession has taken a great load from his shoulders.

Holmes' cell presents an interesting picture. The furnishing is meagre. There is the usual cot and stool, and in one corner under the narrow-grated window is a table on which are paper and pencils. It is here that Holmes sits most of the time hard at work. To a staple in the floor of the cell is fastened a stout iron chain, such as are used to manacle unruly prisoners.

Holmes has taken this chain and arranged it in the form of a cross. At times the eyes that have seen so many

The Gas Tank in the Castle, Chicago

death agonies turn furtively and glance
at the crude reminder of the crucifixion
as though the arch fiend were trying to
gain some measure of forgiveness for
his many crimes. Father Dailey, who is
Holmes' constant attendant, is giving the
murderer what solace he can.

Holmes fully realizes that his time
is growing short, and that the hours
are now slipping away faster than ever.
Once yesterday the murderer turned
and glanced at the calendar. "I haven't
got much time left," he remarked, "and
I still have a great deal of work to
do." When he wrote his statement for
The Inquirer, repudiating the false confessions that appeared in certain papers
he tore off a corner of the paper and
kept it. "The stock is getting short,"
he remarked, "and I must look after
the odds and ends."

AT QUINLAN. ARTICULATOR OF SKELETONS. CHAPPEL

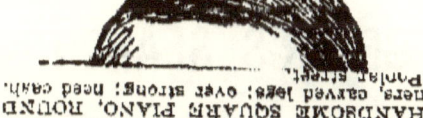

HOLMES' ARREST

How the Insurance Company Worked Out the Great Case.

Soon after the body of Pitezel was discovered on September 3, 1894, and the insurance money paid, Inspector Gary of the Fidelity Mutual Life Association discovered that a fraud had been perpetrated against the company. With special Agent Perry and backed by President Fouse, he started out to unravel the mystery. The task was an enormous one. It took big sums of money. The company stopped at nothing in the way of expense. Agents and Pinkertons were sent out everywhere and Holmes' movements were finally traced. At last the man was captured in Boston after an exciting hunt through New England.

During that chase the insurance people picked up many things that afterwards led them to unravel the great mystery and convict the man of murder. At the time of the arrest the Fidelity people fully believed that Holmes had killed Pitezel, but they did not know the full depths of the man's infamy. At this time even the authorities took little interest in the case.

The belief of the insurance company that Pitezel was murdered and that Holmes was the murderer, is testified to in an affidavit which was made by O. L. F. Perry prior to Holmes' arrest.

From that time on Holmes has maintained his innocence until he made his confession for The Inquirer.

/ / / /

GEYER'S SEARCH

The Detective Writes a Book Telling How He Solved the Pitezel Mysteries.

Up to the time the Supreme Court sealed his fate H. H. Holmes believed that he would escape the gallows. Outwardly his front was as bold as a tion's. In court and out he spun fairy stories to the authorities and mocked them in his sleeve. Had he been dealing with less careful men it is likely that he would even now be a free man.

Holmes was arrested on November 17, 1894, in Boston on a charge of defrauding the Fidelity Mutual Life Association, of this city. On September 3 of the same year the body of the man then known as Perry, afterwards identified as B. F. Pitezel, was found in the house, No. 1316 Callowhill street. As soon as he was arrested Holmes expressed his willingness to tell the entire story concerning it and the collection of the insurance money.

He was permitted to talk, and he proceeded on the first of a series of rambling statements that eventually tangled him up. For a long time he succeeded in keeping the authorities off the right track. But the officials were patient. Link by link they worked on the case, until they finally reached the conclusion that Holmes must have murdered the three Pitezel children.

HIS LETTER TO MRS. PITEZEL.

It was decided to release Mrs. Pitezel from custody in June, 1895, and to take up the hunt in earnest. The day the sorrowing mother left Moyamensing Prison she was handed a letter from Holmes. Viewed in the light of subsequent developments, that letter seems to be as great a series of cold-blooded lies as ever mortal penned.

The document has but recently been made public by Detective Geyer in his book, "The Holmes-Pitezel Mystery." The quotations from Mr. Geyer are also from the same work. It reads:

PHILADELPHIA, June 17, 1895.
Mrs. Carrie A. Pitezel:

Dear Madam: I have been exceedingly anxious during the last few months to communicate with you, but have been headed off in every direction. I learn that you will shortly be set at liberty, and I shall take this letter to City Hall with me and then give it to my attorneys to be sent to you, as the prison regulations do not prohibit my doing so.

I have been repeatedly called cruel and heartless during the past six months

and by those who were at the very time
doing more than I that was both cruel
and heartless towards you. Within ten
days after you came here arrangements
were made with my attorney to furnish
bail for you and a house to live in. We
were refused permission to see you, although you remember coming here from
Boston it was promised I should see
you. Later I offered to make arrangements with your lawyer for the same.
Mr. Barlow, of the District Attorney's
office, told me I could do nothing and
that I need not worry myself about you,
as you are being cared for. Within
three days after you came here you had
been made to believe so much from others that you forgot that for years I had
done all I could do for you and yours
and that it was hardly likely that all at
once I should turn and do all I could
against you.

THREATS OF SUICIDE.

Facts you should know are as follows:
Ben lived West, and while drunk at Fort
Worth, Texas, married a disreputable
woman by the name of Mrs. Martin.
When he became sober and found what
he had done he threatened to kill himself and her, and I had him watched by
one of the other men until he went
home. When we straightened up the
bank account he had fooled away or
had been robbed by her of over $850 of
the money we needed there so much.

Later he wanted to carry out the insurance work down in Mississippi, where
he was acquainted, and I went there
with him, and when I found out what
kind of a place it was would not go any
further with it there, and told him so,
and he said if I did not he would kill
himself and get money for you, etc.
To get him out of the notion I told him
I would go to Mobile, and if I could not
get what was wanted would do so; if
not I would go to St. Louis and write
to him to come. I did not go to Mobile.
Was never there in my life.

When I reached St. Louis I wrote him,
and in the letter he left me after he died
he said he tried to kill himself with
laudanum there, and later I found out
this was so. (Henry Rogers, proprietor
of hotel at Perkinsville, Ala.) Where he

was very sick. He also wrote you he
was sick there. I think you told me.
Here in Philadelphia we were not ready.
He got word baby was sick and he had
to own to me he had drank up the $35
I gave him extra in New York, and then
I told him I would settle up everything,
as if we carried it out he might get to
drinking and tell of it.

He begged me not to do it, and at last
I concluded to try again, but thought
it best to have him think for a week or
two that I was not going on with it, so
he would sober up and be himself. I
blame myself for this and always shall,
for the next day when I went to his
store I found him as I have described,
and Perry or the detectives have got
the cypher slip he left me, or, at all
events, it was in the tin box they took.
He asked me to get you a house in Cincinnati, on account of good schools,
etc., and I did so, but did not dare take
you there after Howe and McD. threatened my arrest, and so made arrangements with Miss W. to live with you.
She took Howard with her from Detroit
because he would quarrel with the girls
if no grown person was with them, and
he wanted his father's watch and Alice
wanted to keep it, and so I took it, telling them I wanted to show it to you and
Dessa, and bought all three of them each
a cheap watch.

When I found the conditions in Toronto were not as Miss W. thought they
were, and I was getting word from Chicago every day that I was being followed, I thought it best to go out of the
country altogether, and the insurance
company know the children, A. and E.,
were at their hotel at 1 o'clock the afternoon you left Toronto, and between
then and when I saw you at 4 o'clock,
at the store where I was buying some
things for them, I had been to my wife's
hotel twice and was with you again at
6.30, and had meantime started the children to Miss W. and eaten my supper.

ACCOUNTING FOR TIME.

From that time until my arrest in Boston if I now could be allowed to sit
down with you and my wife I could
show you where every half hour was
spent. In Boston I received a letter

'from Miss W. that they would leave
there in a few days, and if the detectives would now go, as I beg of them,
they could trace out the New York end
of the matter, and stop all unnecessary
delay and expense. This would spoil
their theories, and would not be a sufficiently bloodthirsty ending of the case
to satisfy them, it seems.

As soon as they got a house and were
settled, they were to send word and
you were then to go to them, and this
was why I wished you to take a furnished house so you could get rested and
not be at hotels. I made arrangements
for Miss W. to tell you all when you
were settled. If you had known they
were following you you would have
been worried, and I think you will remember that I tried to do all I could to
keep you from it and we had to get rid
of the old trunks and get the things
into bundles, so there would be no
checking. There is a bundle of yours
now at the Burlington Depot marked
with the name you went by there, which
I have forgotten.

NEVER QUARRELED WITH BEN.

I was as careful of the children as if
they were my own, and you know
me well enough to judge me better
than strangers here can do. Ben
would not have done anything
against me, or I against him, any
quicker than brothers. We never
quarreled. Again, he was worth too
much to me for me to have killed him,
if I had no other reason not to. As to
the children, I never will believe, until
you tell me so yourself, that you think
they are dead, or that I did anything to
put them out of the way. Knowing me
as you do, can you imagine me killing
little and innocent children, especially
without any motive? Why, if I was
preparing to put them out of life was I
(within an hour before I must have done
it if ever) buying them things to wear
and make them comfortable, even underwear for them to take to Miss W. for
Howard (which I can prove I bought in
Toronto), if, as they would have you believe, Pat had taken him and killed him
weeks before? Don't you know that if I

had offered Pat a million dollars he would
not have done a thing like this? I made
a mistake in having it known that Miss
W. killed her sister, as it tends to make
her more careful about her movements,
but I could hardly do otherwise, when I
was accused of killing them both. Now
after they get done trying to make the
case worse than it is, you will find that
they will trace the children to New York
and to the steamer there. Next to you I
have suffered most about them, and a
few days ago gave the District Attorney all the facts I could, and if nothing
comes of it soon, I hardly expect anything new to occur until I can be taken
to Fort Worth and arrange the property, so Mr. Massie, her old guardian,
can take her part of the money to her
in London. By advertising, if she knows
there is money for her and it comes
through Mr. Massie safely, she will find
some way (probably through her Boston
friend) to get it. As long as there is
nothing to gain she will hardly come out
openly and lay herself liable to arrest.

THE CRUEL COMPANY.

I dislike fearfully to go to Fort Worth
to serve a term, as the prisons there are
terrible. I would rather be here five
years than there one, and in going there
is no better way to have you know that
I am willing to do all I can for you and
yours. I blame the company here for
keeping you shut up six months in this
den, for worrying you about your children not being alive and for their trying
to separate my wife from me, for these
things do not concern them, but I have
never blamed them for otherwise making me all the trouble they can. I would
do the same with another if the tables
were turned.

As matters now stand I have got here,
in Illinois and in Texas, between fifteen
and twenty years of imprisonment
awaiting me. If the children can be
found I want to finish here and in Illinois first, hoping by that time the
Texas matters may blow over or that I
may die; but if they are not found before my sentence expires here, if any
arrangement can be made so papers can
be filed in Texas to bring me back here or
to Illinois, after I have served this first

small charge in Texas, so I do not have to stay and serve the others there until after my Northern term is served, I will go and do all I can to both get the property straightened there, so you can have a small income and arrange for recovery of the children. Ben's death was genuine and you were entitled to the money, and if it had not been for H. and McD. you would to-day have been in Cincinnati with all the children.

About the money, Ben asked me to use most of it to pay debts and arrange so some steady income should come to you from the South. The note you got in St. Louis was made by him in the spring and some money was due on it. We were owing Miss W. about $3,000. I gave $1,000 to her in Detroit (also $400 to Alice in Toronto), and you have no reason to think I was not intending to take care of you then, more than in years before, and now if I can get to Fort Worth without running risk of staying there more than one year I will soon straighten so as to get you money while I am there in jail. Mr. Shoemaker went there two weeks last winter and started matters, but until I can go there and be taken into court nothing more can be done, I fear.

PLANS FOR THE CHILDREN

There are some letters at the City Hall that I promised Alice I would save for her, as I did not dare to let her carry them with her, and if after they get through with them you can get them I wish you would do so. Also Ben's watch. Howard has the other things. I don't know what you will do meantime if you gain your liberty here, but rest assured I will do all I can at the earliest possible moment. So far as the children's bodily health is concerned I feel sure I can say to you that they are as well to-day as though they were with you. Also that they will not be turned adrift among strangers for two reasons: First, Miss W., though quick-tempered, is too soft-hearted to do so; second, if among others where their letters could not be looked over and detained they would write to their grandparents (not to you, as I instructed Miss W. from Boston in answer to her letter to me if she heard of my or our arrest to have the children think we were lost in crossing to London). They have no doubt written letters which Miss W. for her own safety has withheld.

If there are any questions you wish to ask me make a list of them and send to one of my attorneys. I have refrained from asking you any lest you would think that the object of my letter. I have no desire to do anything that will cause your lawyer or the prosecution any unnecessary work or annoyance, and if you write me shall simply answer questions asked. Shall not advise nor question you, nor would I have done so if allowed to have seen you during past months, though it would have saved them much unnecessary delay and expense to have had us eliminate some of the features of the case by comparing memories. I, at least, hope your suffering is nearly ended.

Yours, truly,

H. II. HOLMES.

THE HUNT BEGINS.

Substantially this document presents the case as the authorities knew it when Detective Geyer started on his famous hunt June 26, 1895. Besides Holmes' own statements the detective was in possession of certain clues obtained from a tin box that contained Holmes' letters and papers. Geyer went straight to Cincinnati, where he and Detective John Snooks found the first traces.

"We finally struck a cheap hotel at No. 164½ Central avenue, known as the Atlantic House, and upon examining the register we discovered that on Friday, September 28, 1894, there appeared the name of Alex. E. Cook and three children," writes Mr. Geyer. "The photographs of Holmes and the three children were shown to the clerk, who could not say positively that they were the photographs of the people who had stopped there, but thought they resembled them very much. Recalling to my mind that Holmes had Mrs. Pitezel living in Burlington under the name of Mrs. A. E. Cook, I felt convinced that I was on the right track. The clerk informed us that these parties only remained over night, leaving the following morning. Thanking the clerk for his kind attention we left the hotel and continued our search among such hotels as we had not visited, and

when we arrived at the Hotel Bristol,
corner of Sixth and Vine streets, we discovered that on Saturday, September 20,
1894, there appeared on the register the
name of A. E. Cook and three children,
Cleveland. They were assigned to Room
No. 103, a room which contained two
beds. Mr. W. L. Bain, a clerk at the
hotel, recognized the photographs of
Holmes and the children as the party
who registered there under that name.
The register showed that they left the
Bristol on Sunday, September 30."

The detective then goes on to relate
how they tried to find a house Holmes
is alleged to have rented in Cincinnati.
Summing up this chapter of the work,
Mr. Geyer says:

"Having located Holmes and the children at two hotels in Cincinnati and discovered the two false names he assumed, Cook and Hayes, I felt justified
in believing that I had taken firm hold
of the end of the string which was to
lead me ultimately to the consummation
of my difficult mission. I was not able
to appreciate the intense significance of
the renting of the Poplar street house
and the delivery of a stove of such immense size there, but I felt sure I was
on the right track, and so started for
Indianapolis, from which point several
of the children's letters found in
Holmes' tin box had been dated."

TRACED TO INDIANAPOLIS.

At Indianapolis he arrived on June 20.
"Here," continues the detective, "on
going to the Stubbins House and examining the register, we found that on September 24, 1894, was an entry in the
name of Etta Pitzel, St. Louis, Mo., and
that the hotel records showed she left
on the morning of September 28. Further inquiry elicited the fact that the
girl was brought there by a man known
to Mr. Robert Sweeney, the clerk, as
Mr. Howard, and that on Friday morning, September 28, he had received
a telegram from Mr. Howard, dated
St. Louis, requesting him to have Etta
Pitzel at the Union Depot to meet St.
Louis train for Cincinnati, O. This was
the day Holmes left St. Louis with Nellie and Howard Pitzel, telling their
mother that he was going to take them

to Indianapolis, where they would be taken care of by a kind old lady. Mr. Sweeney fully identified the picture of Alice Pitezel as the girl who stopped at the Stubbins House; also that of Holmes as the man whom he knew as Howard and to whom he had given Alice Pitezel on the St. Louis train for Cincinnati, O."

Further traces of Holmes were found in Indianapolis, and then Geyer went to Chicago and saw a Miss Irons. Janitor Pat Quinlan and others, who gave him information. Detroit was the next point he visited. There he found other traces and also discovered that the boy Howard had dropped out of the story and that Holmes and the two little girls had gone to Toronto.

For several days there the detective was baffled. At last he called in the newspaper men, gave them pictures of the children and told them what he was looking for. All the Toronto papers printed big stories. They soon bore fruit. A man who had rented a house at 16 St. Vincent street to a stranger with two children turned up. He gave the right clue. The detectives followed it up. Photographs of Holmes and the children were promptly identified by those who saw them.

TWO BODIES FOUND.

Then continues Mr. Geyer: "We at once returned to No. 18 St. Vincent street, where we met Mr. Ryves anxiously waiting for our return. Requesting him to loan us a shovel, he went into the house and came out with the same spade he had loaned to Holmes. We rang the bell at No. 16 St. Vincent street. The door was opened by the lady of the house, a Mrs. J. Armbrust. Mr. Ryves introduced us and told her we would like to go into the cellar. She kindly consented and ushered us back into the kitchen. Lifting a large piece of oilcloth from the floor, we discovered a small trap door, possibly two feet square, in about the centre of the room. Raising this, I discovered that the cellar was not very deep, but it was very dark, so I asked Mrs. Armbrust to kindly provide us with some lamps. In a short time she had them ready, and down into the cellar we went. The collar was very small, about ten feet square and not more than four and a half feet in depth. A set of steps, almost perpendicular, lead to it from the old-fashioned trap door in the middle of the kitchen floor.

"Taking the spade and pushing it into the earth, so as to determine whether it had been lately dug up, we finally discovered a soft spot in the southwest corner. Forcing the spade into the earth, we found it easy digging, and, after going down about one foot, a horrible stench arose. This convinced us that we were on the right spot, and our coats were thrown off, and with renewed confidence we continued our digging. The deeper we dug the more horrible the odor became, and when we reached the depth of three feet we discovered what appeared to be the bone of the forearm of a human being.

"Alice was found lying on her side, with her head to the west. Nellie was found lying on her face, with her head to the south, her plaited hair hanging neatly down her back. A messenger was dispatched to Humphrey's undertaking establishment to send two coffins to No. 16 St. Vincent street. In a short time the wagon arrived and the coffins were taken into the kitchen, and we proceeded to lift the remains out of the hole. As Nellie's limbs were found resting on Alice's we first began with her. We lifted her as gently as possible, but owing to the decomposed state of the body the weight of her plaited hair hanging down her back pulled the scalp from off her head. A sheet had been spread in which to lay the remains, and after we succeeded in getting it out of the hole it was placed in the sheet, taken upstairs and deposited in the coffin. Again we returned to the cellar, and gently lifting what remained of poor Alice we placed her in another sheet, took her upstairs and placed her in a coffin by the side of her sister."

BEGINNING OF THE END.

This discovery was the beginning of the end. The story of how Mrs. Pitezel came on to Toronto and identified the remains is one of the saddest incidents in the rest of the narrative. Summing up this part of the case the detective says:

"Nothing could be more surprising than the apparent ease with which Holmes murdered the two little girls in the very centre of the city of Toronto without arousing the least suspicion of a single person there. It startles one to realize how such a hideous crime could be committed and detection avoided. Surely if the investigation and search for the children had not been made by the Philadelphia authorities these murders would never have been discovered, and Mrs. Pitezel would have gone to her grave without knowing whether her children were alive or dead. This was the one consolation she had in the very darkest hour of her life. She knew the fate of her unfortunate daughters, the mystery of their disappearance had been solved, and the only remaining problem was the discovery of her little son, Howard. She could not believe he was dead, and clung fondly to the hope that he would ultimately be found alive.

"Holmes was successful in maintaining the same conditions in Toronto as he had in Detroit. Mrs. Pitezel was at the Union Hotel and Alice and Nellie at the Albion, although each party was ignorant of the proximity of the other."

On the afternoon of July 10, 1895, the bodies were buried and the detective went on to Detroit to take up the hunt for Howard. Finally he returned to Philadelphia, and in August Geyer started out again. This time he was accompanied by Inspector Gary, of the Insurance company. Step by step Holmes' journey was retraced until only forty-eight hours were unaccounted for. These left him in Indianapolis, and there the trail was hotly pressed. On Tuesday, August 27, 1895, they found where Holmes and the boy rented a house at Irvington. There the search was begun in earnest.

HOWARD'S BONES FOUND.

Gruesome relics that told the story of the boy's sad fate soon began to turn up. Some of the children's clothing and trinkets and the long-missing trunk of Mrs. Pitezel were easily found. Then the charred remains of the boy were found inside the stove. When Holmes was putting this stove up he was asked by a Mr. Moorman why he didn't put in.

natural gas. Holmes replied: "I don't think natural gas is healthy for children."

The inquest was held soon afterwards, and in the meantime came the terrible revelations at the Chicago Castle which gave full belief that Holmes was the arch fiend of the century. Holmes was indicted for the murder of Pitezel in September, 1895. His trial began on October 18. The sensational events that followed are already well known. From the hour the verdict was given Holmes has been weakening.

During the time the authorities have pressed their case they have run across various things that led them to believe that Holmes had outside confederates. These friends were aware that all mail sent to Holmes to the Philadelphia County Prison was inspected before delivery to the prisoner and some of it, for proper reasons, never reached the prisoner. One of these friends undertook to divert Detective Geyer from pursuit of the track of Holmes just as he was leaving Indianapolis after his second visit. The detective received at the Spencer House an anonymous letter in cipher, with the key attached, advising him that an important letter had been sent to Holmes to Philadelphia; that the writer was advising the detective at great personal risk and that the letter should be opened and inspected before delivery to the prisoner. The letter, which came in due course, tells Holmes not "to worry about the boy; he is safe and sound," and at first it gave the impression that Holmes had in some way conveyed to an outside party the place where the remains of the boy had been buried, and that the boy's remains had been removed from the place of concealment.

NOT SO EASILY FOOLED.

After careful deliberation, the District Attorney's office concluded that it was a trick or device for a purpose not very clear, and it was totally disregarded, and the search subsequently continued with the result already narrated. This is one of the many letters, some in cipher, which were received, and are now among the great mass of manuscript which has accumulated in the case. Newspapers evidently make their way into lunatic asylums, for letters from the insane came in by the score. The name of Holmes also seemed to become as common as Brown or Smith, for many letters referring to this person and that person by the name of Holmes, and requesting information as to comparisons of points of identity with the prisoner, were received.

One of the letters received in cipher is given below. This letter is very easily read by dropping every other sentence, separated by commas:

"Aug. 2, 1895.

"Friend H. H .H.:—I, and Jim, will not, saw and, split, the wood. They, can't and, don't, want to, know, whether there is, anything, around or, about, the, conservatory or, green house, I, think, will leave, the dog, for, Mrs. John, Cleveland, at Bleak House, to-morrow. Will, join him under, cover, and fix, all, circus board, signs, there. Same, time I will, sigh for, Ponto's fate and yours in his misfortune.

"R. I. T. U. A. L.   Friend,

"I. S. PAGE.

"Friend H. H. H.—I, and Jim, will They don't know anything about the conservatory. I will leave for Cleveland to-morrow. Will cover all signs.

"Same cipher."

Detective Geyer in his book has made a good chronology of Holmes' career. It follows:

Holmes' Chronology.

1860.

May 16—Herman Webster Mudgett born at Gilmanton, N. H.

1878.

July 4—He is married to Clara A. Lovering at Alton, N. H., by John W. Caurrier, Justice of the Peace.

1887.

January 28—He is married to Myrta Z. Belknap under the name of Harry Howard Holmes.

February 14—He files in the Superior Court of Cook county, Ill., a libel in divorce against his wife, Clara A. Lovering Mudgett, praying that their marriage may be dissolved.

1891.

June 4—The said court orders this suit to be dismissed for default of appearance of complainant.

1893.

March—He meets Miss Georgiana Yoke in

Chicago.

September 19—He makes application for a
twenty-year additional insurance for $10,000
in the Fidelity Mutual Life Association, in
which he avers: "Mother died at 56; don't
remember the disease; no acute disease.
Father died at 62 from injury to his foot."

November 9—Fidelity Mutual Life Association
insures Benjamin F. Pitezel in the sum of
$10,000.

Same month Holmes is engaged to be married
to Miss Yoke under the name of Henry
Mansfield Howard.

1894.

January 17—He is married to Miss Yoke in
Denver, Cal., by the Rev. Mr. Wilcox and
they journey on their honeymoon to Fort
Worth, Tex.

January, February, March, April—Mudgett
and Pitezel (the former under the name of
D. T. Pratt and the latter under the name
of Benton T. Lyman), in Fort Worth, Tex.,
where they engage in building a store property on land formerly owned by Minnie Williams.

April—Pitezel leaves Fort Worth and goes to
Chicago.

May—Mudgett and Miss Yoke leave Fort Worth
and journey to Denver, Col.

May 21—They make their appearance in St.
Louis.

June 1—About this date Holmes (Mudgett)
and Pitezel go to Memphis, Tenn. In this
vicinity they first consider the location of
the place where they propose to execute the
insurance fraud.

June 5—Holmes and wife return to St. Louis.

June 15—Holmes purchases a drug store in St.
Louis, Mo., under the name of Howard, upon
which he gave a mortgage.

July 19—Holmes is arrested in St. Louis by
the Merrill Drug Company and sent to prison
under a charge of fraud and for selling
mortgaged property. The man "Brown,"
to whom he sold it, is supposed to have been
Pitezel. During his imprisonment in the St.
Louis jail he meets Marion C. Hedgepeth.

July 23—He is released on bail.

July 20—He is rearrested and again committed
to prison.

July 31—He is again released on bail furnished by Miss Yoke.

August 2, 3 and 4—He is in New York and
Philadelphia.

August 4—Miss Yoke (Mrs. Howard) leaves
Lake Bluff, Ill., where she was visiting, and
journeys to Philadelphia.

August 5—Sunday. Holmes meets Miss Yoke
at Broad Street Station, Philadelphia, and
takes her to a boarding house, No. 1905
North Eleventh street (Mrs. Dr. Alcorn's).
He tells Miss Yoke he is selling a patent
letter copier.

August 9—Holmes telegraphs $157.50 (the half
yearly premium on the Pitezel policy), to
the Chicago office of the Fidelity Mutual
Life Association.

August 17—Pitezel, under the name of B. F. Perry, rents No. 1316 Callowhill street and pays $10 on account of the rent to Walter W. Shedaker, agent.

August 17—Holmes and Pitezel pur hase second-hand furniture of John F. Hughes, No. 1037 Buttonwood street, which was sent to No. 1316 Callowhill street.

August 18—Pitezel calls at the furniture store alone and purchases a cot and some old matting.

August 22—Eugene Smith calls upon Pitezel and sees Holmes pass into the house and go up stairs.

August 22 to September 1—Pitezel is seen in and about No. 1313 Callowhill street by a large number of persons.

September 1—Evening. Pitezel calls upon Holmes at No. 1905 North Eleventh street.

September 2—Holmes leaves No. 1905 North Eleventh street at about 10.30 A. M. He returns about 4 P. M. He tells his wife (Miss Yoke) that the man who called the evening before was a messenger from the Pennsylvania Railroad Company and that he could have an interview with a Pennsylvania Railroad official the next day at Nicetown. This Sunday morning he said he was going out to Nicetown to see the official and that if he was successful, and as their week was up, they would probably start West that night.

September 3—Evening. Holmes and Miss Yoke leave Philadelphia on the 10 23 train and went direct to Indianapolis.

September 3—They arrive in Indianapolis and register at the Stubbins House.

September 4—They take boarding at No. 488 North Illinois street, Indianapolis.

September 4—Pitezel's body found at No. 1316 Callowhill street by Eugene Smith.

September 6—Coroner holds first inquest.

September 5—Holmes goes to St. Louis, calls upon Mrs. Pitezel and tells her to go to Howe with the papers, meaning insurance policy, etc. She takes papers to Howe. Holmes told her that a body had been substituted for her husband and that "Ben was alive and all right," and not to worry.

September 8—Fidelity Mutual receives a telegraphic dispatch from George B. Stadden, manager for Missouri, at St. Louis, stating that "B. F. Perry, found dead in Philadelphia, is claimed to be B. F. Pitezel, who is insured on 044145. Investigate before remains leave there."

About this time Howe writes to the company in Philadelphia, stating that he was counsel for Mrs. Pitezel the beneficiary under the policy, and would come on with a member of the family to identify the body, etc.

September 13—Pitezel's body buried as B. F. Perry in Potter's Field, Philadelphia.

September 5 to September 19—Holmes was with Miss Yoke at her mother's home in Franklin, Ind., leaving her, he said, to go to St. Louis again or to Cincinnati and then to

Indianapolis. At this time Holmes was occasionally with his other wife at Wilmette,
Ill. He was likely with her on September
11. At Indianapolis he tells Miss Yoke that
he had heard from the Pennsylvania Railroad
official in Philadelphia about the order and
they were ready to pay over the money, and
they had directed him to come on at once.
He left her at the Circle Park Hotel, Indianapolis, and went to Philadelphia.

September 17—He writes a letter to Mr. Cass,
Chicago cashier of the Fidelity, stating that
his wife (Wilmette wife) had told him that
information was wanted of B. F. Pitezel,
who was found in Chicago as B. F. Perry.

September 18—He writes another letter to Cass
saying that he overhears the body was in
Philadelphia and not in Chicago, and that
he would go to Philadelphia if his expenses
were paid.

September 19—Holmes leaves Indianapolis for
Philadelphia. He again stops at No. 1905
North Eleventh street; Mrs. Alcorn's.

September 20—He calls at the office of the
company in Philadelphia. No. 914 Walnut
street. He tells Mr. Fouse, president of the
company, that he had corresponded with
Cass. He asks Fouse about the circumstances of the death, which Fouse relates
briefly. Holmes said it was a very peculiar
case and asked Mr. Fouse the cause of
death, etc.

September 23—Alice writes her first letter to
the home folks.

Philadelphia, Pa.,
Corner Filbert and Eleventh streets,
September 20, 1894.

Dear Mamma and the rest:

Just arrived in Philadelphia this morning
and I wrote you yesterday of this. Mr. Howe
and I have each a room at the above address.
I am going to the Morgue after awhile. We
stopped off at Washington, Md., this morning,
and that made it six times that we transferred
to different cars. Yesterday we got on the
C. and O. Pullman car and it was crowded,
so I had to sit with some one. Mr. Howe sit
with some man we sit there quite awhile and
pretty soon some one came and shook hands
with me. I looked up and here it was Mr.
Howard. He did not know my jacket, but
he said he thought it was his girl's face so
he went to see and it was me. I don't like
him to call me babe and child and dear and
all such trash. When I got on the car Tuesday night Mr. Howe ask me if I had any
money and I told him 5 cents so he gave me
a dollar. How I wish I could see you all and
hug the baby. I hope you are hotter. Mr.
H. says that I will have a ride on the ocean.
I wish you could see what I have seen. I
have seen more scenery than I have seen
since I was born. I don't know what I saw
before. This is all the paper I have so I will
have to close & write again. You had better
not write to me here for Mr. H. says that I
may be off to-morrow. If you are worse wire
me good-bye kisses to all and two big ones
for you and babe. Love to all.

E. ALICE PITEZEL.

September 21—Howe and Alice Pitezel called at insurance office. Holmes calls same time. They meet as strangers, although they had traveled together from some point in Ohio to Washington. D. C. Howe and Alice got off at Washington and Holmes took train for Philadelphia. Howe and Alice came to Philadelphia on later train. That day Holmes took Alice out to see the sights of the city and then to Mrs. Alcorn's that night, stating that she (Alice) was his little sister. Alice slept in the third-story next to Holmes' room, which communicated with it. Alice had stopped with Howe at the Imperial Hotel, Eleventh and Filbert streets, from which place she wrote two letters. Following are copies:

Imperial Hotel, Eleventh, above Market street, Hendricks & Scott, proprietors.

Philadelphia, Pa., September 21, 1894.
Dear Mamma and Babe:
I have to write all the time to pass away the time.

Mr. Howe has been away all morning. Mamma have you ever seen or tasted a red banana? I have had three. They are so big that I can just reach around it and have my thumb and next finger just tutch. I have not got any shoes yet and I have to go a hobbling around all the time. Have you gotten 4 letters from me besides this? Are you sick in bed yet or are you up? I wish that I could hear from y u, but I don't know whether I would get it or not. Mr. Howe telegraphed to Mr. Heckert and he said that he would write to you tonight. I have not got but two clean garments and that is a shirt and my white skirt. I saw some of the largest solid rocks that I bet you never saw. I crossed the Potomac River. I guess that I have told all the news. So good bye Kisses to you and babe.

　　　　　　Yours loving daughter,
　　　　　　MISS M. A. PITEZEL.
If you are worse telegraph to the above address. Imperial Hotel, Eleventh above Market street.

Imperial Hotel, Eleventh above Market street, Hendricks & Scott, proprietors.

Philadelphia, 189—
Dear Bessa:
I thought I would write you a little letter And when I get to Mass. you must all write to me. Well this is a warm day here how is it there? Did you get your big washing done if I was there you would have a bigger one for I have a whole satchel full of dirty clothes. I bet that I have more fruit than all of you. Bessa I guess you are without shoes for I guess they don't intend to get me any. H. has come now so I guess I have to go to dinner.

Bessa take good care of mama. I will close your letter and write a little to Nell and Howard next time so good bye love to you with a kiss.

—

Dear Mama:

I was over to the insurance office this afternoon and Mr. Howe thinks there will be no trouble about getting it. They asked me almost a thousand questions, of course not quite so many. Is his nose broken or has he a Roman nose. I said it was broken. I will have to close and write more tomorrow so good bye love to all with kisses to all.

Your loving daughter,
E. ALICE PITEZEL.

September 21—At the conference at the company's office on this day the marks of identification were agreed upon.

September 22—Pitezel's body exhumed at Potters' Field. Holmes finds wart on neck and other marks of identification and says the body is that of B. F. Pitezel. Alice recognizes teeth of her father. He takes Alice to No. 1904 North Eleventh street.

September 23—Holmes and Alice makes affidavits before Coroner Ashbridge that the body found as B. F. Perry at No. 1316 Callowhill street was that of Benjamin F. Pitezel. That evening Holmes and Alice leave for Indianapolis.

September 24—They arrive in Indianapolis. He registers Alice as Etta Pitzel in his handwriting.

September 24—Insurance company pays Howe $9715.85, face of insurance policy, less expenses.

September 24—Alice writes another letter home. The person alluded to in these letters as 4, 15, 3, is the children's cipher for Holmes.

—

Stubbins' European Hotel, one square north of Union Depot on Illinois street.

Indianapolis, Ind., September 24, 1894.

Dear Ones at Home:

I am glad to hear that you are all well and that you are up. I guess you will not have any trouble in getting the money. 4, 13, 3 is going to get two of you and fetch you here with me and them I won't be so lonesome at the above address. I am not going to Miss Williams until I see where you are going to live and then see you all again because 4, 13, 3 is afraid that I will get two lonesome then he will send me on and go to school. I have a pair of shoes now if I could see you I would have enough to talk to you all day but I cannot very well write it I will see you all before long though don't you worry. This is a cool day. Mr. Perry said that if you did not get the insurance all right through the lawyers to rite to Mr. Foust or Mr. Perry. I wish I had a silk dress. I have seen more since I have been away than I ever saw before in my life. I have another picture for your album. I will have to close for this time now so good bye love and kisses and squesses to all. Yours daughter.

ETTA PITEZEL.

P. 9, I go to Etta here 4. 13, 8 told me to
O Howard O Dessa, O Nell O Mamma. O
Baby. Nell you & Howard will come with
4, 13. 8 & Mamma and Dessa later on won't
you or as Mamma says.

ETTA PITEZEL

September 25—Holmes goes to St. Louis and remained there until the 28th.
September 27—Holmes gets $6700 of the in-
surance money out of the $7200 received by
Mrs. Pitezel from Howe. He gives her the
bogus note.
September 28—Holmes takes Nellie and Howard from Mrs. Pitezel at St. Louis. Alice
joins them at Indianapolis and she goes with
Holmes, Nellie and Howard to Cincinnati,
where Holmes registers at the Atlantic House
under the name of Alexander E. Cook and
three children.
September 29—He rents No. 305 Poplar street
from Mr. J. C. Thomas and takes a large
stove to this house. Over night of 28th he
remains at Atlantic House and on the 29th
he takes them to Hotel Bristol, registers
there as A. E. Cook and three children
and remains there until Sunday, September
30, when he left with the children for Indianapolis and registers them at Hotel English as "Three Canning children."
October 1—Monday. Mrs. Pitezel left St. Louis
for Galva, Ill., with Dessie and the baby.
Galva was the home of her parents. Holmes
takes the children to the Circle House, Indianapolis (registers as "Three Canning children"), where they remained until October
10.
October 1—Alice and Nellie write letters as
follows:

Indianapolis, Ind., October 1, 1894.
Dear Mamma:
We was in Cincinnati yesterday and we got
here last night getting that telegram from
Mr. Howe yesterday afternoon.
Mr. H. is going to-night for you and he will
take this letter. We went us three over to
the Zoological Garden in Cincinnati yesterday
afternoon and we saw all the different kinds
of animals. We saw the ostrich it is about
a head taller than I am so you know about
how high it is. And the giraffe you have
to look up in the sky to see it. I like it lots
better here than in Cincinnati. It is such a
dirty town Cin.
There is a monument right in front of the
hotel where we are at and I should judge that
it is about 3 times the hight of a five story
building. I guess I have told all the news so
good bye love to all & kisses. Hope you are
all well. Your loving daughter,
ETTA PITEZEL.

———

Indianapolis, Ind., October 1, 1894.
Dear Mamma, Baby and D.
We are all well here. Mr. H. is going on a
late train to-night. He is not here now I
just saw him go by the Hotel He went some

place I don't know where I think he went to
get his ticket.

We are staying in another hotel in Indianapolis it is a pretty nice one we came here
last night from C.

I like it here lots better than in C. It is
quite warm here and I have to wear this warm
dress becaus my close an't ironed. He ate
dinner over to the Stibbins Hotel where Alice
staid and they knew her to. We are not
staying there we are at the English H.

We have a room right in front of a monument and I think it was A. Lincolns. Come
as soon as you can because I want to see
you and baby to. It is awful nice place where
wa are staying I don't think you would like
it in Cincinnati either but Mr. H. sais he
likes it there. Good bye your dau.

NELLIE PITEZEL.

—

October 6—Holmes rents the house at Irvington from Mr. Crouse (J. C. Wand's clerk).
He said he wanted it for his sister, Mrs. A.
E. Cook and her children, and that she
intended using it as a boarding house.

October 6, 7, 8—Children write letters home.

October 10—Howard disappears on this day.
Same day—Holmes takes Alice and Nellie from
the Circle House.

October 12—Evening. Holmes arrives in De-
troit. Himself and Miss Yoke in one party;
Alice and Nellie in another. He registers
the children at the New Western Hotel as
Etta and Nellie Canning, St. Louis, Mo.
He registers himself and Miss Yoke at the
Hotel Normandie "G. Howell and wife,
Orian."

October 13—Mrs. Pitezel, Dessie and the baby
leave Galve, Ill., for Detroit, stopping in
Chicago. Holmes has written to her that
"Ben" was waiting to see her in Detroit.

October 13—Holmes and Miss Yoke remove
from Hotel Normandie to No. 54 Park Place.
He gave their names as Mr. and Mrs.
Holmes.

October 14—Mrs. Pitezel, Dessie and the baby
arrive in Detroit, and register as C. A.
Adams and daughter at Geis's Hotel.

October 14—Alice writes her last letter.

October 15—Holmes takes Alice and Nellie to
boarding house of Lucinda Burns at No. 91
Congress street.

October 15—About this date Holmes rents of
Mr. Boninghausen the house No. 241 East
Forest avenue. Mr. Boninghausen does not
remember name Holmes gave. In the rear
of cellar under porch of the house Holmes
digs a hole four feet long, three and a half
feet wide, three feet six inches deep.

October 18—Holmes and Miss Yoke leave De-
troit for Toronto, Canada. He tells Mrs.
Pitezel that Ben had gone to Toronto. At
Toronto Holmes registers at Walker House as
Geo. H. Howell and wife, Columbus. Same
day Mrs. Pitezel, Dessie and the baby left
Geis's Hotel, Detroit, for Toronto; were met
at Grand Trunk Depot by Holmes and taken

to the Union House, where they register
under the name of C. A. Adams and daughter.

October 19—Alice and Nellie leave Detroit for
Toronto; arrive in the evening about 8
o'clock; were met by Holmes, who turned
them over to George Dennis, a hotel porter
for the Albion Hotel, and they were registered as Etta and Nellie Canning, Detroit.

October 20—Holmes rented house No. 16 St.
Vincent street of Mrs. Nudel. Said his
name was Howard and that he wanted it for
his sister.

Same day Holmes and Miss Yoke went to
Niagara Falls.

October 21—They returned and registered at
the Palmer House under the name of Howell.

October 24—Holmes borrows a spade from Mr.
Ryvea, No. 18 St. Vincent street, to dig a
hole in the cellar, "for the storage of potatoes." While in Toronto Holmes called at
Albion Hotel for Alice and Nellie every
morning, returning them in the evening.

October 25—On the morning of this day he
takes Alice and Nellie from the Albion Hotel,
paying their account for board in full. The
children disappear.

October 25—He requests Mrs. Pitezel to go to
Ogdensburg. He tells her Ben is in Mon-
treal. He said that he had rented a house
in Toronto, but that two detectives on bicy-
cles were watching it, and it would not be
safe for Ben to visit her there.

October 26—Holmes and Miss Yoke leave Toronto and go to Prescott, Canada; remained
there over night.

October 31—He is found at Burlington at the
Burlington House; registered as G. D. Hale,
Columbus, O. He moved to rooms at Mr.
Aherns, where he gave the names of himself
and Miss Yoke as "Mr. Hall and wife."

November 1—He rents a house No. 26 Winooski avenue of W. B. McKillip under the
name of J. A. Judson, for his sister, Mrs.
Cook.

November 1 to November 16—Between these
dates visited his parents at his old home in
Gilmanton, N. H.; resumes his relations
with his real wife, Mrs. Mudgett. He tells
a romantic story, accounting for his absence
from home.

November 17—He is arrested in Boston.

November 19—He makes his first confession.
He says Pitezel is alive in South America,
or on his way there, and that the children
were with him. He said Pitezel was bound
for San Salvador. That their means of com-
munication was to be in the personal column
of the New York Herald.

Mrs. Pitezel is arrested on the same day.

November 20—Holmes and Mrs. Pitezel brought
to Philadelphia; committed to county prison.

December 6—Mrs. Pitezel makes a full statement to Mr. Fouse and Mr. Perry, of the
Fidelity Mutual Life Association.

December 18—Holmes now says Pitezel is dead
and that the children were given to Miss

Williams, who took them to Europe.

December 17—Makes another confession, declaring that Pitezel was dead and that he had committed suicide.

1893.

June 5—Holmes is tried for conspiracy to cheat and defraud the insurance company and on the second day of the trial pleads guilty.

June 27—Detective Geyer leaves Philadelphia and commences his search for the children.

July 15—Geyer finds the bodies of Alice and Nettie in the cellar of the Toronto house, No. 16 St. Vincent street.

August 27—Geyer finds the remains of Howard in the house at Irvington, a few miles from Indianapolis.

September 12—Holmes is indicted in Philadelphia for the murder of Benjamin F. Pitezel

September 28—He pleads not guilty. The court fixes the day of the trial to be October 28.

October 28—Motion for continuance denied Trial commences and continues until November 2. Jury render a verdict: "Guilty of murder in the first degree."

November 18—Motion for a new trial argued.

November 30—Motion for new trial overruled. Holmes sentenced to be hung.

THE EXECUTION OF HOLMES—SCENE WHILE HE WAS MAKING HIS FINAL ADDRESS
Sketched in the Prison by a Times Artist.

HOLMES DIES
DENYING GUILT

Before His Hanging He Asserts
That He Did Not Murder Any
of the Pietzel Family.

SPOKE CALMLY FROM THE SCAFFOLD

Leaves Minute Directions, Through
Which His Lawyers Believe
They Can Prove Him
Innocent.

HIS BODY BURIED IN CEMENT

The Hanging of H. H. Holmes in Moya-
mensing Prison Yesterday Morning Was
Attended With Few Sensational Features,
But the Condemned Man Made a Cool,
Straightforward Statement From the Gal-
lows Denying That He Had Ever Committed
Murder—The Drop Broke His Neck, But It
Was Fifteen Minutes Before His Heart
Ceased to Beat—He Was in Good Spirits
All Morning and Conversed Freely With
His Friends—Leaves No Money, But a
Mountain of Manuscript—According to His
Own Instructions, His Body is Embedded
in a Ton of Cement in a Vault in Holy
Cross Cemetery—A Truthful Story of His
Remarkable Career.

Holmes walked up the steps of the gallows in Moyamensing Prison yesterday morning more steadily than the priests at his side, and made a speech to the men who had been invited to watch him die more calmly than any man in the little party could have made it. He told them in an unshaken voice that he was innocent of the many crimes charged against him, and repeatedly denied the murder of Benjamin F. Pietzel and the three Pietzel children. His nearest approach to murder, he said, was the criminal operations performed by him on Miss Emmeline Cigrand and Mrs. Julia Connor, the two women who had been in his employ in Chicago.

When he had completed his statement he put his arms around Lawyer Rotan, who stood beside him, and whispered a few last words of farewell. Then he stepped backwards to the centre of the scaffold, submitted quietly to the shackling of his hands, and when Assistant Superintendent Richardson was adjusting the black cap and noose he said, with a slight smile on his face:

"Take your time, Richardson; you know I am in no hurry."

The fixing of the noose occupied but a few seconds, and in muffled tones from under the sombre cap came the words:

"Good-bye—good-bye, everybody."

The murmured responses from the crowd were drowned in the crash of the falling trap doors, and the body fell swiftly downward until the narrow rope grew taut and stopped it with a fierce jerk. It swayed and moved about for several minutes, the hands opening and closing convulsively and the back and

'chest heaving ? them was gradually and
swaying ceased and in fifteen minutes the
flock of doctors hovering about the body
said that there was no life left in it. The
drop fell at 10.12½ o'clock, and the fall
had dislocated the neck.

No autopsy was performed, and the remains were turned over to Lawyer Rotan,
who caused them to be conveyed directly
to Holy Cross Cemetery, where a vault
had already been secured. In accordance
with Holmes' written instructions they.

BENJAMIN F. PIETZEL.

HOLMES DIES
DENYING GUILT

were placed in a large box half full of cement, and on top of them sufficient more
of the same material was packed in, so
as to completely fill it. In this way the
body was incased in a solid block of cement weighing a little over a ton. It will
be buried later.

Holmes left no will, but gave explicit
instructions to Lawyer Rotan as to the
disposition of his small estate. He left
very little money, but turned over a great
many papers and documents, most of
them in the form of letters to be mailed
after his death.

AS HOLMES CHOSE TO DIE

Repudiated All His Confessions, Kissed the
Crucifix, Hugged His Lawyer, Obeyed His
Priests and Made a Speech to Those
Who Came to See Him Hanged.

When the priests left Holmes' cell Wednesday night he was very weak and tear-
ful, but in the light of later events it is
apparent that his condition was the result
of the many excitements of the day,
rather than of a general breaking down,
as was feared. The only man who remained with him was Keeper George
Weaver, the night watch, who asked the
condemned man if he proposed to go to
sleep, receiving a low-spoken reply in the
affirmative. He undressed slowly and
almost painfully, saying very little and
taking but little interest in the conversation of his guard.

"I don't know where I'll sleep to-morrow night," he said, when he had gone
through his brief devotions and stretched
himself on the couch. "But nobody
knows that."

He turned his back towards the light
that was burning just beside the open
door of his cell, and almost immediately
fell asleep. He moved only once or twice
during the next six hours, and did not
wake up at any time. The guard looked

at his recumbent figure, at the piles of papers neatly folded on the little table, at the picture of a woman on the wall, at the crucifix above the bed, at the folded clothes that were so soon to be a shroud, and at the well worn slippers on the floor, which were never to be worn again. He knew Holmes better than anyone else knew him, and he was very heavy-hearted.

Refreshed in the Morning.

When the prison clock struck 6 Keeper John Henry, the day watch, came down the corridor to relieve Weaver, and the two awakened Holmes. They called him twice and then shook him with considerable vigor before his eyes opened and his last night's sleep on earth ended. He sat up and greeted them almost cheerily.

"Good morning," he said, "is it 6 o'clock already?"

"Yes," replied Henry, "how do you feel?"

"First-rate. I was very tired last night and was glad to get to bed. I never slept better in my life."

He made some inquiries about trivial matters, and dressed as unconcernedly as a man might do who had a thousand more toilets to make before he died. The thought that he was now doing every thing for the last time did not seem to affect him at all, and he ordered quite a substantial breakfast. Weaver left and Henry took the guard seat at the door, Holmes resuming work at the almost innumerable letters which he felt himself called upon to write just prior to his execution. These letters are to go to all the women he has married, to most of his relatives and even to the friends of some of his victims. He has written out, also, very minute instructions to his lawyers as to the disposition he wants made of his entangled estate.

MRS. BENJAMIN F. PIETZEL.

The minutes passed rapidly. It was just 8 o'clock when a keeper bearing the condemned man's breakfast came in, followed almost immediately by Lawyer Rotan. The young attorney glanced anxiously into Holmes' face, and when he saw it light up with a smile of welcome his own brightened.

"You're all right," he said. "You look lots better than you did last night."

He Tests His Nerve.

In reply Holmes held out his left arm with the fingers of the hand separated and said:

"See if I tremble."

There was no tremor noticeable, although the guard looked too, and Holmes and his lawyer almost immediately fell into a lengthy and earnest conversation. It concerned the packing of the body after the execution, in cement, a plan that was thought out by Holmes during the long days that he had spent in prison waiting for death. Rotan told him that he had been offered only the day before $5,000 for the remains, and had put the man who made the proposition out of his office.

"Thank you," said Holmes quietly. "I'll see that no one gets my body, either by buying it or stealing it."

A little after 9 o'clock Fathers Dailey and McPake came into the cell and were warmly greeted by Holmes. He was just finishing his breakfast and they remarked that his appetite had not failed him. Superintendent Perkins, Assistant Superintendent Richardson, who was to do the hanging, and several other prison officials stopped on their morning round to visit the condemned man, and he chatted with all of them without the slightest trace of nervousness.

When the breakfast dishes were removed Holmes wrote a few words on a piece of paper and handed it to Lawyer Rotan with the remark that he would never touch pen to paper again. The words were a brief, sincere tribute of personal affection and of gratitude for all that the attorney had done for him. After this last writing Holmes turned himself over entirely to the priests, and from that time on until the drop fell they were always with him. He entered into the ceremonies of the fearful occasion with a solemn face, but did not for a moment show signs of depression.

Gathering of the Witnesses.

While Holmes was on his knees in his little cell saying over and over again his final prayers there was a most business-like activity in the offices and reception room of the prison. The fifty-one people who had been invited by Sheriff Clement to witness the execution had all arrived by 9 o'clock, many of them coming in carriages and leaving in front of the gray building a row of vehicles to help attract a crowd. Those who held tickets of admission were forced to fight their way through this crowd, occasionally having to call in the assistance of a policeman.

On the inside there was dampness in the air and the smell of a prison. The witnesses moved restlessly about from the

stone roadway in the centre of the main
entrance to the reception room, which
opened from it, asking each other if they
had ever seen a hanging before. Most of
them had not. The gathering was a very
curious mixture of youth and old age, the
juvenile newspaper reporter on his first
assignment of the sort rubbing elbows
with the gray-haired physician who had
seen more executions than he had time to
talk about just then.

In addition to the fifty-one people in the
Sheriff's party it was discovered that
some of the Prison Inspectors had taken
advantage of their official position to
bring in between twenty-five and thirty
of their personal friends, who mingled
freely with the other guests. The Sheriff
was very indignant at this, and called
public attention to the fact that, while he
had done all he could do to keep the number of witnesses down, his endeavors had
gone for naught. The question of eject-
ing the outsiders was debated for a few
minutes between the Sheriff and his two
solicitors, and it was abandoned because
of the lateness of the hour.

Swearing in the Jurors.

The twelve men who were to constitute
the jury were called together in the reception room by the Sheriff and lined up before a long table, where they were addressed by Assistant Solicitor Grew. The
latter explained their duties in as few
words as he could, and at the conclusion
he administered the oath which bound
them to report truthfully the cause of the
death they were about to witness. They
all took the oath and signed the pledge.

The jury was composed of Ex-Sheriff
William H. Wright, Dr. Benjamin Pen-
nebaker, Ex-Sheriff John J. Ridgway,
Select Councilman R. R. Bringhurst,
Samuel Wood, Dr. W. Joseph Hearn,
Dr. W. J. Roe, E. B. Detweiler, Dr. M.
B. Dwight, Dr. J. C. Guernsey, James
Hand and Dr. John L. Phillips. It was a
curious coincidence that Samuel Wood, a
yarn manufacturer of Germantown, who
was a member of the Sheriff's jury, and
saw the execution, was also a member
of the jury that tried and convicted
Holmes.

After the swearing in of the jury there was quite a long wait, during which the nervousness of most of the witnesses perceptibly increased. Superintendent Perkins and his assistants, Dr. Butcher and Inspectors Cullinan and Hill made mysterious visits to the gallows and to Holmes' cell, both of which were in the long corridor running north from the reception room. When the door leading into this corridor opened and closed a glimpse could be caught of the scaffold.

The March to the Gallows.

At 10 o'clock sharp President Perkins asked the jury to fall in line, and back of them everybody else took up a more or less favorable position. The door was opened, and down a short flight of steps and across the asphalt pavement the long procession of men with bared heads and grave faces paced slowly by the endless rows of cells. The one in which Holmes stood awaiting his final call and listening to the steady tramp of the men who had come to see him die was closed tight, and in front of it two guards were stationed.

The scaffold reached entirely across the corridor, with a door on one side permitting the witnesses to pass through. When the last man had crossed the threshold of this door it was closed, shutting off all observation. Almost on the instant the door of Holmes' cell opened and he stepped out between Fathers Dailey and McPake, followed by Assistant Superintendent Richardson and Lawyer Rotan. He had demanded the privilege of the latter's presence on the scaffold, and Sheriff Clement gave a reluctant consent.

Superintendent Perkins and the Sheriff walked arm in arm up the thirteen steps which led to the scaffold, and behind them came the chanting priests, whose white robes made even that grusome scene look picturesque. Holmes, when he reached the scaffold, held a crucifix in his hand, and continued praying until the priests stopped. Then he opened his eyes, lifted his head and walked to the edge of the scaffold facing the white faces of the crowd down below. Between him and this crowd was a semi-circle of uniformed guards. A rail reaching to his waist ran around the edge of the scaffold, and on

this he rested his hands as comfortably as
if he was himself a spectator and the rest
of the little party a show.

He Calmly Denies It All.

There was nothing pitiable in the picture made by the condemned man as he
stood looking calmly down upon his audience. His slender frame was clothed in
a loose-fitting suit of black and above the
cutaway coat appeared a white handkerchief loosely tied about his throat. His
face was more than pale—it was yellow.
His brown moustache and hair had been
recently trimmed, but it cannot be said
that he presented a good appearance. The
prison pallor on his face gave one a chill.
He looked dead already.

When he had surveyed the crowd he
began to talk, and his tones were as
steady and smooth as those of an orator
making an after-dinner speech. He made
no gestures, but his words were emphasized here and there, and everything he
said was plainly audible. No one else in
the crowd could have kept as steady a
voice.

"Gentlemen," he said, "I have very few
words to say. In fact, I would make no
remarks at this time were it not for the
feeling that if I did not speak it would
imply that I acquiesced in my execution.
I only wish to say that the extent of the
wrongdoing I am guilty of in taking human life is the killing of two women.
They died by my hands as the results of
criminal operations.

"I wish also to state, so that no chance
of misunderstanding may exist hereafter,
that I am not guilty of taking the lives of
any of the Pietzel family, either the three
children or the father, Benjamin F. Pietzel, for whose death I am now to be
hanged. I have never committed murder.
That is all I have to say."

The Fall of the Drop.

As he spoke the last sentence he turned
half around and put his right hand on
Lawyer Rotan's broad shoulder. He
smiled as he said:

"Good-bye, Sam. You have done all
you could."

He whispered a few other words and

then hugged the young attorney, who almost ran down the scaffold steps when
he was released. The priests motioned
to the condemned man to kneel, and he
did so, still grasping the little crucifix in
his hands. For two minutes his lips
moved in silent prayer, and he arose
steadily to his feet when he had finished.
He shook hands with the greatest hearti-
ness with Fathers Dailey and McPake,
turning again and for the last time to face
the audience as the priests resumed their
chant,

Richardson now stepped forward, and
drawing Holmes' hands behind him dex-
terously handcuffed him. The man stood
as straight and steady as one of the
black beams beside him, looking quietly
upon the last human faces he was ever to
see. Sheriff Clement and Superintendent
Perkins left the scaffold and Richardson
drew the black cap down over Holmes'
face, the latter remarking as he did so:

"Take your time about it. You know I
am in no hurry."

His advice was not needed. Richardson unwound the rope from about the
beam, ran out the noose, and slipped it
over Holmes' head. As he drew it tight
about the neck there came in muffled,
but steady tones:

"Good-bye—good-bye, everybody."

Richardson stepped back and dropped
a handkerchief. The black boards on
which Holmes stood parted in the middle,
and down through the opening his body
fell, stopping with a jerk that knocked
his head to one side and sent his legs
swinging far out towards the spectators.
The horrible contortions lasted for a minute, the body turning round and round
and the legs swaying backwards and for-
wards as if the man were struggling to
break the merciless rope. The back and
chest heaved, the fingers opened and
closed repeatedly, and there were twitch-
ings about the exposed neck.

Dead in Fifteen Minutes.

From this ghastly spectacle most of the
spectators turned to look at the whitewashed walls. Two of them fainted and
one fell, but was quickly brought to his
feet. The dangling body slowly but
surely settled at the end of the rope, and

H. H. HOLMES
From His Latest and Best Photograph.

gradually all movement ceased. Drs. Butcher and Sharp felt the pulse and put their ears over the heart. For fifteen minutes they were unable to discern heart beats, and at the end of that time they pronounced him dead. All the other doctors present did and said the same thing.

ALICE PIETZEL.

The crowd of spectators took to wandering about the corridor, and most of them were relieved to know that the body would not be lowered until it had hung for another quarter of an hour. After life was extinct Lieutenant Tomlinson was permitted to bring in his sergeants and patrolmen and they marched in line by the scaffold, each one critically surveying the corpse. It was about the strangest reception that man could imagine, and it made one shudder to hear the comments. The policemen seemed to enjoy the spectacle.

When the delay began to seem intolerably long Dr. Butcher gave permission to lower the body, and it was let down onto a truck very much like a bag of meal is sprung from a truss. The officials had a very hard time with the rope. The noose had sunk deep into the flesh and did not easily become unloosened, and Superintendent Perkins refused to have it cut off, although Lawyer Rotan begged him to do so. After several minutes of struggling the job was accomplished and the black cap taken off.

To Prove His Innocence.

The dead man's face was a thing too ghastly for description, and even the doctors turned from it. An examination of the neck showed that the axis had been separated from the atlas by the fall, in other words that the neck was broken. No autopsy was performed upon it, and Lawyer Rotan stood by the truck on which it lay to see that Holmes' wishes in this respect were obeyed. While standing there he was asked what the contents of the papers were that Holmes had turned over to him. He replied:

"I have not gone over them yet, but I understand that they are mostly directions to his attorneys to keep up the effort to prove his innocence of murder."

"Does he want that effort kept up?"

"He does and he believes it will one day be successful. So do I."

"Did he leave any money with which to prosecute a search?"

"He did not leave any with me—not one cent."

The arrival of the undertaker's wagon at this point attracted Mr. Rotan's attention in that direction. He superintended the handling of the corpse, and saw that it was well taken care of. As the wagon drove out through the tremendous crowd awaiting it at the west gate the young attorney followed it into the street. He did not return to the prison and it will be a very long time before he goes there again.

It was not very long after the lowering of the body that the crowd of spectators began to thin out. They left the prison one by one, facing all manner of questions when they passed through the mob waiting at the gate, and giving thanks for the privilege of breathing the free air and seeing the good old sun shine once again. Assistant Superintendent Richardson was frequently congratulated on the success of the execution, and in reply he said just as frequently that Holmes was the nerviest of the sixty-seven men he had seen die. Superintendent Perkins said the same, and so did the physicians.

Some of those who witnessed the execu-

tion were: Dr. J. Howard Taylor, Chief
Medical Inspector of this city; L. G.
Fouse, president, and Solicitor Campbell,
of the Fidelity Mutual Life Association;
Colonel J. Lewis Good, of the Board of
Health; Hosie Godwin, of the Sheriff's
office; S. R. Mason, Sheriff of Baltimore,
who said that it would soon be his duty to
hang five men; A. S. Eisenhower, Chief of
the Bureau of City Property; Assistant
District Attorney Samuel A. Boyle, Will-
iam E. Peterson, of the Board of Health;
Detective Captain Peter Miller, Detective
Frank Geyer, Ex-Sheriff Horatio P. Con-
nell, Coroner Samuel H. Ashbridge, Police
Lieutenant Benjamin Tomlinson, Deputy
Sheriff John Ertel, Dr. William J. Scott,
one of the witnesses at the trial; Dr. S. J.
Ottinger, Dr. J. C. DaCosta, Dr. Joseph
Hearn, Deputy Sheriff Williamson, Frank
A. Monaghan, Deputy Sheriff John B.
Meyers, Major Ralph E. Culinan, In-
spector Hill and Prison Agent Camp.

BODY BURIED IN CEMENT

Unique Method of Interment Devised by the Murderer to Protect His Body From Ghouls.

The body of H. H. Holmes reposed last
night in the vault of the Holy Cross Cemetery. All that is mortal of the celebrated
criminal is now firmly incased in a box of
cement, hard as granite, and weighing more
than a ton.

Attorney Rotan arranged for the interment
and followed the expressed wish of Holmes
in every detail. Having a horror of the
dissecting room and knowing that medical
men would like to examine his brain, the
ensuing criminal evolved the scheme of
being buried in a solid ball of cement which
would resist all ordinary agencies of attack
and insure his body immunity from ghouls,
who were not armed with dynamite and
allowed plenty of time for the task of securing the coveted cadaver. Unique in life,
Holmes will be unique in the grave. When
the interment takes place, which will probably be to-day, the incidents of the usual
burial will be absent. The undertaker will
simply have the task of rolling a dead mass
of impenetrable cement, weighing two thousand pounds, into a hole large enough to contain it. There will be no empty coffin for

the cloth to rattle against.

It was a few minutes before noon when Undertaker J. J. O'Rourke, whose office is at the corner of Tenth and Tasker streets, drove to the Moyamensing Prison with an undertaker's wagon. In this wagon was an ordinary pine box in which the body was placed. The wagon was then driven out of the Reed street entrance to the prison and hurried to the yard back of the residence of Mr. O'Rourke. Here was the larger box and five barrels of cement and sand. The mortar was hurriedly mixed and a layer perhaps ten inches deep was placed in the box, which was first put in the wagon in which it was to be hauled to the cemetery. On top of this was placed the body of the felon, attired as he was when he dropped through the trap.

Packing in the Body.

A silk handkerchief was placed over his face and then more mortar was piled into the box. It was packed tightly around the lifeless form and soon covered the still features. After the wondering eyes of two Pinkerton detectives engaged to watch the body had taken the last look that will ever be had of Holmes' body more mortar was thrown into the box until it was full. The lid was then nailed down and the wagon started away for Delaware county, where the Holy Cross Cemetery is located.

It was nearly 2 o'clock when the undertaker's wagon reached the cemetery. There an unexpected delay was encountered. The superintendent, R. B. Campbell, refused to allow the body to be placed in the vault without special instructions from Joseph F. Haley, a clerk in the Cathedral, at Eighteenth and Race streets. In vain Mr. O'Rourke pleaded and exhibited the stub of the burial permit which had been issued by the Board of Health in this city, and the permit from the borough of Yeadon, secured in exchange for the one issued in Philadelphia. Mr. O'Rourke also had a document signed by Father Dailey and known as "Lines for a Christian Burial," a necessary step to secure interment in a Catholic cemetery. Superintendent Campbell was obdurate and said that he had to obey orders.

There was nothing to do but dispatch a man to secure the permit from Mr. Haley. After a tedious wait of three hours the messenger returned and then preparations were made for removing the box and its heavy contents to the vault. To pull the box out of the wagon and let it drop onto the ground was a comparatively easy matter. To move it after it was on terra firma was different.

Mr. O'Rourke, his two assistants, the two detectives and a couple of attaches of the

cemetery took hold and lifted, but the box
did not move. Again they heaved and strain-
ed and succeeded in breaking the handles,
but the hardened cement refused to budge.
The men were in a quandary. They had never
had such a task before and they regretted
that they did not have a block and tackle,
such as is used for moving safes.

Trouble at the Cemetery.

Finally the group of reporters who had
been watching the proceedings came to the
assistance of the men. Thirteen pairs of
stout arms seized the corners of the box,
and by dint of shoving and pulling moved
it inch by inch into the vault. Once there
the vault was closed, and the group of tired
and perspiring workers all left the cemetery,
except the detectives. They remained all
night, keeping a lonely vigil over the vault
in which was the oblong block of cement,
which serves as a shroud for the man whose
name will be mentioned more frequently to-
day than that of any other mortal, living
or dead.

Undertaker O'Rourke does not know when
the burial will take place. Under the cus-
toms of the Catholic church there need be
no more religious ceremonies connected with
Holmes, and it is unlikely that there will be
any. It is probable that Mr. O'Rourke will
delegate the matter of interment to the cemetery authorities, in which case the burial
can be made quietly and without attracting
undue notice. Certain it is that it will be
done at a time when few people will be
around and without any fuss or display. No
more men will be there than will be necessary to move the cumbrous box in which the
body is imbedded as firmly as if in a cast
iron mold.

Before a body can be deposited in the Holy
Cross Cemetery it is necessary that the fee
of $4 for digging the grave and $1 for the
use of the vault be paid. This amount, $5,
was sent to the Cathedral office Wednesday
night by the undertaker. Father Dailey also
called at the Cathedral and explained the
matter so that there need be no hitch.

The lot or grave in which Holmes will
be buried has not yet been bought. This
will have to be attended to soon, as it is
against the law to keep a body more than
three days in the vault. Mr. Rotan will
either select the lot or else will delegate the
choice to Mr. O'Rourke.

As soon as he was notified that the execution had taken place, Undertaker O'Rourke
filed a return of death with the Board of
Health. This was recorded by Registry
Clerk Theodore M. Carr, and in deference
to the notoriety of the deceased, he made the
record with red ink. The certificate of
death, which was signed by Benjamin F.
Butcher, M. D., gave the name of the deceased as Herman W. Mudgett, alias H. H.

Holmes, and further described him as white, male, 35 years old, married. The cause of death was stated as "Hanging according to law." Undertaker O'Rourke in his certificate did not give any occupation for the deceased, and gave the broadly indefinite location, United States, as the place of birth, and named the Holy Cross Cemetery as the place of burial.

CROWMDS WATCHED THE PRISON

Morbidly Curious Persons Lined the Street and Awaited the Springing of the Death-Trap.

As early as 7.30 o'clock the crowd of curious spectators who always congregate on the exterior of Moyamensing Prison when an execution takes place began to assemble and by 9 o'clock the street in front of the prison and all the approaches were lined with people. The driveway that leads to the main entrance to the prison was roped off and a cordon of police guarded the passage way, allowing no one excepting those clothed with authority to approach the gates.

Passyunk avenue, on which the prison fronts, was backed from the railing of the jail to the house fronts on the opposite side of the street, and a ghastly silence predominated that was only broken occasionally by the clang of an electric car bell or the rattle of a wagon's wheels. The multitude itself was painfully silent, waiting for the signal from within the prison walls announcing that Holmes had paid the penalty of his crimes.

By 9.15 o'clock all those who had received cards of admission to the execution had arrived and fifteen minutes later they had all passing within the prison. The crowd without waited patiently for 10 o'clock to arrive and finally when that hour was reached there was considerable speculation as to what time the march to the scaffold would begin. The minutes dragged slowly by to the watchers on the outside, but when at 10.13 there fluttered from one of the prison windows a handkerchief announcing that the trap had been sprung there was a wave of excitement in the crowd and the word was passed from mouth to mouth that the murderer of Benjamin Pietzel had expiated his crime on the gallows.

Although there was absolutely nothing to see the crowd hovered about the entrance to the prison until the undertaker's wagon passed inside, when it became rumored that the body was to be taken our through the rear entrance to the jail. Then there was a rush to the rear of the jail, where the throng of curious spectators waited until the corpse of the murderer, enclosed in a stout box, was brought out in the undertaker's wagon and carried away.

THE CIGRANDS DISAPPOINTED

They Expected That Holmes Would Inform Them Where Emmeline's Body Lies.

Special Telegram to THE TIMES.

ANDERSON, Ind., May 7.

While the parents of Emmeline Cigrand were gratified at the death of H. H. Holmes to-day, they were greatly disappointed and downcast because he did not comply with their pleadings to write them in detail before he died regarding their daughter's demise. They wanted, if possible, to find the remains, if even a few bones, and lay them to rest. They are satisfied that his general confession, in regard to her was not true, even in part. Phillis, her sister, was with Emmeline in Chicago several days before she disappeared, and she says Emmeline was not Holmes' mistress.

Peter Cigrand, the father, was preparing to go to Philadelphia to see Holmes, and, if possible, witness the hanging, but this was made impossible by his being caught in a gas explosion ten days ago and terribly burned.

THE LIFE OF HOLMES

As Soon as He Left College He Took to Murder as a Profession—The Story of His Career in Chicago.

The story of Herman W. Mudgett's life is an old story to most people, but it has been told in so disjointed and incoherent a fashion and with so much that was false or ridiculously exaggerated that it is proper at this time to print as nearly accurate an account of his career as is obtainable. The writer has endeavored to sift the simple truth from the mass of falsehood and fabrication which began with the murderer's own lying statements and which has been added to by many others who are almost his equals in this respect. In the following article that which is known to be true is stated. That which the dead man claims to be true is credited to him, and for the sake of convenience he will be referred to always as Holmes.

He was born in the little village of Gilmanton, New Hampshire, on May 16, 1860. His father was a farmer and his mother up to the time of her marriage had been a school teacher. Both were devout Methodists, and they brought up their three children—two girls and a boy—in that religious belief, Holmes being admitted to the Sunday school when he was but 6 years of age. He was a thin and scrawny child, not at all precocious, but it is recalled now by his old schoolmates that he had a habit of saving his pennies while they spent theirs. He was never a boon companion in play, and before he was 10 years old he was known among his fellows as a serious and solitary youngster, who did not for a moment mind his unpopularity.

He became an errand boy in a photograph gallery, and during nine years acted as clerk in a store, as assistant to a physician and as private secretary to the president of a dental college. He had studied hard at the public schools, had accumulated a little money through his amateur business ventures, and, assisted by his parents, had prepared to enter Dartmouth college. His association with physicians, however, sidetracked him in this ambition, and he matriculated at the University of Vermont, at Burlington, where for one college year he studied medicine. In the following September he journeyed to Ann Arbor, Michigan, and entered the medical college at that place. He was an apt student and progressed rapidly, but before he had been at Ann Arbor a year he formally entered upon the career of crime which ended in Moyamensing Prison yesterday morning.

His First Step in Crime.

It was, perhaps, the dissecting table which gave him his first taste for blood, but his initial crime was a much more commonplace one than murder. He became the agent in Ann Arbor for a medical book published in Chicago, sold quite a large number of them among the students and faculty, and embezzled the proceeds. The publishing firm conveniently failed about this time, and Holmes was never prosecuted. He was graduated in 1884 as a full-fledged physician, and moved to Moore's Forks, New Jersey, where he opened an office as a physician under his proper name.

The practice in the little New Jersey village was not large enough to keep him in food and lodging, and he came to Philadelphia, working for a short time in a drug store on Columbia avenue. Then he found short employment at the Norristown Asylum for the Insane, but it was unprofitable, and he drifted out to Chicago. While at the Ann Arbor University he made the acquaintance of a fellow student from Canada named Paquet. The latter had not prospered since his diploma was granted him, and the two penniless young men began to concoct schemes for defrauding insurance companies. This was in Chicago, in November, 1885, and it was then that Mudgett assumed the name of H. H. Holmes.

The two arranged the details of a scheme to be shared in by an alleged third party living somewhere in a Western State, to secure $40,000 from four different insurance companies located in the East. Paquet suddenly disappeared, and Holmes abandoned the scheme, although he had already purchased a dead body and sent it in a trunk to the Fidelity Storage Warehouse in Chicago. It is only one of the many pathetic incidents in the man's life that on July 4, 1878, he had married Clara A. Lovering at Alton, N. H., the ceremony being performed by John W. Faurgier, a Justice of the Peace. A child was born to them one year later, but Holmes showed no affection for his family, and while in Chicago at this time, after the failure of his first insurance scheme, he filed in the Superior Court of Cook county a libel in divorce against the good country girl whom he had married. This was reached on February 14, 1887, and on June 4, 1891, the Court ordered the suit dismissed because of the complainant's default of appearance.

The Building of "The Castle."

Holmes, in the early part of 1886, opened a drug store at the corner of Sixty-third and Wallace streets, in Chicago, and in connection with it conducted a general swindling trade, victimizing many people in many different ways. He obtained so much money that he was able to purchase the property, and he built on it the five-story structure which has since been known as "The Castle." In this building he caused to be constructed two secret chambers, one airtight vault and a furnace which had all the outward appearance of a crematory. He built the house to do murder in. He calmly and coolly planned it with no other idea in view than that of making a profession of killing people.

The adoption of the profession of murder by Holmes at this point in his life, and after his most uninteresting career up to that time, was not the result of any sudden imgulie. He was of only taking advantage of the opportunities he had been seeking for a number of years, and carrying out the plans which had been maturing in his brain ever since he was first able to formulate the belief that honesty was not the best policy. The stories which he has told of accomplices in his operations in the "Castle" are entirely untrue, except in so far as they concern a professional articulator of bones whose home was in a suburb of Chicago, and Patrick Quinlan, who was the janitor of this human abattoir. The first-mentioned purchased several bodies of Holmes, but says he did so with the thought that he was dealing with a medical student. The second appears to have been one of the few fortunate associates of Holmes who did not meet the fate arranged for him.

The first man killed in the Castle was Dr. Robert Leacock, of New Baltimore, Mich., who had been a student at Ann Arbor, and who is said to have been the man suggested by Pequot as a likely fellow-conspirator. Holmes killed Leacock by giving him an overwhelming dose of laudanum while he was visiting "the Castle," but a compromise was effected with the insurance company whereby the murderer only received a small portion of the insurance money due. Holmes says that this was his first murder, and there is no evidence to prove a previous one.

In the lying confession which Holmes caused to be published on April 12 last he speaks of killing a certain Mr. Russell, a tenant of the Castle, by hitting him in the head with a chair during a controversy over the payment of rent. It was difficult to substantiate this statement for some time, although Holmes tells in detail of the selling of the body to the professional articulator already mentioned. The Chicago police, however, have found that Russell is alive and well in Chicago, and the story has amused them. There is no doubt that Holmes invented the story in order to increase the horrors and consequently the price of his third bogus statement.

The Meeting With Pietzel.

About this time he met Benjamin F. Pietzel, whose home was in St. Louis, whose business was that of a man out of work and willing to make money by any means, and whose confidence in human nature was as large as his capacity for strong drink. He was a country-bred boy who had received no advantages in the line of education. He was married at an early age to a girl from Galva, Illinois, and began life as a farmer in Indiana. Later he moved to Kansas, and when he was forced to leave that State, owing to a worthless mortgage he had secured, he settled in St. Louis. He secured a house for his family in the latter city, and then went up to Chicago to look for work.

He met Holmes when the latter applied to an employment agency for a carpenter to repair certain parts of a glass-making machine that had been placed in the cellar of the Castle by a man named Warner, who had started a company to manufacture glass by some improved methods. Holmes' knowledge of human nature led him to perceive in Pietzel those easy-going qualities which would make him an easy and profitable tool. The temporary employment became permanent, and from that time on until September 2, 1894, when the unfortunate man was murdered by his employer in the house on Callowhill street, this city. Pietzel and Holmes were always together.

Holmes prospered in numerous ways, and on September 19, 1893, insured his life in the Fidelity Mutual Life Association of this city, making the cheerful statement in his application that his mother had died at the age of 58 and his father at the age of 62. They are both living yet. Whatever purpose he had in this was abandoned, however, and he again resumed his occupation of murder. Late in the year 1890 he had opened a jewelry store under "The Castle," and in charge of this he placed Julius L. Connor, having the latter's wife Julia Connor, as assistant in the drug store. The Connors had one child, a daughter by the name of Pearl, who was 5 years old. The family occupied rooms in "The Castle."

The Murder of the Connors.

Mr. and Mrs. Connor quarreled and separated, and the husband went West. Just what relations existed between Holmes and Mrs. Connor after that are uncertain, but a few weeks later he gave both Mrs. Connor and Pearl a dose of poison. It was their bones which the Chicago police found after they had dug up the earth in the basement of "The Castle" and had torn down the wall. In his confession Holmes asserts that about this time he killed a man named Rodgers, of West Morgantown, Va.; a man named Chas. Cole, indefinitely described as a Southern speculator, and a domestic in his employ named Lizzie, but beyond his statement to this effect there is no evidence to show that such persons ever existed.

HOWARD PIETZEL.

Holmes rented rooms in "The Castle" to
Mr. and Mrs. Frank Cook, who were married
in Englewood, Ill., by the Rev. Dr. Taylor
in 1888. They were joined shortly by Miss
Mary Haracamp, of Hamilton, Ont., a niece
of Mrs. Cook, who was a stenographer by
profession, and who later became a clerk in
Holmes' employ. In his confession Holmes
says that these people discovered his guilt,
and that he killed Mrs. Cook and Miss Haracamp. The latter, however, is now alive and
well at Hamilton, and she does not believe
that Holmes murdered her aunt. In his confession Holmes named as one of his twenty-
seven victims Mrs. Cook's unborn child.

One of the numerous advertisements that
Holmes inserted in the Chicago newspapers
applying for female stenographers was answered by Miss Emmeline Cigrand, of
Dwight, Ill., a pretty-faced and unsophisti-
cated girl who had just graduated from a
school of stenography in Chicago. Holmes
accomplished her ruin, but she caused him
a great deal of annoyance, and there is no
doubt that he murdered her in "The Castle"
and attempted to destroy her body in the
furnace. Her relatives kept up a vain
search for her until the discoveries by the
Chicago police convinced them that there
was no longer any doubt of her fearful fate.

Fake Murders and Real Marriages.

Another death at "the Castle" of which Holmes speaks is that of a woman named Rosine Van Jassand, whom he says he killed

NELLIE PIETZEL.

by poison and buried beneath the floor of a restaurant in which she was employed. That floor has been dug up and no body found. He says, also, that he killed a man named Robert Latimer, who attempted to blackmail him, but there is a good deal of doubt about this. His fourteenth murder, he says, was that of Miss Anna Betts, his fifteenth that of Miss Gertrude Connor, of Muscatine, Iowa, and his sixteenth that of an unknown young woman from Omaha, whom he put out of the way in order to obtain a very considerable property in the West. The only one of these people of whom any knowledge has been obtained is Miss Connor, who died an apparently natural death at Muscatine six months after she left Chicago. In the development of his improved glass making scheme Holmes says that he had occasion to kill the man Warner, who invented it, and that the body was entirely destroyed in the furnace.

His long line of murders, real and imaginary, were occasionally broken by marriage. On January 28, 1887, Myrta Z. Belknap, a young woman living at Dion, Ill., became his wife and lived with him at "The Castle" for some time. They did not get along well together, and she returned to her home, where she still lives, and where a girl baby was born to them. Just why Holmes did not kill her he has never taken the trouble to say in any of his varied statements.

Holmes tells of the improbable murder of a young Englishman at this time, but there is no evidence that he tells the truth. It was about the 1st of January, 1893, when he was again out of stenographers, and secured through an intelligence office in Chicago the unfortunate Minnie R. Williams, who had come North from Fort Worth, Texas, to seek employment. Miss Williams was the owner of some real estate in Fort Worth and had graduated from the Conservatory of Music at Boston, but chose to earn her own living for the time being. It was not very long after she entered Holmes' employ that he won complete control over her, and through his promises to develop her property at Fort Worth induced her to deed all her real estate belongings over to him.

Fate of the Williams Sisters.

Miss Nannie Williams, of Fort Worth, Minnie's sister, had an equal interest in the property, and at the suggestion of Holmes Minnie invited her to come North. She did so, was met by him at the depot, taken to "The Castle" and locked in the air-tight vault. Here she died. Just how her sister Minnie was murdered is not clear, although Holmes asserts positively that he ended her life with poison in a hotel at Momence, Ill., on November 15, 1893. He asserts that he placed both bodies in trunks and threw them overboard in Lake Michigan. Whether or not this story is a fabrication, no doubt exists that he did murder the Williams sisters and make away with their bodies. As an illustration of the debonaire style of Holmes' confession it may be said that at this point he mentioned as an incident in his confession the murder of a wealthy visitor to the World's Fair, and adds:

"After Miss Williams' death I found among her papers an insurance policy made in favor of her brother, Baldwin Williams, of Leadville, Colorado. I therefore went to that city early in 1894, and having found him, took his life by shooting him, it being believed I had done so in self-defense. A little later, when the assignment of the policy to which I had forged Miss Williams' name was presented to John M. Maxwell, of Leadville, the administrator of the Williams estate, it was honored and the money paid." That Holmes was as much of a liar as he was a murderer is best evidenced by this ridiculous statement.

Having secured possession of the Williams' property in Fort Worth, Holmes now set about realizing what he could (than it. He had met in Chicago in March, 1893. Miss Georgianna Yoke, of Franklin, Indiana, an estimable young woman, who in the end was partially able to right the wrongs which he heaped upon her by giving testimony at the trial which helped to convict him. It would have been a dangerous matter for him to enter into any new matrimonial alliances in the East, or at any place, under the various names he had assumed, and so he took her to Denver, where, on January 17, 1894, they were married by the Rev. Dr. William J. Wilcox. The name he gave at that time was H. M. Howard, and he was married under it, although he explained to Miss Yoke that his right name was Holmes, telling her—as only he could—that he had a very rich uncle by the name of Howard who had promised to leave him a large sum of money in case he adopted that name.

THE KILLING OF PIETZEL

The Fort Worth Swindles—Flight of the Conspirators—A Prison Conference in St. Louis Overheard—Then the Murder.

During all this time Pietzel had been a quiet and unostentatious tool in Holmes' hands, receiving a regular salary and sending a considerable portion of it each week to his wife at St. Louis. Now, however, came the time of his greatest usefulness, and in January, 1894, Holmes sent him to Fort Worth to see what could be done with the Williams property. Pietzel assumed there the name of Benton F. Lyman, and was shortly joined by Holmes and Miss Yoke, who traveled under the name of Mr. and Mrs. D. F. Pratt. Holmes told Miss Yoke one of his characteristic fairy stories in order to secure her consent to traveling under a fictitious name.

The bogus Pratt and Lyman engaged in the building of a store property on the land formerly owned by the Williams sisters, and indulged in various fraudulent enterprises. One of these was the issuing of a note on May 16, 1894, for $16,000, signed by B. F. Lyman, and indorsed by D. F. Pratt. On this note the pair received $5,000 from Sidney L. Samuels, a lawyer of Fort Worth, who took them to Northern capitalists. The note was supposed to be secured by the Williams property, but this was later heavily mortgaged by Holmes, who also stole a carload of horses and shipped them to Chicago a few hours before he and Miss Yoke left the town forever. Fort Worth to this day has a very distinct recollection of the firm of Pratt & Lyman, and if by any chance Holmes should have escaped execution here he could not have visited Texas with even the vaguest assurance of personal safety.

The escape of the conspirators from Fort Worth caused them to separate for some time. Pietzel went to Chicago and took up his residence at "The Castle," while Holmes and Miss Yoke fled to Denver and rested there in quiet for several weeks. They exchanged a great deal of correspondence, however, and arranged a meeting in St. Louis, where they gathered on May 21 of the same year. Holmes here reminded Pietzel of a $10,000 life insurance policy which the latter had placed on his life at Holmes' request a short time before, and suggested the substitution of a body in order to secure the money. Pietzel acquiesced.

While the details of this scheme were being arranged Holmes could not refrain from indulging in outside jobs, and on June 15 he purchased a drug store in St. Louis under the name of Howard, giving several fictitious papers of no value and a mortgage on the property in payment. For a little over a month he conducted the store and was then arrested by the Merrill Drug Company, of St. Louis, on a charge of conspiracy and lodged in prison. He had attempted to sell the store to a man named Brown, when the former owners discovered his intentions. From July 19 to July 21 he was in prison, but on the latter date he secured his release through bail furnished by Miss Yoke.

A Fatal Conference and Its Results.

While he was in prison, Pietzel called upon him frequently, and the details of the arrangement to swindle the Fidelity Mutual Life Association of Philadelphia out of the $10,000, which on November 9, 1893, they had placed on Pietzel's life, were discussed. Holmes met in the prison the notorious Marion C. Hedgepeth, the man who had just been sentenced to twenty years' imprisonment for holding up a train on the Missouri Pacific Railway. Hedgepeth was consulted in reference to securing a lawyer whose conscience would not prevent him entering into the conspiracy, and he sug-

MISS NANNIE WILLIAMS.

gested the name of Jeptha L. Howe, of St.
Louis. For his advice and for his promise
to keep quiet in the matter he was promised
$500 by Holmes, and it was the failure of
the latter to keep his promise that led directly to his arrest, trial, conviction and execution.

As soon as he was released from prison
Holmes and Miss Yoke came on to New
York. They spent several days in that city
and on Sunday, August 5, 1894, arrived in
Philadelphia and took rooms in the boarding
house kept by Mrs. Alcorn, at 1905 North
Eleventh street. Holmes at that time told
his supposed wife that he was engaged in
selling a patent letter copier, and that the
immediate business which brought him to
Philadelphia was the disposing of a large
quantity of the copiers to the Pennsylvania
Railroad. A few days after he arrived he
telegraphed $157.57 to the Chicago office
of the Fidelity Mutual Life Association in
payment of the half-yearly premium on the
Pietzel policy.

The exact date of Pietzel's arrival in
Philadelphia is a matter of speculation, but
on August 17, under the name of It. F. Pe-
ry, he rented the two-story house at 1316
Callowhill street, paying ten dollars in ad-

vance rent to Walter W. Shoemaker, the
agent. On the same day Holmes and Pietzel purchased a quantity of second-hand furniture from John F. Hughes, 1097 Buttonwood street, and moved it into the Callowhill street building. The two fitted up the
establishment together, and a sign was
placed in the front window announcing that
B. F. Perry was an agent for the purchase
and sale of patents.

Chloroformed While Intoxicated.

Pietzel had by this time exhausted his
usefulness as Holmes' agent, and while the
former understood that a body resembling
his was to be placed in the Callowhill street
store after his departure, the latter had
made up his mind to kill his agent and
gather in all the profits. Pietzel was a man
who drank a good deal, and on Saturday afternoon, September 1, he bought a considerable amount of whisky to tide him over
Sunday. On the following day Holmes
left Miss Yoke at their North Eleventh
street boarding house at 10.30 in the morning and went down to the Callowhill street
building. In the bed room in the rear of
the second floor he found Pietzel in a drunk-
en stupor, and deliberately chloroformed
him to death.

When Pietzel was dead Holmes poured
chloroform over his face and the upper part
of his clothing and set fire to it, breaking the
empty bottle alongside of him in order to
leave evidence that an explosion of some sort
had taken place. He also poured chloroform
in the dead man's mouth, and by pressure on
the chest worked the poison down into Pietzel's stomach. He opened the window shut-
ters so that the sun would shine on the dead
man's face and hasten decomposition. It
must have taken him a very long time to do
all this, because it was not until 4 o'clock in
the afternoon that he returned in a very excited frame of mind to Miss Yoke at their
boarding house.

In the three statements Holmes made regarding the murder of Pietzel the first was
to the effect that the body was a substituted
one obtained in New York and that Pietzel
ad fled. The second asserted that the body
as really that of Pietzel, but that his agent
had committed suicide and he had simply
burned the body in order to give evidence of
a fatal explosion so as to collect the insurance money. The third, in which he admits
the killing, contains the following paragraph:

Holmes' Story of the Murder.

"I first bound him hand and foot and having done this I proceeded to burn him alive
by saturating his clothing and his face

with benzine and igniting it with a match. So horrible was this torture that in writing it I have been tempted to attribute his death to some more humane means—not with a wish to spare myself, but because I fear that it will not be believed that anyone could be so heartless and depraved. The least I can do is to spare my readers a recital of the victim's cries for mercy, his prayers and finally his plea for a more speedy termination of his suffering, all of which had upon me no effect. The chloroform I placed in his stomach after he was dead."

This is all a deliberate lie, because the expert testimony submitted at the trial shows that there was no struggle whatever, and that the clothing of the corpse was in no wise disarranged. More than this, it was proven that the burns inflicted on the body were such as could only result from the contact of fire with a dead person, and neither the hands nor feet of Pietzel had been bound. His murder was a very commonplace one, and it was only the insane desire on the part of Holmes to incorporate sensational falsehood in every statement emanating from him that led him even in the shadow of the gallows to indulge in these ridiculous untruths.

Having killed Pietzel, Holmes and Miss Yoke, whose trunks had been packed in advance, left Philadelphia on the 10.25 train on that fatal Sunday night, and went direct to Indianapolis, where they registered at the Stubbins House. The next day a man named Eugene Smith, who had been employed by Pietzel at the Callowhill street house in this city, discovered the dead body of the man whom he had known as Perry, and the news of his death was sent out through all the papers. Holmes went straight to St. Louis, where he called upon Mrs. Pietzel, to continue his scheme of fraud. Mrs. Pietzel knew that her husband was in Philadelphia under the name of Perry, and had been corresponding with him up to the very day that his death was announced in the St. Louis papers.

FATE OF THE CHILDREN

The Murderer's Desperate Effort to Wipe Out the Entire Pietzel Family, and His Partial Success.

Holmes assured the widow that her h

He then went to Chicago to await developments. Jeptha D. Howe, the St. Louis attorney who had been recommended by Train-robber Hedgepeth, at this point began to play his part in the game by representing himself as the counsel for Mrs. Pietzel, the beneficiary under the life insurance policy, and claiming that Pietzel and the man Perry were one. He made this claim to George B. Stadden, the manager for the victimized Philadelphia insurance company in St. Louis.

The company learned through Holmes' second wife, who was then living at Wilmette, Ill., of the whereabouts of her husband, with whom she had been living when the Pietzel policy was taken out. They wrote to him asking for a description of Pietzel, and he replied very indifferently that while he doubted the identity of the body found, he would, in a few days, stop off in Philadelphia on his way to Baltimore and take a look at it. In the meantime Coroner Ashbridge had held an inquest on September 5, the jury finding that death had been caused by accident, and on September 13 Pietzel's body was buried under the name of B. F. Perry in Potter's Field, Philadelphia.

Having rejoined Miss Yoke, Holmes left Indianapolis on September 19, came on to Philadelphia, and again took rooms at Mrs. Alcorn's boarding house. Mrs. Pietzel was too ill to leave St. Louis for the purpose of identifying her husband's body, but she sent her daughter Alice, then 14 years old, to Philadelphia, in company with Lawyer Jeptha D. Howe. They arrived the same day that Holmes and Miss Yoke did, and took rooms at the Imperial Hotel.

Meeting in the Insurance Office.

The next morning Howe and Alice Pietzel called at the office of the Fidelity Mutual Insurance Company, at 914 Walnut street, and there met Holmes. The fact of the conspiracy was here shown by the fact that Holmes and Howe met as perfect strangers, and were introduced by President Fouse without either giving any sign of recognition, although they had known each other very intimately in St. Louis. During the conference in the insurance company's office the marks of identification on the body were agreed upon.

The next day all the parties interested gathered in Potter's Field and Pietzel's body was exhumed. The late Dr. William K. Mattern, who was then Coroner's Physician, had difficulty in finding the marks of identification, but Holmes located them to the satisfaction of everybody, and the daughter,

Alice, recognized the teeth as those of her father. Holmes and Alice made corroborative affidavits before Coroner Ashbridge at the second inquest, and the company recognized the justice of the claim. That same evening they left for Indianapolis, while Jeptha L. Howe stayed in Philadelphia to dicker with the insurance company. He finally agreed to deduct from the $10,000 the expenses of the investigation, and was given a check for $9,715.85.

Holmes left Alice at a hotel in Indianapolis and went to St. Louis, arriving there September 27. Mrs. Pietzel was induced to give Howe $2,500 of the money sent to her by the insurance company as his fee, and then Holmes secured $5,700 of what remained on the plea that this amount was needed to pay off a note on the Fort Worth property, in which she believed her husband to be interested. Holmes took her to a bank, made an imaginary transaction at one of the teller's windows, and came back with a piece of bogus paper, which he said gave her absolute title to the property out of which he had defrauded the unfortunate Williams sisters.

He Secured the Children.

Then came the worst of all Holmes' crimes. He told Mrs. Pietzel, who was ill, that her husband desired to see his children, and she permitted him to take Nellie, who was 11 years old, and Howard, who was 9, away with him on the pretext that they were going to join their father. He carried them to Indianapolis, where they were joined by Alice, and he registered them at the Atlantic House, in that city, under the name of "Alexander E. Cook and three children." He began at once to look about him for a convenient place to kill the children, but did not find one until October 5, when he rented a cottage in Irvington, a quiet suburb of Indianapolis, saying that it was for his sister, Mrs. A. E. Cook.

Five days later Holmes took little Howard out to the Irvington cottage, having first caused to be sent there a stove and a trunk, which he had borrowed from Mrs. Pietzel. His own description of the murder of Howard is as follows:

HOLMES.

Sketched During His Trial.

"I called the boy into the house and insisted that he go to bed at once, first giving him what I told him was a dose of medicine. It was poison which I had obtained on October 7 at the Ievington drug store. As soon as he had ceased to breathe I cut his body into pieces that would pass through the door of the stove, and by the combined use of gas and corncobs proceeded to burn it." In this statement he unquestionably told the truth, because all that was found of the boy was a few pieces of bone, his teeth and the charred playthings he had taken with him from home. His mother's trunk partially destroyed was found under the front piazza of the cottage.

Returning to Indianapolis Holmes found himself in a dangerous predicament. Miss Yoke came on from Philadelphia to meet him, and he could not tell her of the near approach of the children without arousing her suspicions. So he formed two parties and traveled to Detroit, registering the children at the Western Hotel as Etta and Nellie Canning, and Miss Yoke and himself at the Hotel Normandie as G. Howell and wife. In order to bring matters to an issue and to wipe out at one time what was left of the Pietzel family he wrote to Mrs. Pietzel to bring her eldest daughter Dessa, who was 16 years old, and her little baby, a little over 1 year old, on to Detroit, where he said they would meet their husband and father.

Howard Dead—Then the Rest.

The little family arrived in Detroit on October 14, and were registered by Holmes as Carrie A. Adams and daughter at Gils' Hotel. It was Holmes' intention to kill as many of the party as he could in Detroit, and he rented a house in that city at 241 East Forest avenue. In the rear of the cellar he dug a hole four feet long, three and one-half feet wide and nearly four feet deep, into which he had expected to bury the bodies of the children, but the presence of so many of his victims in Detroit caused him to change his plan. With Miss Yoke he started abruptly for Toronto, Canada, leaving word for Mrs. Pietzel, Dessa and the baby to follow him on the succeeding day, and securing tickets for the two other children on the train with him.

The three different detachments reached Toronto safely, and were again juggled about by Holmes among different hotels. He met Mrs. Pietzel at the depot and assured her that her husband was somewhere near Toronto, but that it would be best for her to remain very quiet until he was located. Holmes sent Miss Yoke on a visit to Niagara Falls and on October 20 rented the house at 16 St. Vincent street, Toronto, giving the name of Howard and saying that his sister was to take charge of the place.

He made a trip to Niagara Falls to bring back Miss Yoke, and on October 24 he went to the St. Vincent street house and borrowed a spade from a neighbor with which to dig a deep hole in the cellar. He said he wanted to bury potatoes. On the morning of the next day he took Alice and Nellie from the Albion Hotel, at which they had been stopping, lying to them about the whereabouts of little Howard, and drove them in a carriage to St. Vincent street. They entered the house which Holmes had rented, and were there murdered that same day. The manner of their killing is described by Holmes as follows:

How the Girls Died.

"I compelled them both to get within a large trunk, which I had caused to be sent to the house, and through the cover of which I made a small opening. Here I left them until I could return, and at my leisure kill them. At 5 P. M. I borrowed a spade of a neighbor, and at the same time called on Mrs. Pietzel at her hotel. I then returned to my hotel and for dinner, and at 7 P. M. went again to Mrs. Pietzel's hotel, where I aided her in leaving Toronto for Ogdensburg, New York. Later I again returned to the house

MISS EMMELINE CIGRAND.

where the children were imprisoned, and ended their lives by connecting the gas with the opening in the trunk. Then came the opening of the trunk and the viewing of their little blackened and distorted faces, then the digging of their shallow graves in the basement of the house, the ruthless stripping off of their clothing and the burial without a particle of covering save the cold earth, which I heaped upon them with fiendish delight."

Inasmuch as there is no gas in the house at Toronto that part of the story is, on its face, a fabrication, and the general belief is that he strangled the children before burying them. Since he made his last confession, however, he has amended it by saying that he had an accomplice in the Toronto murders, who manufactured the gas with which he suffocated the two children.

When he had wiped out this other detachment of the Pietzel family, he set about accomplishing the destruction of Mrs. Pietzel, Dessu and the baby. He sent them to Ogdensburg on the excuse that their husband and father was in that vicinity, and then directed them to go to Burlington, Vermont, all the time following with Miss Yoke and registering her at different hotels and under many different names. He had the audacity at this time to visit his old home at Gilmanton, New Hampshire, and from

November 1 to November 16 he resumed his
relations with his real wife, the first and
only Mrs. Mudgett. The romantic story he
told her of his wanderings is too silly to be
printed.

THE ARREST AND CONVICTION

Last Attempt at Murder Fails and Holmes
Is Taken Into Custody—His Sensational
Trial and What Followed.

At Burlington Holmes rented a house at
26 Winooski avenue, giving the name of J.
A. Judson. Here he placed Mrs. Pietzel,
Dessa and the baby, telling them to await
there the coming of the long dead Pietzel.
He had purchased a package of dynamite
with which to destroy this remnant of the
Pietzel family, and after he left the place
he sent word to Mrs. Pietzel to remove the
package from the garret and take it into
the cellar. Her failure to do this saved her
own life and the lives of her two remaining
children, as was testified to during the trial.
Leaving Burlington Holmes traveled
straight to Boston, and went into a hotel to
register. He had just inscribed his name on
the book at the clerk's desk when a stalwart
detective attached to the Boston Police Department placed his hand on his shoulder
and took him into custody. He was notified
that the charge against him was that of
swindling a Philadelphia insurance company out of $10,000, with a second charge of
horse stealing awaiting him at Fort Worth,
Texas. He was very cool when he received
this news, and he took his arrest with extraordinary composure. The Philadelphia
authorities were notified of his capture, and
they sent a detective on to bring him to this
city, but in the meantime he had divulged
the whereabouts of Mrs. Pietzel.

The latter was arrested at Burlington, and
with Dessa and the baby was brought to
Boston. There they all waived examination
and came to Philadelphia in the custody of
the police of this city, all believing that the
charge against them was conspiracy. Holmes
learned for the first time on reaching Philadelphia that Train Robber Hedgepeth, in
his cell in the St. Louis prison, had waited
as long as he thought he ought to for the
$500 promised him, and when the money
failed to appear he had written a letter to
the Chief of Police of St. Louis exposing the
whole swindle.

Looking Up Holmes' Career.

It is not necessary to recite in detail the story of Holmes' trial. The authorities quickly learned that Mrs. Pietzel was much more sinned against than sinning and ordered her release after a short confinement. Their endeavors to secure proof of a conspiracy very soon led to an investigation into the career of Holmes, and what they discovered has been told in the previous chapters. That the revelations shocked and astounded the civilized world is a fact of too recent memory to bear repetition.

While he was in Boston, on November 18, Holmes made his first confession, in which he declared that Pietzel was not dead and that the body found in the Callowhill street house was that of a corpse purchased of a medical student in New York city. On December 15 he made his second confession, in which he said that Pietzel had committed suicide and that Miss Minnie Williams had taken the children to Europe. He remained in Moyamensing Prison until June 3, 1895, when he was tried for conspiracy and pleaded guilty. On September 12 he was indicted for the murder of Pietzel, and on October 28 was arraigned for trial in the Quarter Sessions Court of Philadelphia before Judge Arnold.

When the trial opened Lawyers Rotan and Shoemaker, for the defense, moved for a continuance, which was promptly denied, and then they both withdrew from the case and from the court. All that day and until the evening of the next day Holmes, single-handed and alone, battled for his life as his own attorney. It was a jury of his own selection that occupied seats in the box, and his cross-examination of the first few witnesses called showed not only a phenomenal shrewdness and nerve on his part, but a knowledge of jurisprudence which astonished the spectators.

The Last Scenes of All.

His lawyers returned to him on the second day, however, and the trial lasted for exactly a week, ending on November 2, when the jury rendered the verdict, "Guilty of murder in the first degree." District Attorney Graham's management of the case attracted the admiration of the entire bar of Philadelphia, not only because of its vigor and carefulness of preparation, but because of the fairness which he showed to the young attorneys representing the prisoner. His final summing up before the jury, however, was one of the most terrific arraignments of a prisoner which has ever been heard in the local courts.

A motion for a new trial was made, and on November 18 Judges Thayer, Willson and Arnold, comprising Court of Common Pleas, No. 1, heard a lengthy argument. Once again the attorneys for the defense made strenuous efforts to secure a postponement, and the bogus affidavit introduced by Lawyer Shoemaker as cause for a continuance later led to his suspension as a member of the bar for one year. On November 30 the motion for a new trial was overruled, and in the presence of a crowded court Holmes was sentenced to be hung.

On February 3 last his appeal to the Supreme Court for a new trial was argued, and on March 4 the application was refused and his fate sealed. The very next day Governor Hastings signed the death warrant and fixed May 7 as the date for the execution. During the time which has elapsed since Holmes has been so constantly in the public eye and has done and said and written so much to make himself conspicuous that it is needless to recount his doings. There is no part of the world to which publications of some sort referring to him have not penetrated, and this fact was one of the few gratifying ones on which he reflected during the last few days of his life.

He loved notoriety.